Game's End

GAME'S END

A NOVEL

Natasha Deen

GREAT PLAINS
TEEN FICTION

Great Plains Teen Fiction
(an imprint of Great Plains Publications)
233 Garfield Street
Winnipeg, MB R3G 2M1
www.greatplains.mb.ca

Great Plains Publications gratefully acknowledges the financial support provided for its publishing program by the Government of Canada through the Canada Book Fund; the Canada Council for the Arts; the Province of Manitoba through the Book Publishing Tax Credit and the Book Publisher Marketing Assistance Program; and the Manitoba Arts Council.

Design & Typography by Relish New Brand Experience
Printed in Canada by Friesens

LIBRARY AND ARCHIVES CANADA CATALOGUING IN PUBLICATION

Deen, Natasha, author
   Game's end / Natasha Deen.

Issued in print and electronic formats.
ISBN 978-1-927855-85-0 (softcover).--ISBN 978-1-927855-86-7 (EPUB).--
ISBN 978-1-927855-87-4 (Kindle)

   1. Title.

PS8607.E444G36 2017   JC813'.6   C2017-902881-2

                                       C2017-902882-0

ENVIRONMENTAL BENEFITS STATEMENT

Great Plains Publications saved the following resources by printing the pages of this book on chlorine free paper made with 100% post-consumer waste.

TREES	WATER	ENERGY	SOLID WASTE	GREENHOUSE GASES
9	4,038	4	271	744
FULLY GROWN	GALLONS	MILLION BTUs	POUNDS	POUNDS

Environmental impact estimates were made using the Environmental Paper Network Paper Calculator 3.2. For more information visit www.papercalculator.org.

Canadä

FSC
www.fsc.org
MIX
Paper from
responsible sources
FSC® C016245

For Johanna Melaragno

CHAPTER ONE

When you grow up seeing the dead, you get used to the tragic ways a person can die and finding their souls trapped between planes. But if the soul in question is the mother who abandoned you at birth, things get a lot more complicated.

"Take a left turn, then we can head up Claxton," I said to Craig as he, Nell, Serge, and I drove on the dark roads. The night ahead of us was typical of Dead Falls before the final winter snap. Cold and sharp, with a sky bereft of stars.

"Claxton's closed," he said. "A tree fell on the road and the crews are still clearing it up."

"Let's do Railroad Road, then." I settled back in the seat.

Craig took the exit off Highway 63 to take us back to town. I pulled out my phone to text Dad and let him know I was with the gang and things were fine, but it was dead. Not surprising. With the supernatural energy created between me, Craig, and Serge, I was lucky my cell didn't explode.

I pivoted to look at my soul-brother. "Can you text Dad and tell him we'll be late?"

Serge nodded and, closing his eyes, reached one hand up to the ceiling.

Nell caught my smirk. "What?"

"He's doing his holy-roller impression to get reception," I whispered.

"He can hear you," said Serge.

"When he's up there, can he get the TV channels from the States?"

"I'm trying to concentrate," he said. "Mocking me doesn't help."

Nell's cell binged with his message. "Who's mocking you, Casper? I'm just saying, if you can get satellite, can you beam in *I Love Lucy*? I miss that feisty redhead." She turned her attention to me. "Do you really want to go left? Or are you just guessing?"

"Psychic magnetism is harder than it looks," I said. "I have to channel my mother's energy."

"Channel harder," she said. "I'm starved."

"She never comes unless you're in danger," said Serge. "Maybe we should do something risky—"

"Like what? Throw me off a cliff and see if she tries to catch me? Anyway, she only shows up when someone's trying to murder me."

"I could murder a large poutine from Tin Shack—"

"Focus, Nell," I said. "We'll deal with your hunger later."

"You could try—"

I felt her wicked grin.

"But they tell me I'm insatiable."

I turned up the heat in the car. "The word you're looking for is 'incurable,' which is followed by 'should be institutionalized.'"

"Don't be snarky with me just 'cause you have mommy issues—"

The radio flipped on. Static hissed, the creepy kind that meant my mother was near.

"Hey, there she is!" said Serge. "Talk to her."

"*Maggie, oh Maggie*," wept my mother.

I twisted the knobs, as though flipping from AM to FM would somehow make her more coherent. "Mom—"

Craig's loud curse yanked my attention away from the radio to him, and then to the figure who stood in our path. A small child, dressed in a bright red coat, was in the middle of the overpass. Thick flakes swirled and, coupled with the glare of the headlights, made her look like a doll lost in the twist of a snow globe.

I leaned forward. "Wait a second...is that Rori—?"

"Rori?" Nell's voice became sharp at the mention of the little girl we'd lost to a vengeful ghost. "Where?"

"Hold on!" Craig downshifted the engine and cranked the wheel. The car swung into a wide arc. Ice and snow spun the tires and sent us hurtling toward the steel girder that separated the road from a certain-death drop to the highway below.

I gripped the door handle and pressed myself into the chair.

Craig ripped free of his seatbelt, flung open the door, and rolled out. He shifted into his ferrier form—an enormous, dark creature with horns, talons, and a serpentine tail. Then he grabbed the car in his massive hands and lifted it over his head a split second before it would have crashed through the railing.

He hit the road hard. The car slammed forward and the airbag deployed, smashing into my face as the seatbelt held fast and dug its straps into my chest. We jerked left, then right, as Craig and the car rocked to a stop.

Nursing what was sure to be a broken nose and two black eyes, I batted the airbag out of my way. "Is everyone okay?"

Serge crawled into the driver's seat. Using his supernatural abilities, he slipped his hand through the cracked dashboard and shut off the car. "What just happened?"

"There was a kid on the road," I said. "I swear—it looked like Rori."

"Seriously? Didn't she just cross over?"

Craig set the car on the road and shifted back to his human form. "It looked like Rori because it was Rori. I know her energy. For her to come back so quickly—something's wrong on the other side." He cast an assessing gaze around the road. "Or on this one."

"I don't see her." Serge stepped onto the highway, and the two of them walked to the spot where the child had been.

"Still think the supernatural life is exciting and glamorous?" I asked Nell.

She didn't answer.

"Nell?"

No answer.

I turned. Her body was flopped to the side. Nell's eyes were closed and her mouth hung open.

"Nell! Guys!" I fought with my seatbelt, then climbed over the centre console.

Craig was already opening the back door and using the flashlight app on his cell to illuminate the dark interior. We crouched over Nell. The wind swept into the car, sucking out the heat, and brought with it a fetid, rotting smell.

I held her shoulder, squeezed, and said her name, but she didn't respond.

"Careful," said Craig. "Don't move her." He unzipped her jacket and pushed it aside.

Serge put his hand on her chest. "Her heart's okay. Strong."

"I'll take care of her," said Craig. "Mags, get us to the hospital."

I was already moving into the driver's seat. After I shoved the airbag out of the way, I started the car. Or at least I tried to. "Serge."

"Yeah?" He crawled into the seat next to me.

"Did you do something? I can't start the engine."

"Lemme see." He slid one hand into the dashboard and, raising the other, wiggled his fingers.

The last time he'd done his holy-roller impression, I'd laughed. This time, I didn't even crack a smile. If it helped him connect to his abilities, it helped us. I shot a worried glance into the backseat of the car. "Maybe Craig should fly her out."

"How will he explain how he got her to the hospital without a vehicle?" Serge slid his hand from one side of the dash to the other. "Besides, she's mortal. He can't go lifting and moving her around. There!" The car roared to life.

I eased us back onto the road, listened to the swish of tires on the icy surface, and tried to find the sweet spot between speed and safety.

"Mags."

Something in the way Craig spoke my name dulled my fear, though it remained sharp enough to cut through granite. "What?" I checked the rearview, but his face was lost in shadow.

"Pull over for a second."

"Are you sure?"

"We might have a problem with the hospital plan. You need to see this."

Serge and I glanced at each other, but I did as Craig suggested. I flipped on the interior lights, then peered over the headrest.

"Look," said Craig. He lifted one of her lids.

Nell's eyes were gone. The whites had turned into a liquid silver with hues of blue. Her pupils and iris were faceted and glittered like diamonds.

CHAPTER TWO

"Is she—isn't that what ghosts look like when they're crossing over?" asked Serge.

"No, she's not crossing over," Craig said. "But she is on the other side." He gently closed her eye. "The question is, why?" He seemed to be asking the question to himself, but he turned his attention back to us. "We can't take her to the hospital. Mortals won't be able to see what we see, but they'll know something's not normal. Her pupils will seem constricted and there'll be rapid eye movement. If they misdiagnose her, it could be fatal."

"What do we do?" Serge asked. He looked at Craig. "Can you heal her?"

"If she was infested with malevolent spirits, yes, but I'm not a doctor. I'm not allowed to do anything with mortals other than take them to the other side."

"What about you, Serge?" I asked. "You helped Rori."

"I started her heart. Electricity is my thing, but Nell doesn't need a shock to her heart. What about her dad? He's a doctor. Maybe if we tell him what's going on—"

"It won't work," I told Serge. "Her dad's pure scientist. We start talking about supernatural forces and he'll think we're high."

"What if Craig shifted to his ferrier form to prove we're telling the truth?"

"Then the doc'll think *he's* high." I moved back into the driver's seat. "Our best bet is to head to the hospital and hope she snaps out of it before we get there."

"I don't understand," said Serge as he buckled his seatbelt. "Why would she be on the other side?"

"Rori was just here." I pushed the speedometer higher and watched the road for black ice. "For sure, whatever's going on with Nell has to do with Rori. They were close."

"How can she be back so soon?" Serge frowned. "Doesn't she get—I don't know—get processed or something?"

"Or something," said Craig. "Processed is a good word for it. She shouldn't be back on this plane of existence so soon. Something's wrong, but I don't know what it is. After we get Nell to the hospital, I want to come back and check out that patch of road. If her presence appeared there, there might be a clue—"

There was a guttural cry from the backseat. In the rearview mirror, Nell's shadowy figure rose, clutched the sides of my seat, and began babbling in a language I couldn't understand. She reached out, grabbed me by the shoulders, and held tight.

"Is she okay? Ow—god! Her nails! Should I pull over? *What is she saying?*"

Nell's voice grew in volume and pitch, until she was shrieking. One final burst of words I couldn't understand, one more squeeze of my arms that was hard enough to leave bruises, and she collapsed.

"Is she dead?" Serge craned his head toward the back.

Silence, then, "Nah, alive and kicking," said Craig. "Just coming out of it."

"What was she saying? Did anyone understand?" I decreased the car's speed.

"Ancient Egyptian," he said. "And she was talking to you."

Trust Nell to bring me back a message from the other world and bring it back in a language I couldn't comprehend. "What's the message?"

"Beware the light. He comes in red."

"Someone wake her up so I can punch her," I said.

"Punch who?" Nell sounded groggy. "Someone get me food. I'm starving."

"You're lucky I don't shove you out of the car. And PS, you need to trim those talons you call nails."

"What did I do?"

"You had a visit to the other side, you came back with a message for me—" I turned onto Running Creek Road "—which you gave me in ancient Egyptian. Craig translated but it's just as confusing in English."

"I came back bringing a message from the other side?"

"Yeah."

"It was probably from your sweatshirt," she said, her voice still foggy. "It wants you to let it go to the great laundry room in the sky."

"Ha ha."

"Seriously. It wants to cross over to a land of needles and looms."

"You're a loom," I muttered. "What happened to you?"

She leaned forward on the centre console. "Where are we going? This isn't the way to the Tin Shack."

"To the hospital."

"For me? I'm fine."

"The jury's still out on that," I said.

Nell put her hand on my shoulder. "Honest," she said. "I'm fine."

"I'd still like to have you checked out."

"Forget it, there are no cute doctors on call tonight."

"Nell—"

"You're worse than my mother. I'm fine. Besides—" She let go. "My dad's a doctor. I promise I'll ask him to give me a once-over."

If there was one thing I could trust in this world, it was a promise from Nell. "What happened just now?"

She leaned back. "Craig screamed—"

"I didn't scream—"

"Craig screamed a manly scream—"

"I can live with that."

"The car rolled..." She faded into silence.

"Then? Nell?"

"Drop your pearls, Millicent, and give me a minute. It's like trying to remember a dream."

For a moment, the only sound was the swish of the tires on the road.

"I was in a field with the brightest, greenest grass I've ever seen. And a sky so blue it hurt my eyes. There was sun and warmth and clouds." She made a soft sound. "And Rori was there, with her wolf. I feel like we talked for years, that I got an entire lifetime with her. I wish—I wish I could remember what she said because I know I asked her a bunch of stuff."

"It sounds nice," said Serge.

"It was. We talked about everything and then I didn't feel sad anymore. Is that weird?"

"No," he said. "I exploded once, and when I came back, it all felt better."

"Me too, I feel better. When I talked to her, I understood why she'd chosen to cross over. There are things she needs to do and she couldn't do them on this plane. And it's so peaceful there, and the love, it's as thick as air. No, wait, that doesn't make sense. But it does make sense. Love is like air and it's so … so tangible … you can feel it, like a physical thing."

"That does sound nice." I felt happy for Nell, for the closure she got. Then I hurt for my mother, who'd died and now lived in torment.

"I remember she said she was watching out for me. And that things would get scary but I shouldn't worry."

I turned onto Tucker Avenue.

"Then she said she wanted you to know something, and she told me it. And then I woke up and told you."

"Craig said—"

"No, wait," said Nell. "It wasn't Rori. She brought me to you and you gave me the message."

"You who?" asked Serge.

"Mags."

"You saw us?" Serge twisted in his seat to look at her. "Like out of body?"

"No, no, Maggie was there, on the other side."

"Wait." I glanced back at her. "I was here, driving the car, but I was also on the other side, giving you some message to give to me?"

"Yeah," said Nell.

"Okay," I said. "I'm done driving. Craig, take over before I run us off the road." We exchanged spots and I seat-belted in next to Nell.

"Let's go to the Tin Shack," she said. "All this visiting other planes has got me starving. I want poutine."

"Get back to me visiting you on the other side," I said. "That's not possible."

"It's possible." Craig adjusted the rearview mirror so he could see me. "You're a supernatural creature and your powers are expanding."

"Are you sure?"

"Of course I'm sure. You see the dead, don't you? That's as supernatural as it gets."

"Everybody's a comedian," I muttered. "I meant about my powers expanding and me being able to be in two places at once."

"Yes and yes. You had a vision of Rori before she died. If you're able to have visions, you're able to exist simultaneously in two places."

"Where was this ability when I had to take gym?" I hunkered in my seat and processed his words. Then I considered his tone. "What are you not telling me about the visions and expanding power?"

He exhaled. "If your future self was strong enough to reach back in time to try and send a warning, then very bad things are about to happen."

"What kind of bad things?" I asked.

"I don't know," he said. "I'm not psychic."

"Do you think this is connected to me trying to find out about my mom?"

"Could be, but it could be something else."

"The only things that have happened in the last couple of months are Serge being murdered—"

"Maybe the bad thing is Serge's parents," said Nell. "They were psycho, and they have hell on their side."

"Doubt it," said Craig. "Hell keeps its souls."

"What about that horde of demons we battled last week?" I asked. "Seems like the underworld is missing a few tenants."

"They were loose in this world until I sent them to the other side," he said. "Anyway, if the message involved Serge, then the message would have gone to him, not to you, Mags."

"But maybe I sent myself a message to give to him," I said. "After all, he has reception issues." I lifted my hand and wiggled my fingers.

"Hilarious," said Serge. "I'll remember that the next time you need me to text your dad."

"Serge died first," said Nell. "Then Kent. Both of those ghost stories are done. Maybe it's about something you're going to do, soon."

"So, what're my options? I stay at home for the next three months until my future self signals the all clear?"

"Whatever it is," said Craig. "You've already opened the door, or else your future self wouldn't have sent back a warning."

"But you said once that time's not the same on that side. Maybe I gave the warning to Nell to prevent what I'm about to do."

"That's fair," he said. "But Rori was on the road—it feels too much like a warning about things that will happen, not a warning to prevent things from happening."

"Great," I muttered. "I have enough power to have an otherworldly meeting with Nell, but I'm too stupid to give her the message in English."

"That's my fault," said Nell. "I tried to tell you, but the words came out wrong."

"That's not on you," said Craig. "The spirit realm has a language and syntax of its own."

Beware the light. He comes in red. "My future self is a moron. I couldn't just give you a name?"

"Maybe you were talking in code," said Serge. "And we have to decode it—never mind. You're not that smart. Ow!" He rubbed the spot on his arm where I'd punched him. "I didn't mean it like that... okay, maybe a little like—" He ducked as I went after him again.

"In your future self's defence," said Craig. "She probably did give you the name, but it's lost in translation from that world to this one. Kind of like how a dream makes sense within the dream, but once you wake up, it doesn't anymore."

"What are you going to do?" asked Nell.

"If it's not something that I do in the future and it's about a door I've already opened, then this must be about my mom," I said. "I want to find out what happened to her, how she died, and why she became The Voice. But now, Rori's come back to warn Nell about things getting scary. Plus, I'm astral projecting and tossing up 'beware of demon' signs. Maybe I should shut it all down. Just forget about it."

"And leave your mom to whatever torment she's living in the afterlife?" asked Serge. "You'd never do it."

"Sometimes trying to avoid your destiny brings you to it," Craig added. "That night, on the bridge, when you and Serge agreed to become guardians, you accepted your fate."

"*My* fate," I said. "Not everyone else's."

"We're all connected," he said.

"So, what's the right answer?"

"Sometimes there isn't one," he said. "Sometimes you just make the choice and go."

"What do I do?" I sat back and closed my eyes.

"The only thing you can do," he said.

+ + +

"Good call on the poutine," I said and used the last fry to scoop up the remaining gravy.

"When stuck between a rock and a hard place, eat carbs." Craig wiped his hand on a napkin and tossed it into the bag at his feet. Then he reached over the car console and nabbed a few fries from Nell.

"Thanks for turning me solid," Serge said around a mouthful of burger. "It feels good to eat."

"What does it taste like?" asked Nell.

He shrugged. "Good but different."

She turned to me. "Does a large helping of cheese curds and starch answer your questions and sooth your troubled brow?"

"My brow wasn't troubled until you started talking about soothing it." I'd managed to not think of my mother during the ride to the Tin Shack's drive-thru, and I'd managed not to think of her when we drove to a deserted section of Dead Falls to eat. And I definitely hadn't thought of her when I was scarfing down the food. But Nell's mention of her killed my appetite. "Short answer: no, I still don't know what to do about her."

"Tell your dad, for one," said Serge.

"I can see that conversation now. Hey Dad, remember how Mom left us right after I was born and you let her go because you thought it would make her happy? Well, she's dead. And not only is she dead, she's one of the lost souls." I held up my hands as though stopping applause from an audience. "Wait. It gets better. However she died, it was so violent and traumatic, she became The Voice, the otherworldly thing that tortures me and, oh yeah, almost killed me once."

"But she didn't kill you," said Serge. "She was trying to help you, it just came out wrong."

"I'm sure that'll make my dad feel better." I shook my head. "No. I can't do it. I won't. He thinks she's off in some sunny location, drinking wine and having fun. Let it go at that."

"Mags, this doesn't feel right," Nell said. "It's you and your dad. You guys don't keep secrets from each other."

Serge reached into the backseat for a napkin.

"It's going to hurt him. He's going to question everything he said and did when she left. And then he'll feel guilty and blame himself," I told them. "He'll never let himself be happy if he thinks she's tormented in the afterlife. He's going to break up with Nancy, I know it, and then everyone's life will suck. That woman's raisin scones make me believe in a divine and benevolent god." I reached into the front seat and grabbed a handful of Serge's fries. "I can handle this. I've got a ghost and a ferrier on my side."

Nell punched me in the arm. "Me too."

"I don't know—"

"I've been to the other side," she said. "And I was strong enough to come back. I've got experience with supernatural stuff and, most of all, I've got pluck."

"Pluck?"

She nodded. "Things always work out for girls with pluck." She held my hand. "I'm on your side and I'll always be beside you, I promise."

"Great, just when I thought my life couldn't get any scarier—ow! Stop hitting!"

"Stop being an idiot," she said. "We need a plan. Craig, can't you do some woo-woo stuff and get us answers?"

"I wish. I'm only allowed access to the souls I transport, plus a little bit of knowledge about the people connected to them."

"But you knew that Serge wasn't supposed to die," she said.

"Only because I was sent here to transport the soul of his girl-friend. Ex-girlfriend."

"Oh, right, I forgot that part," said Nell. "Still, there's nothing you can do? You're ten thousand years old. Seniority has to count for something."

"Nell, I know you want to help—" I held up my hands to protect myself from another punch. "But pluck aside, this is dangerous territory we're wading into." I heard Serge curse. He disappeared into the footwell of the passenger seat.

"More dangerous than the time Tammy and Bruce brought the Ouija board to your house and set free a horde of demonic ghosts? Or the time you made me take you to my aunt's place and her house blew up?"

Before I could answer, she said, "Rori said I shouldn't worry. That things will get scary, but it'll work out in the end. If anything, I'm your lucky rabbit's foot. And I'm even luckier than that, because unlike the rabbit, I still have my foot. Both of them, come to think of it."

"I guess but—"

"It's starting," said Serge. "Whatever you were warning yourself about, it's happening right now."

"Can you feel something?" I asked.

He came into view and pointed at the windshield.

The rest of us glanced at each other, then ducked and looked up, trying to see what he did. Craig got out of the car.

I wrapped my coat around me and stepped into the cold. High against the inky sky, the snow spun in a magenta-hued whirlwind. From its centre, red lightning flashed and dark shadows of souls swam in the eddy.

"I don't see anything," said Nell, coming to stand beside me.

"Craig, can you take Nell home while Serge and I check this out—ow!" I rubbed my shoulder and glared at Nell. "What did I say about hitting?"

"What did I say about plucky sidekicks? You're not moving me."

"Craig," I said. "Help me out."

"If you rub the spot she hit and apply pressure, it'll help with the bruising."

"That's not what I meant."

He shrugged. "I don't mess with plucky sidekicks." He popped a fry in his mouth. "Come on, let's check it out." He stepped toward the light.

CHAPTER THREE

The wind set snow drifting across the hill, but the footing was solid as we made our way into the forest entrance. Craig turned Serge back to his ethereal form, in case we ran into anyone wandering the trails. Then he turned to Nell. "Come by me."

"Why? What's going on?"

"You were on the other side," he said, as he handed me his cell.

I adjusted it so the light shone on them.

He took her face in his hands. His eyes turned red. "I need to see if it left a mark on you."

"Is that good or bad?"

"If there's an imprint, I can shift your perception to see what we're seeing. It'll help protect you." He peered into her eyes. "It's fading, but it's there. Hold on." He pulled her closer, then blew over her face. His breath was smoke and fire, with sparks of blue and white that swirled in hieroglyphs. He stepped back. "How do you feel?"

"The same." She looked around. "Oh, wait. I can see your auras. Mags, you're glowing." She grinned and sidled up to me. "Is that your aura or because you're close to Craig?"

"Nah," I said. "It's just the afterglow of being close to you."

She blinked and tapped my arm with her fist. "I love you, too."

We hurried after Craig and Serge, and Nell flipped on her cell's light. I stumbled over roots and branches, and eventually slid my way down an embankment into a flat clearing. A ghost stood in the centre.

"Oh, he's cute," said Nell.

"Calm down," I said. "He's dead."

"I could make him feel alive again."

I punched her arm.

"What did we say about the hitting?" she asked, but I ignored her and moved closer to the ghost.

He was a couple years older than me, with light brown hair and dark eyes. Dressed in cut-off jeans and a white t-shirt, he didn't seem to notice the winter cold. Which meant he was dead, and he was among the confused dead. I dug my hands into my coat pockets and moved closer. The smell coming off of him was evergreen pine, a sure sign he'd died recently. "Are you okay, sir?"

"Oh, I ain't no sir, ma'am," he said, turning his attention from the barren tree tops to me. "My name's Zeke, Zeke Addison, and I still ain't sure how I ended up here." The ghost left his spot and came over to us. His footprints left no mark in the snow gathering on the ground. The wind created by his movement did nothing to scatter the fallen snowflakes. He squinted to the sky. "Musta been some fall."

Some fall? The area surrounding us was flat and empty. "My name's Maggie, and these are my friends. Can we help you with anything?"

"Nah, I ain't never seen this part of the woods before, but I figure I can get myself back home."

"You've never seen this part of the woods," I repeated. "Because you've never been here. Your accent, you're from one of the southern states in America?"

He nodded. "Land of the free and the brave. The Ozarks are home to me."

"You're not there anymore. You're in Dead Falls, Alberta, Canada."

Zeke's gaze went to each of us, a confused smile forming on his lips. "Y'all are funning with me, ain't ya?"

"I don't joke about things like this," I said.

I felt Zeke considering my mental state. No doubt, he was wondering if he wanted to be in the dark woods, alone, with us.

He came closer, a good sign.

Zeke still hadn't asked how he'd ended up in a small northern town or why he'd suddenly appeared in the middle of the road, in a swirl of purple light. Did the dead not see this plane of existence in the same way as the living? Or did they, like the living, lie to themselves about the reality surrounding them?

I took another breath and tried again to help him cross over. "You mentioned the Ozarks."

But he wasn't listening. He was staring at the sky. "It was a hard fall. I rolled a lot. Maybe I ended up on another trail…"

"In Canada?"

He smiled. "You can keep trying, but I ain't falling for your stunt. Did the boys make you do this?"

"Zeke, what do you see?"

He gave me a sweet smile. "You, all lit up, pretty as a picnic. Warm as sunshine, too."

"What about around me? What do you see?"

"Your friends." He smiled again. "The woods."

"You don't see anything else?"

"What else is there to see?"

Nell's gaze went to the purple-magenta clouds swirling above us. "What about the snow?"

"Ain't no snow."

Nell opened her mouth, but Craig shook his head.

"What was going on before you fell?" I asked.

"Well, it's like this. I was with my boys—Beau, Shortie, and Bubba—and we was at the crick—"

My brain took a second to adjust 'crick' to 'creek.'

He nodded. "It's real beautiful this time of the year. Clear and blue. Anyway, Bubba, he saw a skunk and started jawing about how the critter was better smelling and better looking than his ex, Wanda." Zeke scraped the underside of his jaw. "It's been real bad between them."

"I guessed that from Bubba's comparison."

"Yeah, I suppose that's kind of obvious, ain't it?"

"Happens to the best of us. Keep going."

"I ain't had a date in a long while, and I started talking about how she was kind of pretty, for a skunk. Bubba thought it'd be funny to kiss her. The skunk, I mean. Not Wanda. He'd be real tickled if I did that. But a skunk…"

"You really thought it would be funny to kiss a skunk?"

He nodded. "It seemed like a good idea, at the time."

"Did you do it?" Serge asked, his voice part-horror, part-respect.

"There was a six pack of beer and my family honour on the line."

"Some family," I said.

"Oh, now, when you think on it, a girl and a skunk ain't that different. One's better smelling than the other—"

"I assume you mean the girl," I said.

He nodded.

"Just checking." I wiggled my toes to keep the circulation going.

"—You gotta be nice and gentle with them, but if you treat them right, they'll be okay. The skunk, I mean. Although, treatin' a girl the same way, ain't a bad idea, come to think about it."

I flexed my fingers, trying to get the warmth back. "Then what happened?"

"I don't rightly know. There was a lot of hooting and hollering, and I was crashing through the brush. Then all of a sudden, I was falling and then there was a bright light." He shrugged. "Then I found myself here. Not that I'm not enjoying your company and all, but I can't figure how I ended up here—" He squinted up. "I fell from a hill, and I thought I knew every road and twist in the backwoods."

I figured taking the blunt approach was best. Zeke was great company, but the longer he lingered, the harder it would be to transition him. Besides, my fingers were icicles. I wanted to go back to the car and get more answers from Craig. "It comes down to this: Zeke, you're dead."

His eyelids flickered. "I'm what?"

"Dead."

"Are you dead, too?"

"No."

"Then how come you can see me?"

"It's a talent."

"A talent."

"Like wooing skunks," I said. "I see the dead and I help them move from this existence to the next."

If his smile didn't trumpet his disbelief, the fact that he started scanning for escape did. "I think you're having a little fun with me."

"Okay, it's one big prank. How did you end up here?"

"If I'm dead, how come I don't sink through the ground?"

"Because death is like life. It's going to be what you make of it. You don't sink because you don't think you should sink."

"Maggie—"

"It's snowing." I pointed. "Don't you see it?"

"It's not snowing," he said.

"Then why am I wearing a snow jacket?"

"It's not my place to question a lady's choice of clothing." He leaned in. "But if you're asking, I thought it was odd, but the colour looks real good on you."

"Thanks, but—"

"Not that I don't believe you—" He smiled. "—But I don't believe you."

"Got it. You only have my word." Time to call in the big guns. "See him?" I pointed to Serge.

"Yep." He squinted. "Your boyfriend?"

Craig looked amused.

"Hey," said Serge to him. "I'm not a bad catch."

"You're a great catch," Craig said. "Handsome, funny, smart. You're the whole package."

I glared them both into silence. "He's my brother."

The squint deepened. "He don't look like your kin."

"He's not my real brother, we're soul-bonded."

"If he's not your brother, why do you call him that?" asked Zeke.

"Because." Serge wriggled into the spot between us. "It sounds better than 'hi, meet Serge. We used to go to school together and he bullied me until I wanted to die. Luckily, he was the one who stopped breathing. I helped him figure out that his so-called suicide was a murder, and then we discovered in this life we were both scripted to become guardians. We watch over the dead and living, transition souls from this plane to the next, and make sure the bad spirits from hell stay there.'"

"Yeah," Zeke nodded. "I can see how that's a mouthful."

"If you can see Serge, you're dead," I said. "Because he's dead, and the dead see the dead."

"Are you sure I'm dead? Maybe you're dead and I'm the one who's alive."

I looked to Craig.

"No point in me shifting," he said, seeming to read my mind. "He won't see it."

"Do you see the light that outlines them?" Nell asked.

He nodded.

"The living can't see that."

"No disrespect, ma'am, but I live with fireflies. If the good Lord can make a creature who's able to light up his butt like a power switch, then maybe the glow of you folks is some kind of science I ain't figured out yet."

"That's true," said Serge.

I shot him an exasperated look.

"What?" He raised his hands. "The guy's got a point."

"That's not helpful," I said.

Serge shrugged. "Truth is truth."

"And I'm getting hypothermia," I said. "We need to move this along."

"You dead, too?" He asked Nell.

"Nah," she said. "But I've been to the other side. It's nice. You should go."

"I can't be dead," said Zeke. "When you die, you go to heaven or hell. You don't end up in the middle of the road with a bunch of strangers."

"It doesn't always work that way—" I said.

"It has to. Good people move on. Bad people get punished. If you're neither—if you're not good enough—"

"You're good enough," I said softly. "I've known you for five minutes and I know you're good enough. But I also know you didn't think you were going to die today. Your system's suffered a shock—"

"If it's not about being good or bad," said Zeke, stepping away. "Maybe it's something else. Maybe I'm here for a reason. There has to be a reason. Maybe I'm here to stop a bad thing or to help someone. Life and death have to have purpose."

It was an anguished plea. A flash of connection and understanding lit Serge's face. "Your life has purpose," Serge told him. "So does your death. But you're not going to find the reason here. You have to move on, talk to the higher-ups and see what your destiny is."

Zeke wiped his face. "I've had enough of things just happening because they happen."

Something about the way he said it tweaked me. I took his hand. "What kinds of stuff just happen?"

"Nothing worth talking about. Life just doesn't always turn out like you expect."

"Who did you lose?" Serge asked quietly.

"Who didn't I lose? Ma's finding her end at the bottom of a bottle. Pa's—I don't reckon I know where he's gone."

"Who was the first?" Serge came closer, until we were a quiet triangle of memories and pain, bracketed by the icy night.

"I had this brother," Zeke's face contorted. "I hate that word. *Had.*" He was quiet for a moment. "My little brother, Homer. Cute little cuss. Died on account of the cancer."

"I'm sorry," I said. "It's a terrible way to go, and it's a terrible thing to watch and know you can't stop the pain."

"I lost someone, too," said Nell, coming to join us. "It's not easy."

Zeke knuckled his eyes. "He was the bravest kid I knew. After he—after he left, nothing seemed to matter. What was the point of doing anything other than hooting and hollering? Death was just going to take the ones you loved. And life didn't care about those left behind. It was like, after Homer, Ma, Pa, and I, we all just got in line and waited for death to get us too."

"What did Homer look like?" I asked. "Like you?"

"Homer? Nah, he was better looking than I'll ever be. Dark hair, dark eyes, real chubby. But cute chubby, you know? Baby fat—he got real skinny with the chemo. But he never stopped smiling. He had this laugh when he was real happy—" Zeke broke off, looking around. "Do you hear—I swear I heard him."

"When he was really happy," I said. "You made him happy?"

"I loved him," said Zeke. "I loved him with every beat of my heart. When he died, I died along with him. My little buddy was gone."

"It sounds like he was your best friend," I said.

Zeke smiled at me. "I got him into all kinds of trouble. We stole into old man Jackson's pasture one time, and I pulled Homer up on one of the horses, showed him how to ride bareback—there it is, again! You sure you don't hear—" His gaze went to a dark corner of the forest. "Oh my Lord. Homer? You see him?" He started to cry. "Look how good he looks. He's chubby again." He smiled through his tears. "Can you hear him? He's calling my name. Sweet Jesus in Heaven. Homer! Boy, look at you!"

Zeke turned my way and his eyes were gone. They'd turned into liquid silver and reflected white-blue light.

"Go to him," I whispered.

He moved, laughing and crying at the same time. "He's so healthy. So happy. Lord, Homer, I missed you." He ran to the spot, stumbling over his feet and tripping as he picked up his pace. Zeke dropped to his knees and wrapped his arms around someone I couldn't see.

Pure, white light enveloped him and outlined the silhouette of someone small holding on to him. They began to fade from view.

Nell sniffed. "Too bad everyone can't see this."

Overhead, thunder crackled. Craig looked up.

"Can there be a thunderstorm in the middle of winter?" Nell asked.

"Yeah," he said. "But we're too far north—"

Black lightning flashed, multi-forked and edged in blue.

Craig morphed into ferrier form. "Nell, get Serge out of here! Maggie, don't let any of those things touch your bare skin."

"What? Why do I have to leave?" Serge dodged out of Nell's grasp.

"Because this thing comes for ghosts. Get out!"

"Go!" The boom of Nell's command sent Serge running up the path.

The sky opened into a dark, swirling vortex. Branches of lightning cracked jagged lines. Shadows, made visible only by the supernatural light, formed in the swirling hollow. Beside me, thick spikes formed along Craig's spine.

That was new and creepy. "What is this?"

"No time to explain. Get to Zeke and his brother. Make sure nothing happens to them."

I ran for the ghosts.

"Maggie—"

I looked back.

"Remember, don't let anything touch your bare skin."

Racing to my ghostly charges, I pulled my gloves high on my wrists. I slid to where they knelt. Zeke flickered in my vision, Homer remained an outline.

"What's going on?" Though there was no wind, Zeke's hair waved around his face as though caught in a violent breeze.

"I don't know." I knelt and put my arms around them both. As we connected, the wind rose, clear and warm. Homer morphed from an outline to a fully-formed kid with chubby cheeks and worried eyes. Zeke and I moved so the little boy was protected by both of us.

Lifting my face, I saw the sky from this position wasn't the same. A yellow sun blazed in an orange sky, and from the black centre of the star, the shadows swooped down. I had no idea what they were, but common sense said they were big, bad, and deadly.

I had Homer roll into a fetal position, then Zeke curled himself around his brother. My matchstick figure wasn't big enough to cover them both. Time to fight. I stood over them, yanked on my hood, pulled off my scarf, and hoped the evil things wouldn't go for my face.

I've always wondered why ghosts feel as solid to me as the living, and as one of the shadows flew close, I got my answer. For this moment, for this time. So I could use my scarf as a weapon, wrap it around the shadow and fling it to the side. So I could make a fist and punch the one that swooped close.

It was demonic whack-a-mole, as soon as I smacked one of them out of the way, another took its place. They stank of sulphur and desperate need, and even with the protection of my coat and gloves, I felt their acidic touch. More of them swooped down. My arms were tiring, my legs were losing strength from the countless squats and lunges, and I was sure I'd pulled a muscle—or seven—in my back. I hit and swung and boomeranged until I thought my arms would fly off. From behind, I heard a loud roar, words spoken in a language I couldn't understand.

The shadows exploded, raining black dust. There was a loud crack and a brilliant flash of light burned the sky. The sound of a sonic boom, a high keening. Blistering heat followed by a sharp cold and the pungent smell of rot. The light faded. Nell was beside me. Zeke and Homer were gone. I scanned the landscape. The scarf slipped from my fingers. Craig lay in a pool of scarlet, Serge knelt beside him.

CHAPTER FOUR

The frozen ground bit into my knees as I slid next to Craig, touching his forehead and calling his name. Fallen snow made his blood seem brighter, redder.

"Blood sacrifice." He could barely get the words out. "Didn't work. It took Homer and Zeke."

"We'll get them back."

"Help me," he wheezed. "Before it's too late."

I put my hand on top of his chest, closed my heart and mind to the fear, and concentrated on healing, on the wounds knitting themselves. Serge did the same. The warmth of Nell's fingers closed over mine.

"It can't hurt," she said.

On our knees, the cold and wet seeping in, we sent the energy and light to Craig. After what felt like an eternity, the blood on the ground slid back into his body and his wounds knit themselves clean. His eyes flickered open. "Thanks. Feels better." He took a shallow breath. "Almost back."

"That's a neat trick," said Nell. "Think you could teach it to me? I'd be aces as a doctor if I could do that."

"Only works on supernaturals." Craig grunted and sat up. "Only works for a blood sacrifice."

When he had recovered, Nell and I helped him stand. We got back to the car, put the heat on high, and sat in silence.

"Well, I'm going to ask," she said. "What was that?"

"The cloud felt familiar," I said.

"It should," said Craig. "It's made up of the lost and wandering dead; they're the ones who come to you when they want to transition. They gather when a soul is about to cross over."

"Always?" asked Serge.

"Always," said Craig. "Crossing over is terrifying for some ghosts, and they can't do it. They come and watch, hoping one day to find the courage to leave this plane of existence."

"I've never seen it." I brushed snow off my boots and cranked the heat.

"Your powers are shifting. There's a lot you're going to see now, including soul-eaters."

"Soul-eaters," said Serge. "Tell me more."

"In this life, souls linger for many reasons, both good and bad. They can't let go because of their job, love, terrible relationships— they cling to the things that defined them in life. When another soul crosses over, it acts as a magnet that brings the others. They gather to watch. The collective energy works as a homing beacon. It brings the soul-eaters," said Craig. "I've heard of them, but I've never seen one."

"A soul-eater," I said. "As in, an entity that eats souls."

"Kind of," he said. "Souls and soul collection are complicated things."

"How complicated can it be?" asked Nell. "You die, you cross over—" She glanced at me. "Okay, wait. You die. Sometimes you cross over. Sometimes you get someone like Maggie or Serge to help you cross over." She frowned. "Then again, sometimes you get a ferrier. Or you might linger. Sometimes you group together with other lost souls and terrorize small Alberta towns." She shook her head. "Like I was saying, souls and soul collection are complicated things."

"The only souls that transition easily are the evil ones," said Craig. "They're taken by hell, but that rarely happens. Most people are a mix of good and bad, and even if all you have is one drop of good, there's a chance for redemption. Hell won't come for you."

"And the other souls, the ones that don't cross over?" asked Serge.

Craig sat back. "It depends. Some souls are happy to linger on this plane. But the ones who come when another soul transitions, they're the ones the soul-eater takes."

"Why?" asked Nell.

"Those spirits don't know if they are good or bad, so they don't know where they're going to end up. Or they're afraid of what waits for them on the other side."

"Just talking numbers," asked Nell. "How many of those wandering lost are we talking about?"

"A lot," said Craig. "Which is why we have soul-eaters. They ingest and hold the ghost until a guardian or someone higher can adjudicate their lives."

"And they show up and eat the spectators?" I asked.

"They show up and eat the *spectres*," Nell corrected me. "Who also happen to be spectators. It makes sense, though, it's dinner and a show for the soul-eater."

"Soul-eaters are about efficiency," said Craig. "Tracking lost souls via transition bridges is the best way to do it, and their job is to clear ghosts from this plane. If a soul-eater didn't do it, then this world would be overrun with the lost." He smiled. "There aren't enough people like Maggie to transition and move the departed."

"Why did you make me leave?" asked Serge. "I'm not stuck on this side, and I know what's on the other side."

"You died violently and unexpectedly. And your life was..."

"A hot mess?" offered Nell.

"Conflicted," said Craig.

"That shouldn't matter," I said. "Should it? Like Serge says, he's got purpose on this side and a destiny from the other side."

"But he still fulfills two of the soul-eater's criteria and..."

"...I still struggle with my life and my afterlife," said Serge.

"Exactly," said Craig. "But something's off with this one. It was hungry, but not in the right way. There was a sick need—it wanted Zeke and Homer, but not for their sake. It should never have taken either of them. They were both moving across the bridge to the other side. There's only one explanation for it. The soul-eater came for power."

"Which is another reason I was in trouble," said Serge.

Craig nodded. "Souls are an enormous source of energy. If you could ingest and absorb that power—"

"A ghost a day keeps the doctor away?" asked Nell.

Craig went to answer, but I put up my hand to stop him. "Hold on, by definition, isn't claiming souls for power and preventing them from crossing over the definition of evil? Shouldn't hell claim the entity that's doing it?"

"The soul-eater is still clearing the backlog, which is a good thing—"

"A drop of good," I muttered. "A chance for redemption."

"Those souls aren't crossing over anyway, so while the soul-eater's motivation is corrupt, it's still doing a service for both the living and the dead," he said. "And if you've ingested enough souls—like this soul-eater—you know how to hide in their energy and bend their power to your will."

"Are Zeke and Homer gone?" I asked. "Did I bring them together only to have them destroyed by this entity?"

Craig shook his head. "I don't think so, but I don't know enough about the soul-eaters. I've never had to deal with one. I'm going to go to the other side and look into it." He sat up. "They live in the shadows so there isn't a lot of information on them. Right now, any knowledge would be useful."

"Can I come?" asked Serge. "Something about that energy felt personal, but I can't name it. If I can cross over and look around..."

"Yeah, that's a good idea." Craig held out his hand and Serge took it. "We'll be back as soon as we can." They disappeared to the other side.

"Did you feel anything from the soul-eater?" Nell crawled over the console to the passenger seat. "Did it feel personal to you, too?"

"More than personal, and unlike Serge, I can name it. That was my mother's energy."

CHAPTER FIVE

I came out of the bathroom, tying an elastic band around my braid, and found Serge on the bed. Ebony had curled herself into a ball, and Buddha, his doggy tail covering her, snored beside his feline sister. "How did it go?"

"I had to bail," he said. "I thought the other side would be like a library. Quiet. Orderly. But that place is like Disneyland, the Grand Bazaar, and Grand Central station all rolled into one. Besides, I figured Craig could work faster if he wasn't trying to explain everything to me."

"Did you find out anything?"

"There aren't a lot of soul-eaters because each individual one can ingest an insane number of ghosts. They're supposed to disgorge their souls on a regular basis so they don't build up power, but lucky us, this one is a hoarder." He muted the TV. The cop team on the screen continued to question their suspect, helped by the glare of a solitary ceiling light. "But here's the weird thing. A soul-eater isn't an otherworldly entity. It's someone on this side."

"Someone alive is collecting souls?" I sat beside him. "Is that even possible? You're talking about a corporeal body—a finite capsule. How can it house souls?"

His mouth twisted. "It's confusing, but it has something to do with how a supernatural human is genetically put together. But there's another thing. It was someone like us—like you—a living person who's training to be a guardian."

"It doesn't make sense. It can't be alive. I felt that thing. It had my mom's energy."

He slapped his forehead. "That's why it felt familiar."

"It has my mom." I frowned. "But how can it have my mom? She comes to me in radios and warnings. If she can escape from the soul-eater to contact me, then why does she go back to it?"

"I don't know," said Serge. "Were you thinking about her when we were fighting with it?"

"I'm always thinking about her."

"Maybe it recognized your energy and used the other souls it has to fake your mom's signature and distract you."

If it could hide in someone else's energy, if it could create soul energy, then no wonder hell couldn't find it. And now it had Zeke. It also had a little boy who'd battled cancer then returned from the love on the other side to get his brother, only to be captured by evil.

"Maybe," I said. "But something about it felt too real."

"What if it's her love for you?" asked Serge. "What if she is trapped but her love for you is so strong, she can sense when you're in trouble and warn you. Her love is too powerful for the soul-eater to stop." He sat up. "Maybe that's why her warnings come out wrong, because they're passing through a power-hungry soul-eater first."

"Maybe." I liked the idea of my mom loving me enough that nothing could stop her from trying to take care of me.

"Your mom's warnings might also explain why the entity's here, now. You've transitioned a lot of ghosts and you've never had anything like this happen. But in the last while, you've had two murders, seen hell claim a soul, had a child die and cross over. What if all the convergence of supernatural energy and your mom's warning is what brought him here."

"All good theories," I said. "I wish Craig would get here. I need information." The reminder that I was in the dark with this thing, dependent on someone else for my information forced me off the bed.

"I don't like it either," he said. "Craig has all the institutional knowledge."

I stared at him.

"What?"

"Who knew you were capable of five-syllable words?"

He grinned and wriggled his eyebrows. "I know how to work this tongue into all kinds of multi-syllabic words, and it drives the ladies into the one-syllable ones."

"Oh, god."

"That's what they say."

"Hold on." I held up my hand. "I'm trying to force the vomit back down my esophagus."

He shrugged. "Truth is truth."

"Do you miss it?"

His eyes widened at the question. "Vomiting? Not even a little bit. You have no idea how many nights I got so drunk I had to sleep by the toilet."

It was more nights than I wanted to think about. "Not vomiting, smart guy. I meant, are you lonely?"

"I have you, Craig, Hank, Nell, Nancy—"

Ebony and Buddha raised their heads and looked his way.

"And the dynamic duo over here." He scrubbed the undersides of their jaws.

"I meant the relationship stuff. Do you miss having a girlfriend?" The look on his face made me go over and put my arm around his shoulder.

"I do feel lonely sometimes, really lonely. If you could hold me a little tighter, maybe squeeze those mosquito bites against me."

I shoved him away. "Really? I was trying to have a moment with you."

"I was trying too." He laughed and caught the pillow I threw at him. "Yeah, sometimes I miss having someone. You have Craig, Nancy has Hank, and Nell has—"

"The entire town."

He laughed. "All hail the hive mother." Serge rubbed Ebony's back as she curled on his chest. "What I really miss is the idea of someone. Amber and I were never a couple. I was a beard for her and the reverend—"

Part of me broke for him, for living a life where he could never call the reverend father. Most of me was glad Serge didn't give him that title. He'd been a horrible man, and he didn't deserve any loyalty.

"But for now, I figure it's a good time to work on me, work on this whole guardian thing." He smiled. "I have the faith that one day—"

"The right ghoul will come along?"

He groaned. "You should show me those mosquito bites now."

There was a knock on the door. Dad came in with a cup of tea and a plate of Nancy's cookies. "I saw your shoes at the door."

"Sorry, I was leaving them to dry off."

"And your coat on the floor."

"Also drying."

"Scarf, gloves—"

"Drying, drying—"

"Getting the carpet wet," said Dad as he set the food on the night table. "You slay demons and save souls. How can you leave such a mess?"

"I'm sorry." I reached for a lemon macaroon. "It was a crappy night."

"What happened?"

"Someone stole our ghost."

Dad went still for a moment, then reached for a cookie. "Did you get him or her back?"

"Them, and no. The bad guy took Zeke and Homer."

"That was mean-spirited." Dad took a bite of the macaroon.

Serge laughed.

I said, "You know I'm picking your retirement home, right?"

"I'm sorry." Dad gestured to the bed. "Where's Serge?" A second later his phone beeped. "Ah, okay."

"I like texting to talk to the living," said Serge as he moved out of the way and Dad sat down. "Makes me feel connected."

Dad opened his mouth and I raised my hand. "I feel a dad pun coming, and I'm not in the mood."

"I can't help it," said Dad. "In the last couple months, you've come head-to-head with two murderers, fought a demon, and seen the death of a child. I can't help with any of it. All I can do is throw down terrible puns and fetch Nancy's cookies."

"That's more than you think," I said.

"Tell me everything that happened tonight."

I did, glossing over the more dangerous parts and avoiding mention of The Voice. He worried enough, I didn't need to give him details on what had happened to the woman he'd once loved.

When I finished, he asked, "What's your next move with the soul-eater?"

"Wait for Craig to bring us some intel, then proceed."

"When is Craig back?" asked Dad.

"I'm not sure," I said.

"There's only one thing we can do until he arrives." Dad stood. "Are you coming?"

✦ ✦ ✦

We stepped into the Tin Shack. For a moment, I wondered why Nell, Dad, and Craig figured food was the answer to all my problems. Then I saw the latest sundae promotion on the board and stopped wondering.

Dad pointed to the ice cream. "Caramel ice cream, fudge pieces, caramel sauce, chunks of Snickers and Mars bars, and pecans." He squeezed my shoulder as he took off his glasses and wiped his eyes. "My girl, I think we just found the answer to world peace."

"I'd go for the strawberry shortcake sundae," said Serge. "Maybe the classic banana split." His gaze swept the board. "It's a good thing I'm not solid. I'd order one of everything."

Dad read the texts. "Lean over mine and inhale."

"Now that's mean-spirited," said Serge.

Dad grinned.

"Think we should get a table?" Serge asked.

I glanced at the eating area. The lineup to the cashier was solid but not packed, and there were a bunch of tables free. Still... "Not a bad idea."

I left Dad to the ordering of world peace and got us a secluded table in the corner by the back. The only person near us was two tables ahead, buried behind a newspaper.

"Do you think one day I'll be powerful enough to turn myself solid and eat?" asked Serge. "I miss food."

I met his gaze.

"What?"

"You really are my soul-brother," I spoke quietly so the person near us wouldn't hear. "Of all the things you can be solid for, food is your number one pick."

"Mashed potatoes and gravy." His face went dreamy.

The person at the other table set down their newspaper. Oh, crap.

"Maggie Johnson," said Principal Milton Larry.

The way he said my name was a trail of slime sliding along my spine. "Hello, sir." I glanced at the cashier. Dad was next in line to be served.

"I see you've made headlines once again." He gestured to the paper. "Another murder solved, thanks to your...ingenuity."

I didn't respond.

He stood, slope-shouldered, wispy-haired, and shuffled my way. The smell of his cheap cologne made my eyes water. "What a coincidence. Two murders in the last two months, and you're at the centre of them." His watery eyes took me in. "Funny, isn't it, how death follows you. Death and destruction." He leaned forward. "Did you ever give a thought to the ones left in your wake?"

"I could jolt his heart," said Serge.

No electrocuting anyone.

Nothing too strong. Just enough to make him wet his pants.

Stop. But the thought of the high-and-mighty principal fleeing the Tin Shack with wet pants was enough to make me giggle. I stifled it, but Principal Larry caught the smile.

"Your reaction tells me everything I need to know."

"Sorry, Mags," said Serge.

"I see you for what you are," Principal Larry hissed.

"What's going on, Larry?" Dad came up to the table and dropped his jacket in the seat opposite mine.

"Hank." The principal drew himself up. "I realize this isn't the best place to have this conversation, but I think it's time for you to look for another school for Maggie."

"I don't agree."

"Yes, well, I've had conversations with some of the parents and staff, and they don't feel comfortable having her there."

"Who?"

Principal Larry smiled with the slippery twist of small people who enjoy lording their even smaller power over others. "I'm afraid that's confidential."

"Because it's bull—" Dad glanced at me. "Maggie's never broken any rules. There's no reason for her to leave."

"Our institution grooms a certain kind of person," said Principal Larry. "One of high moral calibre and integrity."

Dad snorted. "You mean like Kent Meagher, who sold drugs and was responsible for numerous overdoses in Edmonton."

"—Maggie doesn't fit—"

"My daughter found out who murdered two of your students."

"She left devastation in her wake! People—good people—are smeared by the things she's done, made guilty by association to the things she's uncovered."

Serge glanced at me. I shrugged. Having people talk about me like I wasn't there was frustrating, and I wanted to stand up for myself. But Dad had a warrior's look on his face, and I wasn't about to wade into his war. Still, I wondered about what the principal said. His tone suggested he was one of the "smeared." If that was the case, then it wasn't smear. It was the truth and he deserved every dirty look tossed his way.

"Like you?" asked Dad. "Are you devastated by Reverend Popov's death? The two of you were close."

"He was a man of God, under extreme pressure."

"If he starts talking about what a good guy the reverend was," said Serge. "I'm going to go poltergeist and spew chunks his way."

Gross, but I like the way you think.

"Spoken like a devotee," said Dad. "My daughter uncovered the dirty secrets of some of this town's upstanding citizens. Things that should have seen the light of day much sooner. Did you know, Larry? Did you know what the great and lauded reverend was doing to his son, to his wife?" Dad stepped close. "Did you know about what he did to Amber?"

"Amber." The principal straightened. "There's a perfect example. Now everyone knows what she did. She will be judged and condemned."

"By who?" Dad unbuttoned the cuff of his shirt and rolled it up. "Who would dare blame Amber for what the reverend did to her?"

Principal Larry glanced down as Dad unbuttoned the other cuff, and he stepped back. "I think it's better for Maggie to go somewhere else."

"She'll be at school tomorrow, and if I hear of anyone causing her trouble..."

"I can't be held responsible for what other people choose to do!"

"Is that what you told yourself when Reverend Popov was beating Serge and abusing Amber?"

"How dare you!"

"I dare."

The edges of Principal Larry's mouth went white. "It's you, isn't it? You're the one who's been going around town, gossiping about me. Saying I knew about the reverend and did nothing!" Rage pushed him forward. "It's because of people like you that I have to carry protection."

Dad smiled. "I have better things to do than gossip about small people."

"I'll get to the bottom of this," he said. "I'll make you pay."

"Get out of my face, Larry, and stay away from my daughter."

The principal moved around Dad.

"In fact, stay away from all of our daughters," Dad called after him.

Principal Larry froze for a moment, then scuttled to the exit.

"I don't know if you should have done that," I said, watching as the patrons of the restaurant set down their phones and picked up their burgers. "I'm pretty sure that whole thing was videoed."

Dad took out his cell, looked at the screen, and laughed. "Just saw Serge's text. I was trying not to vomit on Loser Larry, too."

"Neat, right?" Serge grinned. "I've figured out how to text so only some of the living can get it. Now, I don't have to be so careful when I'm talking in public."

"You, without a filter," I said. "That's not scary."

Tucking it back in his pocket, Dad said, "I don't care if the entire town caught me and the principal on video. There's something off with him, and if it wasn't for his family being the founders of this town, he would've been run out by now. His father got him the job of principal just so his idiot kid had something do in the morning. Everyone knows your vice-principal's the one who does all the work."

"Thanks for sticking up for me," I said.

Dad smiled. "I suppose I might have been hard on him. I guess it's not fair. He has no one. But I have you, my girl."

"I love you too, Dad."

He smiled.

"Especially when you come bearing food."

"Remember these moments when you're picking my nursing home. The food order should be ready by now. Let me check." Dad turned, then stopped as Ralph, the owner of the Tin Shack walked up with a tray of food in his hand.

"Here you are." He set it down. "And here you are." He handed Dad a gift card for the restaurant.

"What's this for?" asked Dad.

"For what you did with Larry." Ralph's face creased in disgust. "I'm sorry for what happened to the Popov kid—"

Serge looked up.

"—And I'm sorry for what his father did to him."

"He was never my dad," mumbled Serge.

"—But Serge terrorized my Mindy. Bullied her."

Serge went white. "Mindy. I remember."

"I heard she's in a prep school in Edmonton," I said.

Ralph nodded. "And in therapy. Between the school and the doctor, it's expensive and we're barely making ends meet, but it's worth it to see her smile again." He turned to me. "Don't you let that jackass tear you down. Nobody said anything about not wanting you at the school. That's just him being pissed because you took away his god and now he has no one to worship. People never liked the reverend or the principal, and with all the secrets surfacing, Larry can't hide behind his family's pedigree anymore. You're a good girl, Maggie." He nodded at us, then left.

"The principal's wrong about you leaving destruction in your wake," said Serge. "Ralph's right, you're a good person, Mags, you try to do right. When I was alive, all I did was hurt people. I'm sorry I won't be able to make it up to Mindy. To everyone."

"It's not—the reverend and your mom played a giant role in some of the choices you made," I said.

"Yeah, but they were still my choices." He stood. "I'm going to go home. I'll see you two later."

He blipped out. Dad and I finished our meals, then stood to leave. As I walked out the exit, I caught Amber Sinclair and her mom coming in the other set of doors.

Dad saw them too. "That's not your doing."

"Maybe." But for good or bad, everyone in town knew about the reverend and Amber. Everyone whispered and judged her mom, May, for not seeing it, for not protecting her daughter from it. What would happen once Amber had the baby?

I may have brought the reverend to the light and to justice, I may have taken down the bad guy, but Principal Larry hadn't been all wrong, no matter what Serge said. I left destruction in my wake. And now, the entity I battled wasn't simply one of flesh and blood. He was supernatural and his powers were stronger than a man standing at a pulpit.

I had a duty to save Zeke and Homer, to find out if this soul-eater had my mother too. But there would be a cost to this, and I wondered who would pay it. I pulled my collar against the wind, stepped around the blond man coming in, and followed Dad into the night.

CHAPTER SIX

"**F**eeling better?" I asked Serge as I came into my room.

He nodded and muted the TV. "I can't undo the past, but I can work on the present and change the future. That's my focus. There are a lot of Mindys out there. I can do something good for them."

"I like that plan."

"But if you want to give me a hug and make me feel better—"

"I'm full of sundae, burger, and fries. Keep going and I'm going to throw it all up on you."

He laughed, then grew serious. "You know I'm just using Mindy as a place-holder. I mean anyone in trouble. Albert, John, Kia, Lonnie."

"Yeah, I know."

"Kayley, Madison, Emily—"

"What is wrong with you?"

"I don't know." He rubbed his chest. "I feel like I'm caught in a loop. Sure you don't want to give me a hug and make it all better?"

"Stop. Just stop."

He grinned.

I did too. Hard to believe when he was alive, I would've run the other way if I saw him coming. That we'd been enemies. I sat next to him. "I've been thinking."

"I thought I smelled smoke."

"Focus. The soul-eater came because of Zeke—" I spun my hands. "—But there's a good chance this thing has my mom."

"And now it's coming for you. If it has your mom, it would have her memories of you. It knows how to get you."

"Except I'm alive, and soul-eaters want ghosts. What would it do with me?"

"That's the question," he said. "Unless he was coming for me."

"Why didn't he come the day you died then?" I asked. "I don't think it's about you. I'm not even sure it's about me." I crawled on the bed. "I can't fight the feeling that there's another reason this thing is here."

"You're overthinking its motivations. It's here for you. The night we saw Rori on the road, your mom sent you a warning."

"'He's coming, Maggie, he's coming for you.'"

"Right. What if she was warning you about the soul-eater?"

"Soul-eaters come for souls. I'm still alive."

"But the soul-eater is a living person," he said. "All he has to do is kill you and your soul is up for grabs. You're a guardian-in-training which means you have powers. Plus, they're growing."

"In other words, I'd make a tasty treat."

He put his arm around me. "He won't get you, I'm here."

"Just to confirm, that's supposed to make me feel better, right?"

"You're hilarious."

"You're a guardian, too," I said. "Maybe he missed his chance when you died. Maybe he's coming for you now."

"I'm not worried."

"No?"

"I'm a man with a plan."

"Let me guess. Your plan is to toss me in front of you, then run?"

"I thought I'd kick you in the shin first, really make sure you're down before I escape."

The jokes helped, but they didn't make me feel better. "A soul-eater has taken two of our charges and now it's after me or you, or both of us."

"He's our biggest and baddest bad guy yet."

"I get that he clears the bottleneck of wandering souls, but how do the higher-ups not see the bigger picture? Why don't they take him out?"

"Maybe we're the ones they'll use to do it."

This was driving me nuts. There were too many things that didn't make sense, too many things still hidden in shadow. Now, that shadow was growing and I feared it, like the soul-eater, would consume everything it touched.

+ + +

I came out of the bathroom, rubbing the last of the lotion into my hands. A shadow flickered in the corner of my eye. I thought I heard the echo of my mother's voice as I stepped through the threshold into someone else's room—one that belonged to a small child. Blue walls, shiny white shelving, and toys stacked in precise lines. I stepped on to the lush carpet, checking for signs of life. No one was there. I turned to go back to my bathroom, but found a wall where the door had once been.

This was either the most vivid dream, ever, or I'd transported into someone else's life. Transportation wasn't part of my gifts, but considering everything happening, I supposed it wasn't out of the question. Trust my luck to end up in someone else's house and their kid's room, too.

I'd heard that pinching yourself was supposed to wake you from a dream state. Three attempts later, all I had to show for my efforts were arm bruises destined to turn purple. I tried psychically calling for Serge, but as soon as I opened my mind, I knew it was futile. The connection between us usually hummed and vibrated in a four-dimensional experience of light and sensation. Now, there was no bridge, just emptiness. Whatever was going on here, dream or reality, I was on my own.

Opening my mouth and yelling "hello!" seemed stupid and dangerous. If I had crossed time and space and ended up in someone else's house, there was no need to bring attention to myself and let the homeowners know a stranger was in their house. I doused the lights, then crept to the window and looked out.

Homes lined the streets, lazy plumes of smoke rising from their chimneys. A thick layer of snow painted the rooftops and glittered silver. Wherever I was, it wasn't Dead Falls. We hadn't had this much snow and I didn't recognize the road. And wherever I was, it had to be a big city. Only a heavily populated area could justify the giant homes I saw.

I felt in my pockets, hoping I'd left my cell in one. No luck. For a psychic chick who had tackled demons and murderers, I was as prepared for the surprises of life as a half-naked girl in a B-rated horror flick. There was no clock in the room, but the dark night suggested the family would soon be coming to bed. I considered hiding under the bed, but discounted it. Ditto with the closet. Those were the top two places a kid checked for monsters.

My only solution was to sneak to the front door and hope I didn't get attacked or shot on the way there. Maybe the parents left their phones in their coats, maybe their car keys. Either way, there were more options for escape on the main floor than in their kid's bedroom.

I cracked open the door and peered through the gap. A staircase stood to my left, the open doors of two bedrooms and a bathroom on my right. I scuttled on all fours and peeked through the railing. The stairs swept to the main floor. On its right side was the front door and the main room. Both were unoccupied. I couldn't see anything else. The house was quiet, and I hoped that meant the family was out. Staying on all fours—like somehow being low to the ground was the equivalent of being invisible—I snuck down the stairs.

So far, so good. No cats or dogs greeted my movements. The house was well made—no creaks or groans from my weight on the steps. I reached the last stair and noticed a small table on my left, complete with a purse and keys. Not so good. Someone was home. Time to find a hiding spot. I wasn't sure where the hallway led, but there was a light in the distance and common sense said to stay in the shadows. I stood, debating my options and cursing my lack of genius.

Then I heard the sound. A small shift, a quiet creak. Whoever was in the house was in the room with the light and too close for my comfort.

"Don't move."

I froze at the female voice.

"Don't even breathe," she said.

The quiet menace in her voice raised the hair on my skin. I couldn't see her in my peripheral vision. Where was she that she could see me but I couldn't see her?

"I'm tired of you not listening to me."

My heart risked a faltering beat. She wasn't talking to me. I eased the keys from her bag, then searched for a cell, with no luck.

At least I had one possible means for escape. I slipped the key ring into my pocket.

"How many times do we have to go through this?"

"But, Mommy—" The small voice of a little boy, fearful.

"I told you, pick up your toys and put them away. Care for them. I don't work hard for you to treat your toys with disrespect."

"I didn't mean to break it—"

"Don't you even think of crying."

I flinched and imagined her son doing the same.

"But I didn't mean it, Mommy."

"You never mean it."

Fear held me—I was in an unknown city, in a stranger's house, and far away from anyone who could help. But there was another feeling, one that melted my icy insides. Anger. I'd seen that kid's room. At most, he would be eight years old. Whatever toy he'd broken, whatever mistake he'd made, he didn't deserve her fury.

I recognized her tone. When he'd been alive, that was the default emotion Serge used on me. Wrath. Hate. And it always led to violence. If I was going to be arrested, so be it. No way was I going to stand in the shadows and hope she wouldn't take her anger to the next level.

I moved fast but quietly. My gaze glanced off the table. I grabbed her purse in case I needed a weapon. Some envelopes spilled out of the open compartment, and I caught her first name: Jennifer. Good. If I had to yell to catch her attention, screaming her name would be an effective way to surprise her.

Domestic violence, the abuse between people who know each other, was the deadliest, the most unpredictable. Memories of Serge in his previous incarnation filled my inner vision. The ugly twist of his mouth, the mottled red of his skin, the way he'd flex his fingers, and I would hope he wouldn't tighten them into a fist.

I hovered in the doorway, hunched close to the floor, and peered out. The mom stood in stilettos and a black pencil skirt, silk blouse, and glittering jewelry. And she loomed over her son. Small, dressed in cowboy pajamas, dark hair like his mom's. He held a toy car in one hand. In the other hand was the door to the car.

I'd had similar toys when I was small. Dad was all about cool toys, whether they were marketed to boys or girls. I remembered that brand of car. They broke all the time. After the fifth time taking it to Dad, I'd learned how to reattach the door by myself.

"Talking to you doesn't do any good," she said. "So, the time for talking is over." She grabbed a wooden spoon off the counter.

"No! Mommy!" He flung one hand out in protection, used the other to shield his face. The speed at which he did it told me this wasn't the first time Mommy had put hands on him.

If she was going to hit anyone, it was going to have to be me. I ran for them and threw out my hand to her just as she brought the weapon down. I caught the force of the handle, crying out as the pain ricocheted its way down my arm.

I pulled the spoon, but it was locked tight in her grip. Her face was rigid in a rictus of rage, but what freaked me out was that the rest of her was stuck, too. Frozen in the moment. I yelped and stumbled back. Did I do that?

I spun to the child, crouching next to his cowering form. "Hey, are you okay?"

He didn't answer but kept his face buried in the crook of his arm.

"Honey, it's okay."

The boy lifted his head.

"Hi, I'm Maggie." I went to touch his arm and found my hand passing through his body. Well, that wasn't good.

"Mommy?"

"I don't know what happened to her," I said.

He stared past me. No. He stared through me. "Mommy?"

Fear is a multifaceted thing, and this prism had me locked in five levels of hell. I flashed back to when Serge had first died and then appeared to me. How I'd pretended not to see him and taken pleasure in his terror and confusion.

I'd thought Karma was a bitch then, and I had confirmation of it now. I was cut off from anyone who could help me, lost in a house and a city that wasn't my own, facing down a violent mother and a terrified child, and no one could see me.

CHAPTER SEVEN

Light appeared behind me. Its radiance filled the space and cast forward its shadow. I turned, holding my hand up as protection, then dropped it when I realized no protection was needed. The light was from the other side, full of love and peace, and from the doorway created, a creature stepped through.

It had no face, no shape save the general form of a human outline, but I'd seen it before. The shape in my bathroom. Though its skin held the smooth sheen of a polished pearl, there was no sense of delicacy. It exuded strength. Instinct and memory of my mother's warning made me stand and step out of its way.

The boy raised his hand toward it. "Who are you?"

"My name is Serena. It's time to go, Matty."

My brain told me she wasn't speaking English but Ancient Greek. I didn't know how I knew that, let alone how I—or Matty—was able to understand her.

"Mommy's mad again. She'll be really mad if I go—" Even as he spoke, he rose and came to the creature.

It reached out to him, its form outlined in golden light, its skin catching and reflecting a rotating spectrum of color. "Come. Let us leave this place."

"I'm tired," he said.

"You won't be anymore."

He took her hand and the energy that infused Serena turned his cheeks golden and outlined him in the same yellow aura as the creature.

Serena bent to him, wrapping Matty in a hug. The light grew and intensified until I had to hold my hand to my eyes or risk blinding myself, and still it grew. I felt the heat, the cool, I felt the call of the other side and found myself stepping into it.

"Guys love strong, silent girls," said Serge. "But the mime act is annoying. It's your turn to choose what we're watching on TV and playing mute isn't going to work. So, is it a lawyer solving a murder or a doctor solving a murder? In the meantime, check this out—" He gestured to the TV. "The guy's sending an SOS with a mirror and moonlight. I love '80s television. It's like a drug trip without the drugs."

I blinked and, dropping my hand, found myself standing in the threshold of my bathroom door. Serge lay on my bed, the animals curled at his feet. He held the TV remote in his hand and was gesturing with it. "Well?"

"What just happened?"

"Are you kidding?"

"No."

He must have caught the tone in my voice because he shut off the TV. "Mags, you okay?"

I shook my head. "I don't think so. Have I been here the whole time?"

"What?"

"Did I leave the room at all?"

"No." He dragged the word out into four syllables worth of concern. Serge set down the remote and moved his hand over my cell. A flash of white light appeared in the space between the phone and his palm. He stood and came my way. "We were talking about which show to watch. I wanted a cop show but you said you wanted something lighter. I asked you to choose. You came out of the bathroom and said, 'what I really want is,' then you stopped talking and stared at me for a few seconds."

"That's it? I zoned out for a few seconds?"

"Yeah, Mags—" He took my hand and led me back to the bed. "What happened?"

Craig appeared in front of the window. "You texted?"

"That was me," said Serge. "Something's happened to Maggie."

"What?" The question had edge. He sped toward us. "What happened?"

I sat on the bed and they crouched in front of me, scanning my face as I told my story. When I finished, they sat back and looked at each other.

"Well?"

"It sounds like you're describing a serengti," said Craig. "One of the mermaids. They all call themselves Serena. It's odd this one didn't have a face—they're among the most beautiful of the supernatural creatures." He frowned. "More than odd. It's weird she's faceless."

Serge's eyebrows rose to his hairline. "Mermaids? Aren't they water-dwellers?"

"Yes," said Craig. "But supernatural creatures can exist in many forms, in many dimensions. The mermaids are protectors of children and animals, especially when the child or animal's life will end violently. It sounds like Serena came to Matty and took him. His body remained behind, its systems in play for the mother's final act, but his soul was gone, free from the trauma of his death."

"That's a little bit of good news," I said. "Serge, hand me my cell."

He did.

"The mom's name was Jennifer." I punched in the search terms: Jennifer, Matty, domestic violence. "Got it." I clicked on the first link and scanned. "Looks like Mom was convicted of his murder, life sentence. It happened in Vancouver...fifteen years ago."

"You went back in time?" asked Serge. "How is that possible?"

"Because you're a supernatural creature," said Craig. "You can exist in many times and space."

"To recap, I wasn't smart enough to give Nell a proper message from the future, but I was powerful enough to dive fifteen years into the past."

"Don't be so hard on yourself," said Craig. "Your powers are growing, which makes them unpredictable."

"But why would I have gone there?" I asked. "Is it a warning or just my powers acting up?"

"I don't know," said Craig. "You and the serengti are similar, you're both protectors. But for a serengti, their charge is the most important thing and they will protect them at any cost."

"That sounds like Maggie," said Serge.

"*Any* cost," Craig repeated. "Their morality isn't like ours, which means they have no problem crossing lines we wouldn't. Because of that, they straddle both light and dark."

"If they're all named Serena, does that mean they're female?" I asked. "I was thinking of Nell's warning—"

"He comes in the light," said Serge.

I nodded.

"A serengti begins life as a human of any gender, but once they transition, they're female."

"Besides, the mermaid isn't the one to fear," said Serge. "You wouldn't hurt a kid or an animal, and that's the only way one of them would go after you."

We talked for a little longer but got nowhere.

"I bet we could find out stuff if we went to the other side," said Serge.

"It's not a bad thought," said Craig. "Mags, I've been thinking about you and your mom. Do you know anything about her?"

I shook my head. "Dad never talks about her."

"You're saying he's been *dead quiet* about her?" Serge grinned.

"That was so bad I felt it in my teeth," I said. "But yeah, quiet as the grave. Why are you asking?"

"Since Serge and I are going to the other side, I thought we might see if we could find some information on her," said Craig.

"I thought you weren't allowed to see anything concerning me," I said.

"I'm not, but I don't like what's happening. Something terrible's going to go down and my instinct says your mom's part of it."

"I wish I could help," I said. "But I don't know her name, I don't even know what she looks like."

Craig gave me a quick kiss. "It was worth a try."

"Let's go," said Serge. "I bet we can find something."

The guys left. Sleep wouldn't come and I was alone in the dark, wondering about the connections that bind us, even when we can't see them.

CHAPTER EIGHT

Nell was waiting for me in the kitchen when I came down the next day. "Thought we could grab some Tims," she said. "I'm in the mood for a double-double. Any progress on the soul-eater?"

I caught her up on what we'd learned.

"So, you've got nothing."

"Less than nothing. I feel—"

"Stupid?"

"Thanks."

"Why waste a bunch of words when one word will do? How stupid do you feel?"

"Stop it. How am I supposed to stop this thing and free the souls, and then save my mother?"

"One thing at a time, kitten."

Dad came down the stairs. "Hi Nell, I didn't realize you were here. Did you want some coffee?"

"We're going to get some at Tims—hang on a second," I said. "Dad, didn't you let Nell in the house?"

"Nope." He went to the coffeemaker. "Just got out of the shower."

"How did you get in here?" I asked her. "Nancy's on night shift."

"One word," she said as she headed for the stairs. "Pluck. You coming or what?"

Dad raised his coffee in salute.

I grabbed my coat and bag.

"Is Casper joining us?" Nell asked.

"He's with Craig on the other side." I tucked my keys in my pocket and went outside.

Nancy was pulling into the driveway. "Hey kid," she said, after she'd parked. "Your dad around?"

"Yeah, having coffee."

"Hold up a sec." She glanced at the front door. "What happened last night?"

"What do you mean?"

"Milton Larry came down to the station, ranting and raving about your dad threatening his safety."

"That's not true," said Nell. "He threatened Mr. Johnson."

"How do you know that?" I asked.

"Pluck."

"I swear to god, Nell, you tell me that one more time—"

"It's online." Nell peeled her gloves off with her teeth. "I bookmarked it." She took out her phone and opened the video for Nancy. "Your dad is fierce. He's all polite and low-key, but check out the look on his face. He could take out Loser Larry barehanded."

"We really have to talk to your dad about his tendency to channel General Sherman every time your safety or reputation's on the line," said Nancy as she handed the phone back. "I calmed Larry down, for now. But Hank's got to lay off on challenging that lunatic."

"Good luck with all of that," I said. "Did you know Principal Larry's carrying a gun?"

"A gun? You sure?"

"Maybe a knife. He told Dad he was carrying protection."

Nancy's lip curled into a sneer. "Larry is an overgrown kid from one of the richest families in town. He doesn't need any more protection than what his parents and siblings offer. No matter what he does, he'll always be covered by them."

"And he's the principal of our school," said Nell.

"We should go," I said. "He hates me enough that if I walk into class a second late, it'll be detention."

"Be careful with Larry," she said. "That guy's wound tight, and you're the one who ended his hero."

"I'll protect her," said Nell.

"And who will protect the principal from you?" Nancy went into the house.

Nell and I headed out and drove the icy roads to Tims, then to school. Traffic was busier than usual. Even though the delay could risk me getting detention, I was happy for the extra time away.

"Your almost-mom's not wrong," said Nell. She pulled into the parking spot and left the engine running. "Loser Larry has a way of looking at you that makes my skin crawl. He hates you."

"He'll have to get in line." I sipped my coffee and reached for a chocolate Timbit.

"It's going to get worse. You haven't been to school for a couple of days, and in that time, you solved another murder. Your cred is growing and he's just a little man with an even smaller—"

"Nell."

"—Life." She took my hand. "Don't be alone with him. Even if he calls you into his office, get someone to go along. Someone who's alive. I love Casper, but he's not much help if Larry's throwing down and you need a witness to back up your story."

"Maybe he couldn't corroborate." I unbuckled my seatbelt. "But I bet if he turned solid in front of the principal that would take care of business."

Nell cut the engine. "All I'm saying is be careful."

I didn't argue, but what Nell didn't know was that the hate was mutual. Part of me wanted the principal to try something, just so I had an excuse to vent all my anger. Most of me was smart enough to stay away from anything that would put me on that tempting path. Still, I wasn't afraid. Whatever Principal Larry started, I would finish.

✦✦✦

"Maggie!" Tammy appeared in a whirlwind of flannel and floral perfume and wrapped me in a vice-grip of a hug. "I haven't seen you in ages." She pushed me away and gave me an accusatory glare. "We've been texting and texting—" She gestured to Bruce, who stood behind her. "—And you don't answer."

"My phone died." Crap and I'd forgotten to charge it.

"Everything in this town is dying," said Bruce, prying Tammy away and giving me a hug. "How are you?"

"Okay, I guess."

"I can't believe what's happening. Serge, Kent, now Rori." Tammy's eyes misted. "It's like something has it out for the kids of Dead Falls."

"Yeah," said Nell. "The adults, 'cause they're the ones behind all those deaths." She glanced down at her phone and frowned. "Nancy just texted me. She says you're supposed to call her."

I took Nell's cell and stepped away. Nancy picked up on the first ring. "What are you and Serge up to?"

"I don't understand."

"Why is he surfing police resources, looking up your dad?"

"Uh—" Crap. He must be back from the other side and following up on what he'd found out about my mom.

"Uh-huh. I just got a call from Frank, who wanted to know if I was rethinking my relationship with Hank."

"What did you say?"

"I told him it was background stuff to keep Larry happy, and he bought it."

She didn't sound super mad, which was a good thing, still... "You make the best lasagna I've ever tasted."

"Nice try. I'm not above grounding you."

"I'm sorry." I glanced over my shoulder, but no one was paying attention.

"Don't push it. Do I want to know why you're doing background checks on your father?"

"Uh, eventually, but for now, it's best if you have plausible deniability."

"Fine, but lay off on using my resources for whatever you're up to."

"Yes, ma'am. Hey, about your lasagna, that would be so good for dinner—"

"Go to class." I heard the smile in her voice as she rang off.

"Everything okay?" Nell asked when I handed her the phone.

"Some technical stuff, no big deal. What did I miss?"

"There's a lot of talk—" said Tammy.

"Gossip," said Nell.

"Talk, gossip. Everyone's freaked out about the murders and

what's going on in town. They think Dead Falls is cursed." Tammy stopped and waited for my reaction.

"Who's 'they'?"

"Kids, mainly, but a few parents," said Bruce. "That's why Tammy and I thought it would be a good idea to start a support group."

"That makes sense—" I said.

"For ghosts," said Bruce.

"—And that makes less sense," I finished.

"See what happens when you're gone," murmured Nell. "They lose whatever common sense they had."

"Face it, stuff's going down," said Bruce. "We can either bury our heads in the sand or deal with it."

Cripes. The last time Tammy and Bruce tried to help, they brought a Ouija board to my house. As soon as it was under my roof and the game had connected to the combined energy of me, Serge, and Craig, a group of poltergeists had been unleashed.

"How are you going to face ghosts?" I asked. "Or have a support group for them?"

"Don't be silly," said Bruce. "The group is for like-minded individuals who want to communicate and start friendships with those on the other side. Maybe if there's more understanding of their culture and ours, there would be less anger from the—"

"Alternate-life groups? Those on the faint end of the heartbeat spectrum?" offered Nell.

I elbowed her in the ribs. "Stop helping."

"What?" She grinned. "You haven't heard the best part."

"Best part?"

"We want you to be the president," said Tammy.

"Me? Why?"

"You're a death magnet," said Bruce, then grunted when Nell caught him in the stomach with her elbow.

"Be sensitive," she said. "Sensitive."

"I know you like the sound of that word, but I don't think you know what it means," I said to her.

"I may have said it wrong—" Bruce eyed Nell and stepped out of her range. "But face it, Maggie. Death follows you. Have you ever considered you might have psychic powers?"

Thank god I'd finished my coffee or else I'd have choked on it. "Uh—"

"We should continue this conversation later," said Nell. She pointed to some kids who stood on the outskirts. A few of them were recording us. "Somewhere private."

"How about my minivan tonight?" asked Tammy. She smiled at me. "We can get some food from the Tin Shack and hang out."

"Sounds good," I said, watching as Nell strode over to one of the kids and plucked his cell phone out of his hand.

"Hey!"

"Just checking what you're taping. Calm down."

"I have a right to record anything in a public space," he said.

"No, you don't. Cells aren't allowed to be on during school hours." She tapped on the screen.

"Don't erase it!"

Nell used her small size, dodging out of the guy's way, then spinning from his grasp. "I didn't erase anything. I did send myself some of your more interesting photos." She tossed the phone at him.

He grabbed for it, accidentally flipping the phone back at her.

Nell caught the cell and, taking his hand, pressed it into his palm. "I see you video-taping me and mine again, and those photos go straight to your momma."

He muttered something as he turned away.

"You know what you are?" I put my arm around her shoulder.

"Plucky?"

"The pluckiest. Come on, let's get to class." An eraser whizzed by our heads and slammed into the locker.

"What did I say?" In one swift move, Nell grabbed it and swung to face the kid.

He raised his hands. "Prove I did it." He turned his back on her.

She whipped it at him, hitting him square in the back of the head.

"Hey!"

"Prove she did it," I said.

He glared, but did nothing as we walked away.

I smiled at Nell, but the churning started in my stomach. This was too much like what had happened at all the other schools. Dead Falls was the place I'd managed to avoid the label of "freak," and that was in large part because of Nell.

If kids were losing their minds over me, that was fine. I'd lived through worse. But if they turned on her...I flashed her another smile as she looked my way, but the shadow was expanding, gaining weight and substance, and bringing with it bigger, badder things.

CHAPTER NINE

Bigger and badder happened two hours later. Lunchtime. My locker. Shaving cream oozed out of the vents, and the only good thing about it was that it hid the slurs written over the door in black marker.

"Those jerks," said Bruce. "When I find them—"

"Don't sweat it," I told him. "It's a locker, and it's not even mine. It's property of the school." Big words and a casual smile to cover up the sick feeling inside. A crowd of kids gathered around us. Among them, the guy from earlier. The one who had taken the video. He smirked and lifted his cell.

My raw emotions must have worked like a beacon because Serge appeared next to me. "You'd think being dead would give me a pass," he said. "But you should have heard the riot act Nancy gave me once she found me in the house."

How did she find you?

But his attention was on the locker. His face turned scarlet. "Who did this?" He swung around. "Tell me who did it and I'll grab their—"

How did she find you?

"Mags, there are bigger things to deal with right now."

I'm trying to keep it together. Look around, we have an audience. I can't cry in front of any of them.

"She texted me and asked where I was."

That almost made me smile. *Next time you're hiding from the fuzz, don't answer her texts.*

Nell and Tammy came up with Mr. Donalds, the janitor. He inspected the locker as he set down his bucket and sponges. "Never thought I'd be cleaning your locker like this, not since Serge died."

"Sorry about all the graffiti," said Serge.

That was ages ago, I told Serge. *Don't give it a second thought.* "I can clean this up," I told the janitor. "I'm sure you have other stuff to do."

Nell eyed the kid with the phone. Her mouth went into a flat line and she took a step toward him. I grabbed her arm and pulled her back. "It's not worth it," I said.

She gave me a long look but stood down. "Is it me or is it cold in here?"

"It's cold as cold can be."

She took out her phone and checked her texts for Serge's messages.

I bent down to get the rubber gloves, but the janitor stopped me.

"You have enough to deal with," Mr. Donalds said. His baby face turned pink. "I'm sorry for this. You'd think they'd be happy you found that little girl's body, and she wasn't left alone in the fields." He smiled. "Go ahead and have your lunch. I'll take care of this."

The jerk with the cell gave me a big smile, turned, and walked away as Craig came up.

Craig took in the locker, then the kid.

"Can your boyfriend cast spells?" Nell whispered.

I shrugged. "Why? You want to put a hex on the guy?"

"I think Craig's already on it." She nodded in his direction.

I turned and saw what she meant. His gaze was on the kid, and I could see his lips moving. I stood and went to him.

"Hey, you're back. What's going on?"

"Shouldn't that be my question?" he asked. "I know that guy destroyed your locker. It's all over his face."

"Everything's fine," I said. "What were you doing with that kid? Casting a spell?"

He blushed. "Hardly." He wrapped his arms around me. "I saw your locker, I saw the kid, put it together, and wanted to go nuclear." Craig's hold tightened. "But you are strong, Mags, and I'm sure me stepping in like some caveman boyfriend would be the last thing you need. You got stuff handled."

"The moving lips—?"

He laughed. "I guess I was casting a spell of sorts. I was whispering, 'Don't be a dick, Maggie will ask for help if she needs it. Don't be a dick. Don't be a dick.'"

"He's right," said Bruce. "People are being stupid, don't let it get to you."

"Easy to say, hard to do," I said. "Especially when the mob is destroying my locker."

"It's just a matter of time before they come after our stuff," said Nell. She turned to Tammy. "You might want to park outside of the lot for a while."

"No problem," she said. "Bruce and I could use the extra exercise."

I was uncertain how I felt about their casual display of loyalty. For sure, I was all for having the group support me. But giving support was a lot harder when people were chucking stuff at your head or bashing in your windows. Not for the first time, not for the last time, I wondered if it had been a wise or rash decision to make friends.

"I know what you're thinking." Serge took my hand. "But even if they bail, at least you had them for a little while."

I don't know if that makes it better.

"I'm dead and Mr. Donalds remembers me because I wrote graffiti on your locker and did my best to screw up your life. No one will ever remember me with kindness. They won't even remember me with mixed emotions."

I'm sorry for that—

"Don't be. Those were my decisions, and this is what I deserve."

It might be the consequences, but you don't deserve all the blame.

He smiled. "Want to know what I found out before Nancy shut me down?"

I nodded.

"You guys moved a lot."

I know that, smart guy.

"Yeah, but I didn't." He grinned. "I told you, I was going to tell you what I learned, not what you knew."

Is that it?

"Your dad doesn't have much of a credit history," he said. "It's not weird, but it's unusual. Do you know why?"

I shrugged. *No, is that a big deal?*

"How did he buy the funeral home in town if he didn't have money to back him up?"

Think he's a mob hitman in hiding and he got the money as a retirement gift?

"Your dad, a hitman? He cries at cute animal memes," said Serge. "I doubt he'd know which part of the gun to hold. Nancy shut me down, but I've got enough to start backtracking your life and see if I can find out anything about your mom." Serge blipped out.

The rest of lunch was uneventful. Visual arts class was first up that afternoon, and Mr. Parks was setting up a silent film when the intercom crackled and the droning voice of Principal Larry filled the room. "It has come to my attention that one of the lockers in this school has been vandalized."

All heads turned in my direction.

"This is unacceptable. Lockers are school property, and when you damage them, it costs time and money to repair. That money comes out of a tight budget—"

He went on about the lack of funding and cuts to programs, but the message was clear. The principal didn't care that I was the victim, he wasn't going to look for the culprits, and the subtext was in bold font: Maggie Johnson was a fair target, just don't mess with school property.

Mr. Parks tossed me a sympathetic smile. "I'm sure he'll come around to talking about you soon."

I doubted it.

Principal Larry prattled on when there was a sudden scuffle and muffled shouts from the intercom. Someone—the principal—cursed, then yelled, "Ow!"

"Listen, you flaccid, little meatballs—"

Nell. I was up and grabbing my books.

"Go! Go!" Mr. Parks waved me to the door.

"You're bullying Maggie because she's been at the centre of two murders, two accidental deaths, and one questionable death," said Nell.

Nell, trying to help and instead making me sound like the grim reaper.

The principal must have grabbed for the mike because there was another round of muffled thumping.

"Think it through, airheads," said Nell, as I sprinted down the hallway. "If Maggie is the angel of death, if by some weird alignment of the planets she's able to command the other side, do you really think it's a good idea to anger her?"

More scuffling, more cursing from Principal Larry.

"Behave, because unlike Loser Larry, I will be looking for you," said Nell. "And you won't like what happens when I find you." She finished the last part as I staggered through the office door. Nell smiled at me and held out the mike. "Did you want to add anything, Maggie?"

I shook my head, too out of breath to speak.

"Young lady!" Principal Larry smoothed the strands of his toupee back in place. "Your conduct is outrageous—"

I lunged for Nell and slapped my hand over her mouth, but she elbowed me in the stomach and reared on the principal.

"My conduct? My conduct?"

I grabbed for her again, but a pissed-off Nell proved faster and more agile than my winded self.

"You're supposed to be an educator. You're supposed to ignite our love of learning and sense of connection. Instead, you watch as people set us on fire to see us burn."

"She's overwrought," I wheezed, pressing the stitch in my side. As soon as I'd found Zeke, Homer, my mother, and brought the soul-eater to justice, I was getting a gym membership. "I'll take her home."

"Your friend has a good idea," he said. "Possibly the only good idea she'll ever have."

The scene flickered in my vision. For a moment, the serengti appeared beside the principal. I put a vice-grip on Nell. "Let's go."

"No! Not till I'm done."

"You're done," I told her. Then I called Serge to me.

He appeared and took in the scene. "Want me to hold him down while Nell pummels him?"

I saw Serena. She only comes when a kid's going to be hurt. Cover the principal's heart. If he makes a move to Nell, zap him.

"Or you." Serge strode to where Principal Larry stood. "He touches either one of you, and he's got a one-way ticket to the Great Beyond."

"You had a chance to stand up for Maggie and Serge, and you did nothing. Especially for Serge," said Nell. "If you'd helped him instead of licking the reverend's boots, he'd never have gone after Maggie. He'd still be here."

"That's enough." The principal's face went leather tight. "You apologize for that or you're suspended."

"I won't!"

"Let's go, Tiger," I pulled her out of the office. "Walk it off."

"Your friend can leave the grounds, Miss Johnson, or I'll call the sheriff to remove her."

"She's leaving," I said. "You don't need to call Nancy."

"Yes," he said. "But you're not. School is in session and you have a class."

"I'm not abandoning her," I said.

"Do it, or you're expelled."

Serena appeared again, flickering like a half-formed thought.

Do you see her? I asked Serge.

"No."

"Miss Johnson, make your decision."

"I'm not leaving my friend." My voice sounded like I was underwater. I felt like I was underwater. Heavy and light, both at the same time.

"This world doesn't revolve around you," he said.

"It doesn't revolve around you, either."

His face went scarlet. "Miss Johnson—"

What was going on with me? If Dad heard me disrespecting the principal like this, I'd be grounded for eternity. So why did I hear my voice saying, "You're a hateful man. I'm glad people see you for what you are and I'm glad your family's status can't protect you anymore."

He blanched.

"Maggie!" Serge grabbed my hand, and suddenly, the fog cleared.

The principal reached for his desk and pulled it open. I caught a flash of something dark, with a muzzle.

I grabbed Nell and got us out of the office before the principal went nuclear.

CHAPTER TEN

"**Y**our dad's not going to ground you for a week," Nell said as she pulled into Golden Chicken Market and did a double take at the parking lot. "What's with all the cars?"

It was a good question. The lot was almost full and most of the vehicles had rental stickers. "Maybe there's a wedding."

"If so, it must be someone important." She maneuvered the car into a spot and cut the engine.

"Time to find something to bribe my dad with before he grounds me." I unbuckled my seatbelt.

Her cell binged, and she checked the text. "Nancy says she'll look into what we say is in the principal's desk, but she figures he'll have moved the gun by the time the deputy gets there."

"Which one is she sending?"

"Andrews," said Nell.

"The adorable one with freckles? She should've sent Frank. That guy's big enough to intimidate."

She climbed out of the car. "Anyway, your dad won't ground you because one, you didn't say anything to Loser Larry that didn't need to be said, and two, you're ghost-hunting."

I got out and shut the door. The rotting scent hit me again. "They need to do something about the old mill. The smell coming off it is deadly."

"Tell me about it," said Nell. "When the wind hits just right, the stink can bring tears to your eyes." She sniffed the air. "You must have super-human smell because of your woo-woo abilities. I got nothing."

As I followed her into the store, my gaze caught a dark sedan with a blond guy inside—the same guy I'd passed leaving the Tin Shack the other night. He caught me looking and drove off. "Dad's big on respect of elders, even and especially the ones you can't stand." I swung wide of a group of customers clustered around the fresh bread. "But you're right about the ghost-hunting. He won't ground me. Worse, it'll be two weeks with no dessert."

"I'll smuggle you chocolate cake."

I caught a few of the people in the store watching me. A couple of them had their phones out. "In the meantime, let's go. I need all the help I can get when it comes to not getting a Dad glare." And that meant getting in his good books by picking up a bag of his favourite dark-roast coffee. I headed for the coffee and tea aisle, spotted the woman standing in front of the bean grinder, and came to an undignified stop.

Nell crashed into the back of me, then peered around my shoulder. "Let's go," she whispered. "We'll wait in the frozen foods—"

The woman turned and laid eyes on us.

I straightened. "Mrs. Pierson."

Nell lifted her hand.

The three of us stood there, locked in a bizarre high noon, with no bad guy and no sheriff in sight. Just a bereaved mother and two girls who had answers to her daughter's afterlife, but no way to tell her.

Mrs. Pierson stared for a long moment, then moved our way. Her gait was uneven, but her makeup and clothing were impeccable.

"Nancy Drew and crew," she said, and I smelled the traces of alcohol on her breath. "Any more murders solved?"

Nell opened her mouth and our long friendship told me she was going to offer condolences. I put my hand on her arm to stop her. Nothing we could say would make it better.

"The wonder girl, solving all the murders, walking away smelling like a rose, while the rest of us dig graves."

"I'm sorry for your loss," Nell said. "But Rori was a loss to me, too."

"She wasn't your daughter."

"She was like a little sister."

"Then you should have done a better job caring for her," said Mrs. Pierson.

That was ironic or stupid, or both.

"You should have found her sooner. Found her before I had to bury—" Her voice broke on a sob.

Instinct made me reach for her. Grief made her sink into me. She wept silently, as if the heartbreak was so great, it defied sound.

"I'm sorry," I said. "We're all hurting."

She pushed away and shook her head. "You didn't lose your husband, your daughter, your reputation. I have nothing. You don't know my hurt." A hard light came into her eyes. "Amazing how you escape. You survive the fall off the bridge, but Reverend Popov dies. You survive the push down the hill, but my daughter loses her life in a field. One day, Maggie, you will hurt like I do. One day, you'll know pain." She pushed me away.

"Give me your phone," I told Nell. When she did, I called Nancy and told her to swing by the market, that Mrs. Pierson was probably drunk and needed a ride home. Then I got the coffee for Dad.

"That was wrong of Mrs. Pierson," said Nell. "It's not your fault."

"She's hurting," I said. "I can't take it personally."

"But hoping for your pain—that's a little intense for a woman wearing cotton candy-scented lip gloss."

I had no answer and no idea how I felt about any of it. Time to change the subject. "Sure you don't want to get your dad anything to offset his straight-A daughter being suspended? We can swing it by the hospital."

"Nah," she said. "I texted him. He's busy and doesn't like to be disturbed when he's at work. Anyway, I got it handled."

"You were born having it all handled."

"You know why?"

"I swear, if you say it's because you're plucky, I'm dropping you in the nearest snowbank." I paid for the coffee and got Nell to drive me to the funeral parlour.

"It'll be fine, and that's not just me saying that." She put her hand on mine. "Rori said."

I left her and went to find Dad in his office. As I stepped inside, I caught a flash of dark. The sedan from the market, with the blond guy at the wheel, drove slowly down the road. I frowned, then dismissed the coincidence as the reality of a small town. People ran into each other all the time. Look at what happened with me, Nell, and Mrs. Pierson. I let the door shut behind me.

CHAPTER ELEVEN

"I'm not surprised." Dad handed me a cup of coffee. "It was always a matter of when, not if, Larry lost his mind with you. Are you suspended or expelled?"

"I don't know."

"Don't worry. It'll be fine. You won't be either."

"I'm not grounded or cut off from desserts?"

"I hate to admit it, but I'm tempted to give you an extra helping. That guy's such a—" He caught himself before he swore, then lifted his mug in salute. "Don't make a habit of it, though. Respect people, Maggie, even when they don't agree with you, and especially when they're being idiots. Hate and anger come from a place of powerlessness, don't give them yours."

"Am I allowed to give them something to chew on, in addition to my respect? Like maybe a knuckle sandwich for Principal Larry?"

His grin flashed. "Don't be disrespectful."

"I wouldn't have minded a suspension. I could use the days off," I said. "Trying to figure out—" I swallowed my words before I mentioned my mom and her connection to the soul-eater. "—What's going on with the entity that stole Zeke and Homer."

"I'm sure you'll figure it out."

He seemed relaxed so I took a breath and prepared to tell him about Mom. Dad cleared his throat, a sure sign he was about to say something big. I decided to let him go first. "What?"

"This thing with that horde of ghosts who had the Meagher boy—"

"The Family? What about them? Craig sent them to the other side."

"It's about the night they broke into the school." He set down his mug. "One of the guys was showing me a video—" He stopped talking and played with his cup.

"Of the Tin Shack?"

"No, the other video."

"Serge in the trunk of my car?"

He shook his head. "You haven't seen the other one?"

"You're freaking me out," I said. "What's going on? Show me the video before I lose my mind."

"Watch." Dad pulled out his phone and called it up.

I took the cell.

He leaned over and took back his cup of coffee.

The footage was surprisingly clear. Someone had recorded the town meeting the night that the ghosts had tried to take possession of the townspeople. The footage showed Principal Larry, droning on about useless crap no one cared about. His speech was interrupted by the hissing and shrieking of the microphone and speakers. By virtue of my cursed gift, I could also hear The Voice—my mother—wailing my name.

The person recording the video panned the audience, then honed in on me as The Family descended in a red haze. They separated into wisps and went after the crowd. To those with non-supernatural eyes, it would have looked like flickering lights and lightbulbs popping. The crowd, infected by the psychic energy and sick on paranoia, screamed, surged, and ran for cover.

"The guys here say it's become a virus," Dad said.

"You mean viral." There were too many people that night, too many with their phones out for me to know who was behind this video. But their hand was steady. Amidst all the confusion, they recorded like a professional, and I wasn't sure how I felt about that.

"Virus, contagious, viral. Whatever," he said. "Look at the title of the video. They're convinced our town is cursed by spirits and haunted by ghosts, and that you're at the centre of it all."

"They're not that wrong," I said. "We've had more murders in the past few months than in the last twenty years, and I've been in the middle of all of them."

"Whoever this TruthOuts45 is, he's posted it as proof that ghosts exist. The comment section is…well, it's disturbing," said Dad. "There a lot of moles out there."

"Do you mean trolls?"

"Who are the disgusting pieces of flesh that post cruel comments?"

"Trolls."

"Then trolls. There are a lot of troll comments. Some people are really angry. They think you and whoever took the video did it as a prank, but there's a fair number of people buying what this TruthOuts45 is saying." Dad paused the video. "I've already been fielding calls from news outlets in the big cities. They want to know more. They want you."

"Famine, war, and melting snow caps, and the news outlets want to turn our town into a sideshow."

"Not the town, my girl. You."

"What are you talking about? The entire town's in the video." But even as I said it, I was thinking about the rental cars at the market, about the unfamiliar faces in the bread aisle, the people with their phones out and their attention on me.

"But you're at the centre, you're the focus of the shot."

"Maybe I'm the only one that TruthOuts45 could track ."

Dad pushed the phone at me and started the video, again. "Look closely. The reporters are coming for you."

I squinted and hovered over the screen. Partway through the video and I still didn't see what he did. "I'm lost." I paused it. "What is it that sets me apart?"

Dad hit the play button. "Look at your face. Then look at everyone else's."

"I don't see it? Am I glowing? Is there an aura?"

"No, honey," he said. "It's your expression. People are panicking. They're screaming and running. Not you. You look—"

"Like I know what's going on," I said. "I'm too calm."

He shut off the video. "I've done my best to protect you. You're almost a legal adult, but I've never treated you like a child. If you want to face the coming media storm, then I'll support you. But as your dad, I'm telling you, this is dangerous. The more the world knows about you, the more the crazies can find you. People are either going to learn about your gift, then hound you for the secret knowledge you possess or they'll persecute you for having an ability they fear. Those who don't believe your gift will use this video to vilify you for perpetrating a prank that could have caused serious injuries and traumatized spectators." He fiddled with his phone. "I think the three of us—four, where's Serge?"

"Home."

"You, me, Nancy, and Serge should get out of town for a while, go on vacation. Maybe Craig should come, too. Take the supernatural population of Dead Falls down a notch for a while."

"Nell will want to come too," I said. "It'll be a caravan."

Dad took off his glasses and rubbed his eyes. "This is your decision. We have to protect you and your gift. Once the media puts your face and name together and starts backtracking your life..."

He didn't need to finish because I knew what would happen. My secret would be outed. For sure, there would be questions about the weird things that followed me. Questions about the sudden, midnight moves. Oh, cripes, and the sausage incident.

"There are crazy people out there," he said. "I don't want them to find you."

The crazy had already found me, though Dad didn't know all of it, yet. The soul-eater was out there. So was the blond guy following me from the market to the funeral home. This town was small and the mix of supernatural and mortal was dangerous. If there was a confrontation, the damage would be catastrophic. "We should go, at least for a few days."

"You'll talk to Craig and I can talk to Nell's folks—"

"No," I said. "Let me."

"They're more likely to let her come if they get the invite from an adult—"

"I don't want her to come."

He didn't need to ask for an explanation, the surprise on his face asked for him.

"There's a spirit hunting ghosts," I said. "The less people I have to keep track of, the better."

"But if this thing is going after the dead, what's the issue with Nell? She's alive."

"She'll want to help. I can't risk her life, no matter how plucky she thinks she is."

"You don't want Nell with you?" Dad leaned back, then forward. "The girl is a five-star general in a cashmere sweater. What are you not telling me?"

Everything, including news about your ex-wife. "Nothing. This thing is dangerous, and it might have the ability to mess with the living. You're my dad, you've lived this with me. Nancy's a cop. She's got training. Nell's as mortal as mortal can be. Besides, there's heat coming down on me already. It might be good for her to not associate with me for a bit."

Dad nodded. "I understand." He refilled his coffee. "I talked to an old friend in Florida. He's going to help." Dad flashed a quick smile. "I went ahead and planned, in case you were onboard with a sudden vacation. Nancy and I have some last-minute loose ends to tie up. I think you should go ahead. Gregory will meet you at the airport, it's all arranged—"

"Who's Gregory?"

"A friend. He's going to help."

"Why have I never heard of him until now?"

Dad smiled. "Because we spend most of our time dodging poltergeists and jumping out of the way of flying flatware."

"Really, how did I not know about this guy until now? Am I a terrible daughter?"

He came around the desk and hugged me. "He's not someone I talk about, and you're the best. I'd rather focus on your life than mine, anyway."

He spoke with love, but his words hit hard. Dad's life revolved around me. No surprise he didn't have time to talk about his old friends, let alone visit them. Once this thing was over, I was going to make sure he had a life, one that didn't involve worrying over his daughter.

"He has a condo in Miami. It's the perfect place to lay low. You go with Craig and Serge," said Dad. "We'll follow." He stood. "I'd like you to get going as soon as you can. Pack tonight, then head out tomorrow morning."

"That's sudden—"

"The reporters are coming, and god knows what else. I need you to get away from here, fast."

I nodded, thinking of the guy in the sedan.

He handed me the keys to his van and I headed home. Paranoia had me checking the rearview mirror, then switching streets and routes when I spotted the blond guy in the sedan behind me. He turned off on Parsons Avenue.

I looped the streets then headed home. As I shut the car door and headed up the driveway, I heard a voice behind me.

CHAPTER TWELVE

"That was a lot of maneuvering for a simple ride home." The man stood on the pavement, watching me.

"Who are you?"

"Carl Reid." He started up the driveway.

"Mister, I asked for your name. I didn't invite you to come closer."

He stopped, smiling as though my warning was adorable.

"Why are you following me?" I scanned for his car. Nice trick. He'd parked on a neighbour's driveway and used their truck to partially hide his vehicle.

"Who says I am?"

"I do."

"My car? You must be mistaken. There are a lot of cars like mine on the road."

"I saw you a couple of days ago. You were also at the Tin Shack," I said. "You were there the night me and my dad went in for a sundae. Earlier today, you were at the market, then the funeral home."

"You must be mistaken. I was never there." He started up the drive.

"I'm a lot of things, but I'm no liar. Get back or I call the cops, Carl."

My anxiety seemed to amuse him. He smiled and said, "I have a few questions. Once you answer them, I'll be on my way."

"And I have great lung capacity. Want to see what happens when I start screaming, and my neighbours come out to find you with me? This town is friendly, but they don't like strangers and they don't like strange adults with their children." Big talk. It was a roll of the dice if the neighbours would hear, let alone help.

He held up his hands in a surrender gesture and walked backward. "I've been tracking this story, Maggie, I've been tracking you, and you can't run and hide forever. This isn't like the time in Calgary. Or Vancouver. Or Victoria."

I grew colder with every city he mentioned and more fearful of this stranger who'd tracked my life.

"Your past is catching up with you. So are your actions. Yours and your dad's."

"I don't know what you're talking about."

"Sure you do. I see it on your face. You have abilities. You have a power the world could use."

My brain froze, my mind went blank, unable to think of a comeback.

"You owe it to the living to show them the world of the dead."

That thawed my brain. "I don't owe anyone anything, least of all you. Go away before I call the cops."

"Maggie—"

An SUV drove by and slowed, then came to a stop in front of my house.

"Next time." Carl turned and went back to his car.

A red-headed woman got out of the SUV. "Maggie Johnson? My name is Rachel Ambury. I'm with the *Toronto Gazette* and I wondered if I could ask you a few questions."

I walked in the house and closed the door, but watched them through the side window. Rachel went over and tapped on Carl's car window. He drove off. After a minute, so did she.

Once I'd made sure neither of them was coming back, I locked myself inside. Then I forced myself away from fear. Being scared wasn't going to solve anything. I had to divide up my priorities. There was packing, figuring out how to tell Nell that she wasn't invited, and coming up with a plan to defeat the soul-eater, then my mother. First thing, pack. It would give me time to calm down.

No, wait. First thing, text Craig and tell him what was going on. I plugged in my phone and shot him a message. Rather than texting back, he appeared in my room. By the time I finished explaining everything, my hands had stopped shaking.

"Your dad's right," he said. "You have to get out of here. I don't know what's worse, the reporter or the serengti stalking you—"

"I'm more frightened of the reporter."

"Me too," he said. "The serengti is probably bonding with you because it perceives a common thread, that you're both protectors over the living. But the reporter—" He moved away from me. "I don't like this."

I waited for him to continue, but he stared out the window. "Craig?"

"I have to make a decision," he said, turning to me. "But there's no good choice."

"What are you talking about?"

"If I stay here, to help with the reporter and the serengti, I can protect you," he said. "But I won't have any answers about *why* any of this is happening."

"Option two?"

"Go to the other side, break the rules, and get answers." He watched me. "But it leaves you and Serge alone, and it leaves me vulnerable if I'm caught."

"How vulnerable? What will the higher-ups do if they catch you?"

He shrugged. "Something little, something big. I'm not worried about myself. Being a ferrier is a multi-lifetime job."

"We're safer if you stay, but the danger for everyone is greater if you do," I said. "We need answers." I took his hand. "You *should* go to the other side, but I don't like the idea of putting you in a bad spot with your handlers."

He wrapped his arms around me and gave me a kiss.

"What is the right answer?" I asked when he pulled away.

"Sometimes there are none," he said. "Sometimes we make a decision, then we make it right."

"I'm okay risking big," I said. "But not with your supernatural life."

"My life and destiny are mine to risk." He stepped back. "Getting some answers is more important than anything the future might hold. If you need me, send Serge, okay?"

I nodded. Craig kissed me once more, then he disappeared.

I stepped from my room and found I was no longer in my room.

Of all the crappy timing. I was in a locker room—the boys' one, judging by the smell of dirty socks and ripe cheese.

"Look, it's the freak."

The deep voice sounded at the same time its owner rounded the corner. A large guy with red hair, wearing a hoodie and a mean-ugly expression.

I glanced behind me and he laughed. "The freak doesn't know he's a freak."

Two guys came up and flanked him. I stepped back, slipped, and put out my hand to catch my balance. My white hand. I tried to snatch it back and give myself a quick once over, but the body wouldn't respond. I was possessed by someone else, or maybe I was possessing him. Either way, I had no control over what was happening to me. The kid I was in looked down.

I was a guy. Skinny, barely any hair on my chest, but thankfully, a towel wrapped around my hips. "Look." My voice was high, squeaky. "I don't want any trouble."

"We're not going to give you any trouble." The redhead smiled. "The bell's going to go soon, and you seem like you're running behind. Thought we'd help you get clean."

"I'm fine," said the body's owner. "I just got out of the shower."

"Maybe, but you still smell of freak."

"Leave me alone, okay? I didn't do anything to you!"

Their hands were on me before I even registered they'd moved. One of them ripped off my towel, the others grabbed my arms and hauled me backward. I bore down and lurched forward. When that didn't work, I kicked the guy in front of me. Hard. In the crotch. He howled, clutched himself, and pitched forward. The redhead's fist came up, hurtling my way.

Then it froze.

Just like last time. They were locked in the moment. I wrenched free, stumbling toward the light that beamed in.

"Zach, my name is Serena. I'm here to take you away from this pain and torment."

The same serengti, but this time, the creature sounded tired.

"What am I doing here?" I asked, but trapped in the body and consciousness of Zach, heard him ask, "What are you doing here?"

"This life has been torture for you," said Serena. "I'm here to take you away from it." She took my—his—hand, and tugged. His soul broke from the body, the sound and sensation like strips of Velcro being released. They moved toward the light, but I sensed an anger simmering in Serena, especially when she looked back at the bullies frozen in their rage. She pulled Zach's hand once more, and we stepped into the light.

CHAPTER THIRTEEN

"**Y**ou're doing it again," said Serge, snapping his fingers in front of my face.

He came into sharp clarity—blue eyes, freckles—along with the comfortable mess of my room. I swallowed a sob and threw my arms around him. "I'm so glad you're back."

"Whoa, Mags." He held tight. "What's going on?"

"It happened again—I was pulled into Serena's world."

"Are you okay?"

"I'm freaked out that this thing can pull me into its world so easily. This time it was a kid named Zach."

"Are you okay?" He pulled away and made eye contact. "Are you?"

I shook my head. "There's too much happening. My mom, the soul-eater, Screna, all the crap going down with the townspeople. And why is Serena beaming me into scenes with those kids, with Matty and Zach? Is it related to the soul-eater? Is it just random, or is it some other thing I have to deal with?"

"*We* have to deal with. Take a breath. Tell me what happened just now."

"Zach was at school. It must have been right after gym class, because he'd had a shower and was in the locker room. I don't know where it was, but their mascot's a knight." I had to pack. I had to catch Serge up on everything he'd missed. I had to talk to Dad about Mom. I had to figure out Matty and Zach. There were too many things I had to do and not enough time to do any of them.

"You look pale, which is saying a lot."

"I was in his body and mind. God, Serge, he was so scared of those guys."

"Sit down. Take a minute."

I grabbed my tablet and started searching. "The main bully's hair was from the '90s. Plus, I know the mascot. I bet I can find him."

"You can look for him later."

"If it's connected, then we need to get the information before I forget the details." Several search terms later, I had what I wanted. "Zach Bryant, seventeen, drowned by a pack of bullies. It happened in 1998."

"Didn't you say they were in a locker room? How do you drown in one of those?"

I scanned the article. "They held him under the shower head, with the water on full power. According to this, he struggled and in the fight, they either dropped him on the ground, or they smashed his head into the wall. He lost consciousness, they left him under the water, and he drowned." I shoved the tablet aside.

Serge lay on the bed and covered his face with his hands.

"What?"

"I feel sick."

"Like a group of errant souls is looking to add you to their mix, or maybe just one super bad guy who's still living?"

"This isn't about The Family or the soul-eater," he said. "This is about that poor kid drowning." He uncovered his face. "This is about all those years I was the bully. All those times I got off on hurting people."

"But you don't anymore," I said. "And you're on another team, one that steps in to help."

"I guess." He sighed. "It still makes me feel sick." He rubbed his face. "Speaking of which, do you have any cuts on your skin?"

"That was an abrupt topic change—wait, is this another set up for one of your juvenile boob jokes?"

"I don't know what hurts more," he said. "That you think I'd joke about your safety, or that I'd joke about boobs."

"No cuts."

"For sure?"

"Promise," I said. "Why?"

"When you were battling the soul-eater, Craig said not to let any of them touch you. I wondered if maybe it had."

"Hold on." I went to the bathroom, stripped down, and checked my body. When I came back, I said, "Nope. Nothing."

"Too bad. I asked Craig about why there shouldn't be contact. He said the soul-eater could track you through your blood, like a homing device."

"I'm fine."

"Seems like it."

"Why don't you sound happy about it?"

He sat back. "Because if it had been a soul-eater tracking you, we could have bled it out of you. And it might have explained you jumping around with the serengti. Like maybe the tracking makes you glow like a runway and the serengti found you that way. But if Craig's right, and this is really about a growth of power and this thing connecting to you because of your mom, then we're in a ton of trouble. Your powers are unpredictable. Plus, whenever the serengti takes you on the field trips, you go to places I can't follow."

"I'll get a handle on my powers, in time."

"We don't have time," he said. "If you're stepping through doorways and walking into the past, then what happens if we're in the middle of a fight and you blip into another moment?"

"So far it's only happened when I'm literally walking through a door. As long as we keep the fights away from doorways, we're fine. You think the soul-eater will meet us in the alley for the big rumble?"

"It's not funny."

"C'mon, it's a little funny," I said. "And we need all the funny we can get, 'cause the living world is freaking me out."

"The afterworld is no picnic, either. Do you think there's a connection between the serengti and the soul-eater?" he asked.

"I've been wondering the same thing, but I don't think so."

"The soul-eater can mimic different energies, right? Do you think he can pretend to be Serena?"

I shook my head. "No, they're definitely separate entities. Serena's emotional. I didn't feel anything from the soul-eater except a desire for power."

"Too bad," he sighed. "It would have been great to take out both of them with one action."

"You and I don't have that kind of luck," I said.

"It feels like things are spiraling down."

"It gets better, or worse, depending on how you look at it." I updated him on Craig, my conversation with Dad about the video, and the trip to Florida.

"You're right not to involve Nell," he said. "But you know she's going to kill you when she finds out you cut her from this."

"I'd rather have her mad forever than dead for all eternity."

"What are you going to tell her?"

"Nothing. I'm going to wait until I'm in Florida, then text. She can't kill me if I'm hiding in another country."

"It's Nell. She can do almost anything."

"Don't remind me." I stood. "Time to get packing."

"Did you talk to Hank about your mom?"

I shook my head. "It all got turned around so fast, and he was so worried about me being outed, I got caught up in his emotion." I caught the thoughtful look on Serge's face. "What?"

"Do you think mimicking energy is as simple as that? Getting caught up in emotion?"

I shrugged. "I've never tried to match anyone before."

He held out his hand. The TV turned on. Stretching out his other hand, he shut off the laptop. "Craig had me practise centring myself. I bet it could work for you and help with your powers. Take my hand."

I did.

"Now, close your eyes and focus on me."

I repeated his name in my mind. Calmed my breathing. He always felt solid and warm to me, but now, he felt bigger and warmer. The scent of him surrounded me, like the earth after a fall of rain.

Then I sensed it, saw it. Behind my closed lids, an electric rope of colour and light, twisting and turning on itself. In my mind's eye, I reached out and touched it. My fingers slid into it. "Can you feel that?"

"Yeah."

So weird. So weird to be so connected with a guy who'd spent his life hating me, and his afterlife protecting me. The rope in my fingers flickered, thinned. I panicked and grabbed for it.

"Ow!"

My eyes snapped open.

Serge held the side of his torso. "That hurt."

"Sorry, I was losing the connection and grabbed for it."

He grinned. "I guess guys aren't the only ones with performance anxiety."

"Ha ha."

"You know what this means?"

"I think so, but I'd like to hear what you think," I said. "Why don't you explain it back, so we can make sure we're on the same page?"

He sighed, exasperated. "If you can learn how to hide in my energy, then it's another level of protection. Plus, if the soul-eater can hide in other energies, maybe there's a way to track it."

"If there was, you'd think the higher-ups on the other side would've figured it out by now. Face it, looking for the soul-eater will be like trying to find a needle in a haystack. Wait," I corrected myself. "That would actually be easy to do. You'd bring a magnet. Finding this guy is more like finding a needle in a haystack of needles."

He swore.

"It was a nice thought." I put my hand on his shoulder. "But it was never going to work."

"I'm trying not to freak out about everything," he said. "Could you not harsh my buzz with the truth?"

"Hiding in your energy—it's like I'll be invisible," I said. "And if I hide in your energy, and you hide in my energy, the soul-eater will be too confused to find us."

"If we do it right, then your dad won't find us, either. No more having to unload the dishwasher or clean the bathrooms."

"We'll be rebels, riders on the ectoplasmic storm." I looked at him. "Better?"

"Much."

"Good. I'm going to get packing."

"I'll help," he said, with a lecherous wiggle of his eyebrows. "We should start with your unmentionables, which I'm more than happy to mention."

I rolled my eyes and punched his shoulder. Secretly, his words made me happy. If he was relaxed enough to make stupid jokes, then it couldn't be all bad. I headed to the bathroom to grab my shower stuff. After a quick hesitation at the doorway, I stepped through.

And found myself still in my house, in the bathroom.

Tightness eased from my chest. Maybe this was a sign. Maybe things were finally going to start untangling themselves and I'd get the answers I needed, soon.

CHAPTER FOURTEEN

The next morning, I woke to the bing of my cell, puffy eyes, and a pounding headache. Fumbling in the near dark, I groped for the phone. It was a text from Nell.

REMEMBER WHAT RORI SAID. IT WILL ALL WORK OUT.

Coming into the kitchen, I saw Dad and Nancy sitting at the table. Dad rose and wrapped me in a hug.

"Did you tell Nell anything?" I asked. "Because she sent me an odd text."

"I didn't give you away," said Dad.

"She phoned me," said Nancy. "I ducked her call. Then she stopped by the station. That girl's a pint-sized bloodhound. I thought she was going to throw me in a headlock, but I didn't give anything away, either."

"You carry a gun and a taser," I said. "And you have a hundred years of being a cop."

"Careful on calling me old," she warned.

"I'm not worried," I told her. "If you can't take on Nell, I'm safe."

"I never said anything about using traditional weaponry. I'm just saying it's in your best interest to remember who cooks." She glanced at Dad. "And who could be cooking. Remember that the next time you want lasagna."

"Hey!" He put his hand over his heart. "I can cook."

"Didn't you once burn water?" she asked.

"I didn't burn—Maggie was grappling with a ghost that had an unusual phobia—"

Nancy turned my way.

"Allodoxaphobia," I said. "The fear of opinions. She veered toward poltergeist when I tried to tell her she needed to move on."

"How did you transition her?"

"I started yelling, 'is that really—? It can't be! I can't believe they're here!'" I plucked a grape off Dad's plate. "She saw her mom and moved on."

"And the water in the pot boiled over," said Dad. "It did not burn."

"Still," I said to Nancy. "Your threat is made, and I apologize, even though I wasn't calling you old. I only meant you had extensive experience." I reached for a crepe. "Even if you're scared of Nell."

Nancy moved the plate out of my way. "Big talk from the girl who won't tell Nell what's going down."

"I'm not scared of her. I'm terrified, and I'm okay with that."

"Way to own your truth and be accountable to yourself," said Dad.

And that made me think of the secret I was keeping from him about my mother. "There's something I need to tell you."

"Is this about your cell?" His eyes went wide behind his metal frames. "Geez, Maggie, tell me you didn't wreck another phone!"

"First of all, no, and second, at a time like this, you're really worrying about my cell?"

"If your supernatural gifts included knowing the winning lotto numbers, I wouldn't have to worry."

"It's not about the phone."

"Then what is it?"

"It's about my mom."

He stared at me from over his cup of coffee.

"What?"

"I wish it was about the phone." He set down his mug.

"I have to tell you—we have to talk about her."

"Is your phone working?"

"Yes, that's not the—" I noticed Nancy rising from her chair. "You don't have to leave."

"This is family stuff."

"Which is why you should be here," I said. It took a second for the words to register, and another second for her to process what I'd said.

Then she was out of her chair, holding me tight to her. The wool of her sweater tickled my nose. The scent of baking and her soap undid my heart.

"You're my family too, kid. I'm so proud of you, I know you're going to do big, amazing—"

"I swear to god, I'm barely keeping it together. If you make me cry—"

She gently pushed me away. I turned back to Dad.

"Those phones are expensive," he said.

"Are you still riding me about that? Oh, wait, you're deflecting."

"I'm not sure that's the word for it."

"There's another word," I said. "But saying it will get me grounded. We have to deal with what's coming, and that means acting like adults."

"Don't talk to me about being an adult," Dad said. "I pay my bills. And yours. Like the phone—"

"Dad!"

"Go easy on me," he said. "Deflecting is harder than it looks."

"What's going on?" Serge came into the kitchen.

Dad read his text, opened his mouth, and I raised my hand. "We're not playing this little game."

"He asked for an update—"

"Which I'll give him, later," I said. "In the meantime, we need to talk about Mom."

Serge sat down.

"It's not fair I don't tell you about her," said Dad. "But it's too painful. Your mom made her decision when you were born and she was—"

"She's dead."

He stilled. "What?"

"She's dead."

"Did she—" He hesitated. "—Did she come to you?"

"Sort of..." Now it was my turn to hesitate. "She's The Voice."

Nancy choked down the food in her mouth. "She's the what? That thing that almost killed you when you were trying to solve Serge's murder? And the thing that knocked you down the hill when Kent died is your mother?"

I nodded.

She made the sign of the cross against her body. "I gotta get to confession and ask forgiveness for thinking my mother was bad."

"Are you sure?" Dad asked. "I knew your mom and she was kind, loving—"

I reached over, took his hand. "She's in a really bad place."

"What are you going to do about it?" he asked. "Are you sure she's—" He couldn't finish.

"I don't know how she died, but it was horrible."

Dad turned away, but I saw the pain on his face.

"We have to help her," said Serge.

Both Dad and Nancy checked their texts.

"It sounds like the right thing to do," said Dad. "But you don't know what you're stepping into."

"If it was you or Nancy on the other side, I wouldn't hesitate." I didn't tell him the other part, that guilt was a giant motivation for me. I hated that the resentment I'd felt towards my mom had been based on the only fact I had: she'd left me when I was a baby.

"Maybe there's a good reason you're hesitating," said Nancy.

"Nancy's right," said Dad. "I don't like what your mom's... become...but if you're right about how she died, no good is coming from you trying to find out. What if it was gang related? What if she saw a crime? You start asking around and who knows what's going to crawl out from the dark."

"Bad things, but I can't leave her."

"When she left," Dad said. "I promised her I would take care of you. I promised her I would be all you needed so you would never want to look for her—"

"That's crazy," I said. "Every kid is going to wonder about who their parents are. How am I any different?"

"She had to leave, it was the right thing for her—"

"Why would she even put that on you—being enough so I would never look for her? And what about her? Wouldn't she want to know how I was doing?"

"She trusted I would take care of you. I'm sorry she's in a bad place, but you need to leave her alone," Dad said. "If the roles were reversed, I'd rather live in torment than think I'd put you in any kind of danger."

It didn't feel right, but I'd just turned his world sideways. Maybe he'd come on board after he'd had time to think. "Maybe I can't find her, okay, but the soul-eater is coming after Serge and me. My powers come from her side. If I could talk to an aunt or uncle…"

"She was an only child."

"Parents?"

"Dead."

"I know when you're lying."

He held up his hands. "Probably dead."

"Maybe not as dead as you think. Anyway, she had to have some other family. Even if I can't have a moment with Grandma and Grandpa, I can—"

"No, Maggie," he said. "Leave it."

"But they have answers."

"You've never needed them before."

"The soul-eater might have her," I said. "And it's torturing her."

Dad's face went ashen. "I'm sorry for that. We'll figure this out in time."

"We don't have time," I said. "Bad things are coming for us, and my mother's family might have the answer. Serge and I can end the soul-eater. The souls deserve their freedom."

Dad stood. "I made a promise, and promises don't stop, even in death. She said take care of you, protect you, and I will."

"I'm sure she didn't think her life would end the way it did." Nancy held out her hand to both of us. "Maybe there's room to—"

"No," said Dad. "This conversation is over, Maggie."

And it fell into place, her not asking for updates, Dad not wanting me to look for her. "She never wanted me, did she? That's why you don't want me talking to her family, because they'd tell me that, wouldn't they?"

"No, my girl, that's not true."

"That's why she left, that's why she made you promise not to let me look for her."

"It's not like that—"

That's not what his face said.

"You're lying. Don't lie to me."

"It's not that your mom didn't want you. It's just that your birth… complicated things for her."

A complication. For her. Not him. Just her. I stood, pressing my hand on the table to hold balance. "I'm going to my room."

"It's coming out wrong," he said. "Your mom loved you."

I waved down his words and mumbled some nonsense about wanting to get on the road because of early sunsets. A quick shower, then I was pulling on my clothes and not caring about how the fleece-lined sweater stuck to my wet skin.

"Maggie?" Dad knocked at the bedroom door.

"Did she want me or not?" I swung it open.

"Her family wasn't going to be happy about it," he said. "But she wanted you. If she didn't care, why would she keep an eye on you all these years?"

"The other side has a way of clearing the brain."

"I don't know what to do," said Dad as he came into my room. "Your mom had her reasons for making me promise what I promised."

"Like she had her reasons for not wanting me?"

He sighed as he sat on the bed. "That's not the full truth."

I waited.

"Your mom was the one with the power. She struggled with it all of her life."

"Her parents couldn't help?"

"They didn't have the abilities she did, and their religious beliefs told them to fear her and her gifts. She learned, young, to hide them." His smile was brief.

This was the most he'd ever talked about her. I kept quiet, unwilling to break the fragile space between us.

"You are so much like her. Every time you speak, every time I see you." He took my hand. "You are everything that was beautiful and good about your mom."

Tears blurred my vision.

"Your mom became powerful, but it came at a cost. It wasn't just about the souls. It was about the living. She was able to see people in all the ways they were, all the ways they could be. It began to destroy her." He squeezed my fingers. "Then you came along. She sensed you would be even more powerful than she was."

"And she left?"

"Her abilities were tearing her apart. She tried medication, meditation—nothing was working. She could no longer tell what was true reality and what was possible." He went silent and for a while, I thought he wouldn't say anymore.

"She asked me to care for you, asked that I wouldn't tell you anything about her—"

"Why?"

"She didn't want you to look for her, and she didn't want her family making you feel as though there was anything wrong with you." Dad let go of my hand.

"I'd rather she had stayed, even if she was troubled."

"She left to keep you safe, and I made a million promises to her to protect you. This is as much as I can tell you without feeling like I've violated everything she and I were to each other."

"But bad things are coming and she's trapped. Maybe her family changed how it felt about psychics once she left. There's no way Mom was the only one with abilities. There might be a sister or someone who can help me."

"Let me think on it," he said.

"That usually means no."

"Not this time. I have to be careful," he said. "She's gone from this world. I have no way to talk to her and make her understand any of the decisions I've made."

"But, Dad—"

"I know." He raised his hand as he stood. "But this is more than you and me. This is her and me, and a lifetime of love and trust that was between us. Give me some time."

I wanted to point out he'd had seventeen years, but that seemed snarky. So, I nodded.

He kissed my forehead and left.

I grabbed my stuff and headed downstairs.

"You have everything you need?" Nancy asked. "Clothes, toothbrush, emergency credit card, phone?"

I nodded.

She handed me a cell, then another. "To hold you until we get there."

"It should be tomorrow or the day after," said Dad. "Gregory will meet you at the airport."

"Don't talk to any strangers, ghosts, or—"

"Dad." I took his hand. "I've got this. We've got this."

Tears misted his eyes. "I don't think we've ever been apart."

"And we never will be," I said. "It's you and me, against the world."

He hugged me tight. "Stay safe, my girl."

Serge came in through the front door. "I really like messing with electronics. I warmed up your car."

I grabbed my stuff. "Thanks."

"Not that you need it," he said.

"Why? It's freezing." I opened the door and came face to face with Nell.

"I've got all the gear stowed in my trunk," she said. "We can swing by Tims on the way out of town." She grabbed my bag and headed to her vehicle.

I spun to face Nancy and Dad. "You told her?"

"I didn't say a word," said Dad.

"Me either." Nancy raised her hands.

"Hey!" I called after Nell. "What makes you think I'm letting you come?"

She smiled. "First, you're not letting me do anything. And second, I do what I want. You know why?"

"I'm terrified to ask."

"Because I'm plucky. Let's go."

"Is there any use in arguing with you?"

"It's a chance to exercise your lungs."

"What about your dad and mom?"

"They're fine," she said.

"You don't even know where we're going."

She pulled out a credit card. "I'm sure they'll take plastic."

"This is dangerous," I said.

"And Rori said not to be afraid and that everything would work out. Have faith."

"Nell, no." I glanced back at Dad and Nancy, who watched, waiting to step in. Dad pulled out his phone, pointed at it—code that he was phoning her folks—then turned away.

"This is dangerous," I repeated.

"You can join me," said Nell. "Or I can track you. Either way, you need a team, and I'm part of it."

"Her dad says it's fine." Dad came to the head of the stairs.

"So? Tell her she can't go," I said.

"You tell her."

Nell smiled.

He shrugged. "I can't stop her if her dad won't. Besides, it might not be a bad idea to have—"

"Some muscle on board?" asked Nell.

"—A friend," finished Dad.

"How is that possible?" I asked her. "How can he just let you do this?"

"How does your dad let you do what you do?"

"I have powers."

"And I'm plucky."

"Nell—"

"You're my best friend, Maggie. Where you go, I go."

"Nell—" The look on her face stopped my lecture. "Come on, let's go."

CHAPTER FIFTEEN

Nell stopped at Tims and got us a box of Timbits and coffee to go. I tried to pay, but she shut me down with a look scalding enough to leave third-degree burns.

"You need to conserve your energy," she said.

"Money's not energy."

"You never know when you might have to get a disguise." She handed me a cup of coffee. "Something that's a little less hobo chic."

We drove to the Edmonton airport. A twenty-minute line-up to get through customs and security, a thirty-minute delay because my passport wouldn't register properly on their computers, a fifteen-minute talk with a customs guy who was big and stern enough to make me feel like a toddler, another ten-minute conversation with another giant customs guy to get clearance, a three-hour wait for the plane to arrive, then we were in flight. I tried to concentrate on the movies and, when that failed, tried to lose myself in a book, but the questions kept rising. By the time we landed, I was mentally exhausted.

"Ladies and gentlemen." The captain's voice came over the intercom. "We're just having a brief discussion with the tower. We apologize for the delay, and promise to have you on the skyway, shortly."

Shortly turned out to be a ten-minute wait.

"I wonder what's going on," said Nell, craning her head to see above the headrest.

"Probably just problems with the hydraulics of the skyway," said the guy next to us. "It happens a lot."

"Too bad they don't let us use the slide," said Nell.

"Mags." Serge knelt beside me.

"Nell, turn on your phone, and see if we missed any messages," I said.

"Okay, but we'll probably get better reception in the airport."

"Turn it on." I jerked my head to the side. "I feel like there might be something coming through."

"Oh?" Her gaze flicked to the empty aisle. "Oh."

Once she'd turned it on, I opened the mental bridge between Serge and me. *What's going on?* I bent forward and played around with the items in my bag.

"I don't know, exactly, but something bad," he said. "The cops showed up at the house. And by showed up, I mean they broke into the house."

Nell's cell binged and she read the text.

What cops?

"Frank and the other one, Maureen. They came in, and I heard them talking, saying they had to find you." The freckles stood out on his skin. "I don't know why they'd just barge in like that, but they grabbed Nancy's go bag and were talking about her going to Edmonton—"

The whirr of the airplane door halted his conversation.

There was a problem with my passport.

"You don't think you have the same name as someone wanted by the FBI or anything?" asked Nell.

"No. I mean—no, if there had been a real problem, they would have stopped me before the flight." I glanced at the guy on the other side of the aisle, who was watching and listening. "I'm fine." I smiled.

He didn't smile back.

A minute later, two cops stepped through the plane's door. One of them whispered to the flight attendant, who picked up the intercom phone and said, "Magdeline Johnson, could you come to the front, please?"

I stood, pretending not to see the gawking faces of the other passengers.

Nell stood and followed me down the aisle.

"Magdeline?" He studied my face for any deception. "We need to see ID, please."

I dug into my bag, painfully aware of my shaking hands, and showed him my driver's licence.

His gaze flicked to Nell, who showed him her identification. Her hands were steady.

"We only want Miss Johnson," said the bigger cop, looking from me to her.

"That's her." Nell pointed. "And I go where she goes."

He opened his mouth to argue, took a longer look at her, then decided against fighting.

"What's going on?" I asked. "I haven't done anything wrong—"

"We just need to talk to you for a moment," said the smaller cop. "Somewhere private."

"No way." Nell held up her hand. "She stays in public view."

"Listen, young lady—"

"No," she insisted. "You listen to me. My mom and dad have all kinds of political connections. Whatever's going on, you do it in a public place, or you let us call a lawyer, or the Canadian consulate."

While the two of them engaged in a stare-down, I went back to Serge.

What exactly did Frank and Maureen say?

"It's terrible for Nancy," said Serge. "I wonder who'll take over now. Dead Falls won't be the same."

Oh, god, what happened? Man, alive. *Did you see Dad?*

Serge shook his head.

"Come on," said the big cop, eyeing the passengers recording our exchange. "Let's get out of here, and let these people disembark."

Judging by the looks on their faces, my fellow passengers were happy to stay seated and be part of the drama. The small cop stepped out of the plane, while the big one waited until Nell and I filed out and took up the back.

Once we were off the skyway, the little one picked up speed.

"There." Nell pointed at the glass enclosure that held the smokers. "It's public and everyone can see us."

"Miss—"

Nell ignored him and, grabbing my arm, strode to the smokers.

The small officer sped ahead of us, stepped inside, flashed his badge, and cleared them out within a minute.

The big cop looked at Nell. "Good enough?"

She nodded. "I don't like this," she whispered to me. "They're being way too nice."

I followed the cops into the room.

"There's been an incident back home," said the big cop.

Nell's eyes clouded with confusion.

"Incident?" I repeated.

The cop and his partner exchanged a glance.

"It's about your father," he said, his voice soft.

"My dad?" I asked as my stomach dropped out from under me. "What happened?" I was having a hard time breathing. The cigarette smoke filled my lungs and clogged my throat. "Was there an accident?"

Another shared glance.

"What happened to my dad?"

Nell clutched my hand.

"His vehicle was found on the side of the highway." The cop's eyes filled with sympathy, and I knew his next words before he spoke them. "I'm sorry, Maggie, your dad's dead."

CHAPTER SIXTEEN

I barely tracked the next—minutes, hours, days, eternity—that followed his announcement and the bits of information the cops knew. Serge cried. Nell cried. I retreated into a cold, quiet place where there was no sound, save the dull throb of my heart.

Dad couldn't be dead. Impossible that someone had shot him. It was a mistake. It had to be. I was a psychic, I was his partner against the world. If anything had happened to him, I would've felt it. If anything had happened to him, he would've come to me.

I stayed in denial, dumbly following Nell and the cops. They made flight arrangements and I nodded at the right times, showed my ID at the right times, said my name at the right times. Serge stayed by my side, talking, though I didn't hear a word. Nell brought coffee but I couldn't get my fingers to work, to curl around the cup.

The flight came and I was fine. Fine through the pre-check, through the flight, through the touchdown and unloading. But when we came through the doors into the main area of Edmonton International Airport, when I saw Nancy, her pale face among the crowd, then I knew. Dad was gone. I was alone without him in this world and, worst of all, he had gone into the next one without ever saying goodbye.

✦ ✦ ✦

He lay on the metal slab, grey skin, the thin morgue sheet pulled to his neck. The clock on the wall said it was a minute past midnight. My first official day without my dad.

"I'm so sorry, Maggie," said Hinton, the new coroner.

I ignored his sympathy. "Dad really liked you. He thought you gave the job dignity." I tried to put feeling in my words, but emotion seemed incapable of breaching the cold dead inside me.

"The medical examiner will come up from Edmonton and do the full autopsy."

"Autopsy." I repeated the word.

Nancy, standing beside me, put her arm around my shoulder. Compared to the chill of the room, her touch felt as hot as hellfire. "I have connections with the office." Her fingers dug into my skin, and I was grateful for the physical pain. "They'll be here in a couple of days."

"It's nice of them, but not necessary," I said. "We know someone shot him." Put a gun to his chest and pulled the trigger.

"No one in town could've done this," Hinton said. "Everyone loved your dad."

Not everyone. Not Mrs. Pierson, who blamed him for allowing me to investigate the death of Kent Meagher and—in her mind—destroying her family. Not Mrs. Sinclair or her daughter, Amber, who held him responsible for their loss of income and status in the town. Not Principal Larry because Dad stood up for me when the administrator wanted to run me out of school for being the freakish daughter of the town's undertaker.

"I bet it was one of those big city folks driving through to get to the Northwest Territories for some kind of communing with nature," said Hinton. "All that crowding and skyscrapers. Road rage is just part of their everyday commute." He maneuvered his bulk around the table to stand in front of Nancy. "The guys will find out who did this." His tone was overly optimistic.

She nodded.

"Tragedy can make men rise to the occasion. I'm sure Frank will find skills and abilities..." He trailed into silence.

"I'm sure Frank will do his best," Nancy said.

Her voice was faint lightning in the storm raging inside me. Frank could do whatever he wanted, but I was going to find out who did this to my dad, and I was going to make them pay. Then I was going to find my dad's spirit and demand an explanation for how he could leave this plane of existence without coming to me.

Hinton cleared his throat. "In the meantime, we should start planning his funeral." He stepped back, putting his hand on Dad's shoulder.

"Did he want a military funeral? They might pay for a portion of it, too." His cheeks reddened. "I'm not the funeral director—"

In unison, we turned and looked at Dad. Ironic. The guy who could answer the question was on the slab.

I tuned back into Hinton's question. "Why would he want a military funeral? He wasn't military."

Nancy's head went back. "Kid, what are you talking about?" Her eyes narrowed, as if gauging me for shock.

"Dad wasn't in the service."

"He was part of the CSOR, the Canadian Special Operations Regiment." She glanced at Hinton, then stepped close and whispered, "It was one of the reasons he was okay with your extracurricular activities."

My dad, part of an elite fighting unit. "The guy who burned water?"

"Hardly anyone knew," she said. "He didn't like to talk about it, but yeah, he was part of the military."

"He had a tattoo," Hinton added, as if that explained everything. As if it made it all right that an entire part of my dad's life had been kept from me.

"Can I have some time alone with my dad?"

"Sure thing, kid. I'll keep them away until you're done. I phoned Gregory and let him know what happened, but it was a fast call, and I promised I'd touch base with him, again. I might as well do that, now." Nancy squeezed my hand, then stepped aside as Hinton led her out.

I stood, staring at the familiar but foreign face. My dad and not my dad. "Why didn't you find me? Why aren't you here?"

I took a few deep breaths and tried to channel the growing power inside me. But no matter how hard I looked at Dad, I saw nothing but the crushing sense I'd failed him.

I closed my eyes and called Serge, and wished Craig was back from the other side.

"Mags." Serge grabbed me and held me tight. His gaze went to Dad and he started to cry. "Hank was really good to me." He tightened his hold. "I can't imagine what it's like for you. We'll get through, I promise. I won't leave you, and we'll find the guy who did this."

"Keep holding me like that, and there won't be much for us to go through. You're crushing my chest."

"Sorry." He let go.

"Tap into your frequency," I said. "Tell me what there is to see. I tried, but I'm not getting anything."

"You're grieving," he said. "That's bound to affect your energy channels."

"Maybe." Maybe I just wasn't powerful enough. "Do you see any abnormalities?"

"Like what?"

"Like a supernatural signature?"

"You mean the soul-eater?" He circled the table. "You think it took your dad?"

"Dad wouldn't have left without saying goodbye, or giving us a message. That thing must have him."

"It's not going to have him for long." Serge closed his eyes and raised his hand to the ceiling. He took a couple of breaths. Then a few more.

Hyperventilating. At least I wasn't the only one.

When he opened his eyes, they glowed like sapphires caught in the light. "I see something. A mark, on his forehead."

"Where, exactly?"

He pointed at the space between Dad's eyebrows.

"What kind of mark is it?" I strained to see what he saw, but my efforts only made my eyes jiggle.

"It makes no sense."

"Just tell me."

"It looks like one of those bugs from when I was camping," he said.

"That's even less helpful than what you said before."

"I'm trying to remember the name. Give me a second."

One Mississippi. "Well?"

"Ha ha. Give me five."

After a three-count, he said, "It reminds me of a weevil. Not exactly, but sort of." He blinked and his eyes returned to normal. "We don't know what happened with your dad. Maybe he and his killer were fighting, and the bug got in the way. And when your dad died, it died too and this is the psychic imprint."

"It's cold for bugs to still be out. Can they even leave psychic marks? That seems like higher-life-level stuff."

"Don't knock the bugs," he said. "If every bug drops dead today, then the whole world's dead in a matter of weeks. That's high-life level to me."

"I guess, but it's too cold for beetles," I said. "And it's a supernatural mark. Especially considering the location. A bug imprint, tattooed on his third eye."

"A destructive bug," said Serge. "Weevils destroy crops. They took out the wheat stores on the Henderson farm a couple years back." He scanned Dad's forehead. "What do you think it means?"

"Maybe the soul-eater marked him." Maybe he cursed my dad, too, with the mark. I shoved the thought down and away. Dad needed me to save him and solve his murder. Getting emotional and freaking out wasn't going to do any good for anyone. "Did you see anything else?"

He shook his head. "No, I'm sorry. I wasn't much help."

"You were. We know whoever killed Dad had supernatural abilities." I gestured to his forehead.

He smiled bleakly. "Now all we have to do is find a guy with a thing for bugs."

That tweaked me. "Didn't Principal Larry have some kind of insect degree?"

"Yeah, but if he's supernatural, then I'm alive."

Fair enough. I went to the door and called back Nancy.

"Did you get anything?" she asked. She took my hand.

"Nothing," I said. "But Serge is here—"

Her cell binged. She glanced at it. Read. "I'm sorry for you, too. He was a good guy to all of us."

I gave us a moment, and gave Nancy an extra one for not coming apart when she talked. "Serge found a supernatural mark on Dad's forehead."

"The guy who did this has abilities." A shadow flickered across her face.

"What?"

"Nothing."

"Don't lie to me," I said.

She hesitated, then, "We don't know why your dad was targeted. The other officers think it's random, Hank being in the wrong place at the wrong time. But, kid, what if it was something else?" Her fingers hovered over Dad's forehead. "What if it was a supernatural killing?"

"Hitmen from the other side?"

"No, someone who's like you, but not like you," she said. "There are all kinds of people flocking to Dead Falls because of the video. The media's here, ghost hunters. What if the guy who took out Hank has abilities and recognizes the two of you are the same? But what if that person is possessive about their power? What if they were jealous, and came for you, but found your dad, instead?"

I didn't even want to think of Dad being the conciliation prize for a psycho. "Why? It's not like the other side is some ivy-league college and only a few of us get the choice spots. There shouldn't be a need to compete."

"In this day and age, we shouldn't have people running around murdering each other at all," she said. "But here we are. I'm not saying that's the case," she continued when I remained silent. "But we can't discount anything. Not until we have more information."

I agreed, but her theory added another person to the line-up of people who hurt my dad because of me.

"Frank's here." Hinton came into the room, the deputy on his heels.

"If I can see the mark," said Serge. "Maybe there's a psychic trail, like a vapour or something I can follow. I'm going to head out." He frowned. "I wish Craig was back. Mags, call me if you need anything."

His words binged on Nancy's phone.

"I don't like you playing Scooby Doo," I said.

"Sorry?" Hinton asked.

"Nice to see you," said Nancy, pointing at Frank. "She was saying nice to see you."

Hinton nodded as Frank said, "It's nice to see you too, Maggie. I'm sorry it's under these circumstances." His gaze went from me, and his pity was a palpable thing that stretched and suffocated. "Nancy, I'm sorry for your loss."

She nodded.

"I've got some paperwork." Hinton drifted away.

"What's the point of us being a team if we can't divide the work?" Serge asked me. "I'll be fine, I promise."

"You holding up okay?" Frank asked the question, but I wasn't sure who he was asking, me or Nancy.

"We've all got our roles to play." Nancy looked up from her cell to me. "And we all need the place to play it."

Serge smiled and stepped back.

Don't move.

"Come on," said Serge. "Didn't you hear her? Nancy's okay with it."

"I didn't realize you were here until Hinton told me," said Frank. "I should leave you alone. I only wanted to pass on my condolences."

Just because she said—

"Hang back for a bit," she said, and we knew she meant Serge.

"The trail could be getting cold," he said.

It's too dangerous for you to be out there, alone.

"I don't imagine you have any updates, but what have you found out, so far?" asked Nancy.

"Ah." Frank took off his hat and scratched his grey chin stubble with the back of his hand.

"Spit it out," she said. "Maggie and I have people to meet up with and things to sort out."

"I understand where you're coming from, Nancy, but this thing with Hank..." He trailed off and waited for her to finish his sentence.

She stared at him.

"You know how it is with family..."

If she stared any harder, she was going to split him in two.

"Damn it, Nancy! You know I can't give you any information. You're the grieving widow!"

"Tell me what I want to know," she said. Her voice was quiet, the kind of quiet that made the hair on my arms stand up.

Frank stepped back. "I only came to get an update from Hinton. To see if he had anything to say about Hank."

"He has nothing to say," she said. "But I'm listening. Talk."

"You know procedure. I can't—"

"Who's going to tell on me?" She stepped towards him. "You?"

"I don't want any trouble—"

"Then talk, Frank."

He dipped his head. "We don't know much. There was a set of tire tracks, good tread, probably a sedan. The guys are running it down."

"It was snowing," she said. "What about footprints?"

"The perp used a shovel or something to blur the prints." Frank glanced at me, then went back to talking to the floor. "Hank saw the attack coming." He went to the table on which my dad lay, pulling back the sheet as though he was doing something holy. "His hands. Your dad put up one hell of a fight."

The world blurred. When it cleared, I moved with Serge to the table and examined Dad's hands. Bruised skin, red cuts, swollen fingers.

"Hank hit the guy hard enough to break or fracture bones," Serge said, gesturing to the wounds.

Nancy read the text.

Can you be sure of that?

"The reverend liked to hit," said Serge. "I learned to hit back."

"If it wasn't for the guy having a gun," explained Frank. "Hank would've won the fight. I'm sure of it."

"Years of military training can't be forgotten," murmured Nancy, tucking the phone in her pocket. "But did he fight a stranger who ambushed him, or a friend who betrayed him?" She trailed her fingers along my dad's knuckles, then turned to Frank. "No one's walking around sporting injuries?"

He shook his head. "No visits to the emergency."

"Principal Larry has a gun," I said.

"He was the first guy I went to," said Frank. "But his skin's unblemished."

"Maybe he hired someone else to do it," I said.

Frank shuffled. "We're considering everything, I promise."

Maybe it wasn't anyone local. Maybe it was the soul-eater, and he was injured, Serge spoke in my mind, *but he used ghost energy to heal himself.*

So even if Dad put up a fight, nothing's showing.

The town's overrun with people ghost-hunting and reporting on ghost-hunting. It could be anybody.

Do you think the healing might leave a psychic mark?

Maybe.

Then we should take a walk around town. I stepped back, keeping an ear out as Nancy and Frank discussed the bullet.

"Straight to the heart, but he shot Hank from behind, the coward—"

"We'll know the calibre of the bullet once the medical examiner gets here—"

The sudden vision of Dad's chest cracked open, his skin pulled back, made me nauseous. I moved to the door and left Nancy to the details. On the other side, I found Nell and her dad.

She grabbed me and held on tight.

I forced a smile I didn't feel and directed it to her dad. "What's up, Doc?"

The smile he gave me looked like he'd dead-lifted it, and it dropped off his face as soon as it appeared. "God, I'm sorry, Maggie." He wrapped his arms around Nell and me.

We stood for a moment, me loving that they'd shown up without asking. Me, envying Nell because at the end of all this, she'd go home with her dad. I'd never be able to do that again.

"Can I go see him?" she asked after we broke the hug.

I nodded. "He'd like that. Nancy and Frank are still in there."

"I'll be respectful—"

"You never have been before," I said. "Why start now?"

She gave me a weak smile and left.

"Your dad was one of the best men I knew," said Doc.

There seemed to be more he wanted to say, so I stayed quiet.

"I don't know how to say this—"

Uh-oh. "Just say what you have to say."

"Hank had a heart of gold, but let's face it, owning a funeral home in a small town doesn't exactly set you up for life." Doc put his hand on my shoulder. "You're family—" He glanced up as Nancy came out. "—If we can help with the funeral, or anything else…"

"Thanks, Daniel," Nancy said. "That's generous."

"I'm sure the military will step in, too," he said.

"Did everyone in the world know Dad had been in the service, except me?"

"Other than Nancy, I'm the only one he told." He made eye contact with me. "We had a special bond—each of us having strong, dynamic daughters will do that—and I trusted him to look after Nell when she was in your care. He never let me down; he was a second dad to her. I can never take Hank's place in your heart or your life, Maggie, but if you ever need fatherly advice—"

I hugged him tight and tried not to bawl. "Thanks, Doc." I forced a smile, then went to tell Nell goodbye.

"You're the luckiest person I know," she said when she saw me.

"We really need to work on your vocabulary."

"You are." She held up her phone. "I was talking to Casper. He thinks the soul-eater thing has your dad—"

"And is probably torturing him," I said.

"Don't think about that. Focus on this. It's not about *if* you find the soul-eater and bring the reckoning, it's *when* you find him. Your dad's freedom is just a matter of time."

"And this makes me lucky because...?"

"Because once he's free, he's by your side until you die," she said. "You will never have to say goodbye to anyone you love."

"It's a nice thought, but that's not a hundred percent certain. Dad might cross over."

"Your dad would never leave you," she said.

"He died without telling me." My voice cracked. "He died without saying goodbye. My powers are growing. He should've been able to reach me. At the very least, I should've been able to sense the danger."

"Don't be a princess," said Nell. "He died and that piece-of-crap soul-eater probably sucked him in before he could do anything. And you didn't sense anything because you're powerful, but you're not the *most* powerful."

I blinked back the tears and nodded. Solve the mystery now. Lose my mind later. "Serge saw—" I looked around the room, then peered through the door at the adults in the other room.

"Wow, must be pretty good intel if you're checking for eavesdroppers," she said.

"It's not that. Serge is gone." I caught her up on the supernatural tattoo and Serge wanting to play the dead world's version of private detective.

"That idiot! He went off alone? And you let him?"

"I didn't let him," I said. "He snuck out."

"I'm going to get the two of you babysitters," she said. "You obviously can't be left unsupervised. Come on, let's go get him."

sing the psychic link was the fastest way to call Serge to me, but standing still was driving me crazy. At least driving around the town searching for him felt like I was doing something. "Let's find him the old-fashioned, mortal way," I said.

One step out of the morgue doors and I regretted my decision. Flashbulbs flashed in my face. Questions assaulted my ears.

"Who killed your father?"

"Did he send you a last message?"

"Did your father tell you he loved you?"

"Is a spirit behind the death of your father?"

"Tell the truth."

The last voice was Carl Reid's.

"Tell the world what you can really do," he said.

I blinked but white spots stayed and kept him hidden in the dark crowd. People surrounded Nell and me, and I didn't recognize any of them. In the background, more figures, but they were too far away for me to know if they were familiar.

"I just—can I get—?" No one was letting me pass. They crowded closer.

"I got this," said Nell. "Get behind me." She pushed in front of me, grabbed my hand, and barreled forward.

The crush of people pushed in. I yelped as someone grabbed my arm and a shock of electricity ran through me.

"What was with you yelling?" Nell asked after she'd shoved me into the passenger side of the car, then climbed in the driver's seat.

"I don't know." I took off my coat and checked my arm. "I think one of them might have tried to taser me."

"You're kidding."

I shook my head. "I felt it. Electricity."

"That's not a taser," she said. "Those things make you pee your pants."

"Yeah, well that run-in almost made me pee my pants. I'm sorry."

"Sorry? Why?" She laid on the horn to make the reporters move. None did.

"I'm supposed to be protecting you—ow! Would you stop hitting me?"

"Sometimes I protect you. Sometimes you protect me. It's called friendship. You have enough going on, without adding more weight on your shoulders." She laid on the horn, again.

A couple of deputies came out of the station next door, saw what was happening, and cleared the crowd.

"Anyway, the day I need you to save me is the day—" She stopped. "Forget it, that day's never coming. Let's find Serge." Nell drove through the streets, starting with Running Creek Road. The headlights of her car lit up a figure walking along the shoulder.

"Is that—?" She flipped on her blinker, honked the horn, and pulled over.

Craig turned, waved, and jogged toward us.

I wasn't sure what to do. Part of me wanted to run into his arms and hide from the world. Part of me wanted to keep my distance because if I started crying I'd never stop.

He climbed into the backseat before I could decide. "Nice timing." He buckled in. "It's freezing out there."

"Why didn't you ferrier yourself home?" Nell pulled back on the road.

"There may be a problem with that," he said.

"Jet lag from being on the other side?" she asked. "Or lost in thought over what you found out?"

"I didn't have a lot of luck with finding anything," he said. "I tried to access Maggie's files, to see what the connection between her, her mom, and the soul-eater is. I also wanted to see if I could find out more information about the serengti."

"Did you find anything?" I asked.

"No, and I don't like this. Bad things are going to happen if we don't stay on top of it."

Bad things had already happened. I told him what happened with Dad. Then he was unbuckling my seatbelt, pulling me over the console, into the backseat, and into his embrace. His tears mixed with mine.

"I'm so sorry," he whispered. "If I'd stayed—"

"I told you to go," I said. "This is my fault. His death—"

"None of you ninnies is to blame, so stop with the self-pity crying," said Nell. "This is the fault of a bunch of evil guys. Someone was going to die and I'm super pissed it was Mr. Johnson. Did you get any answers at all, Craig? Anything that can help us figure out who's behind this?"

"Yes and no." He leaned forward. "I got some answers, but the higher-ups caught me sneaking around. They weren't happy." He settled back in his seat. "They've suspended me for the next thirty days."

"That's good," Nell said. "That means you can help us—"

"And they turned me mortal."

The car went silent.

"What does that mean?" I asked.

"It means I'm not of much help to give you answers. I can't remember what I found out because the mortal brain can't contain all my lives or knowledge. It's out of my reach."

Of course. Of course the answer would be there, but the higher-ups would keep it from me. They wouldn't stop a soul-eater, they wouldn't warn me about my dad or tell me about my mom, but they would throw up obstacles. When Serge had died, one of the supernaturals, Hera, had come to us. Twice. She'd explained what was going on with me and Serge. My dad was dead, and she was nowhere to be found.

Craig reached forward and put his hand on my shoulder. There was love in the touch, a connection for a lost friend, and it took everything in me to keep it together.

"Call Serge," said Nell. "We can't waste time driving around."

I did what she asked, and Serge appeared in the backseat beside Craig.

"The entire town is out," he said as he buckled into the seat. "I went to the Tin Shack and listened. Everyone's talking about Hank, but no one knows anything." He did a double-take with Craig. "Whoa, dude. What happened to you?"

"Got caught going into Maggie's files. Suspended for thirty days—"

"Cool," said Serge. "You can help—"

"And turned mortal for that time."

Serge swore. "That explains why you look different."

"Let's go to the crime scene," I said. "Maybe there's some psychic clue left. Does anyone know the location?"

"I do," said Nell.

Of course. That girl knew almost everything.

Nell flipped on her signal and headed to the location. Police tape and barricades blocked the entry to the scene. Nell cut the engine and we got out of the car.

"This is an active crime scene." The deputy came toward us. "You'll have to—oh, Maggie. I'm sorry. I didn't realize it was you."

I tried to remember his name, but my brain was wet cotton.

"Jack Andrews," he said. "We met a couple of times when you were at the station."

"Right. I'm sorry. Of course, I know you."

"You have nothing to apologize for," he said. "I'm really sorry about what happened. Frank called in some help from the other towns. We'll find this guy. No one hurts one of our own."

He spoke, and his words of comfort, the desperate need I had for kindness, were like a physical cut to my skin. "Thanks."

"What are you doing here?" he asked, his gaze took in Craig and Nell.

"I wanted to see—"

"No, you don't," he said. "The crime scene guys are still here and—" Pain flickered in his eyes. "—Nothing's been cleaned up."

In other words, my dad's blood was still on the road.

"I'm going up there," said Serge. "There has to be something."

Find us when you're done.

He nodded and went through the barrier.

"Can you tell us anything?" asked Craig. "I know there are rules about what you can and can't say, but—"

Andrews took a quick breath. "I liked your dad, Maggie. Hank was a good man."

The tears rose and burned my eyes. I blinked them back.

"From the tire tracks, footprints, and stuff left on the road—" He stepped close and dropped his voice. "—I think someone was pretending to have car trouble."

"It was a fake flat tire," said Nell. She caught my gaze. "What? I hear things."

"Did you hear who did it?"

"If I had, the cops would be shovelling his bloody body parts off the road," she said.

"Nell's sources are right," said Andrews. "We think Hank pulled over to help, and that's when it happened. I was one of the first guys on the scene. Your dad put up a fight, but no one can stop a bullet."

The sudden image of my dad's final moments crushed me. Craig took my hand.

"We're running down the tire tracks. The footprints are too messed up to be of any use." He looked over his shoulder. "I should check in with the rest of them. I wish I could let you up, but rules are rules."

Yeah, and not once had any of those rules worked for me. The principal's rules had allowed for bullying. The other side's rules had taken Craig's power, knowledge, and left a soul-eater on the loose.

"You should go," said Andrews. "The longer you're here, the more trouble I'll get into."

"We'll go." Craig pulled me back. "Thanks for talking to us."

He nodded. "Maggie, I don't know…I don't know what your family's plans are, but if you need help with anything, you'll let me know. Okay?"

"I will." I forced a smile that hurt my face and put out my hand. "Thank you, Deputy Andrews."

He took it, but rather than shaking my hand, he pulled me into a tight hug. There was support in his embrace, a sense of connection and empathy, and it hurt so bad I could barely breathe. "We'll find who did this," he said. "I promise."

I thanked him and pushed away. Turning, I opened my mind to possibilities and tried to tap into any supernatural energies around us. Crying could wait. Falling apart could wait. Right now, I needed all the clues I could get about the soul-seeker.

I opened my eyes. Oh, crap. Not again. The serengti had pulled me into its world. I blinked, then blinked again. My eyes adjusted to the darkness and I realized I was on a highway. Somewhere rural because all I saw were darkened fields, highlighted by a bright, full moon. Yeah, it had to be countryside—there were too many stars for me to be anywhere near a city.

In the distance, I heard the rumble of an engine. I looked behind me. A car but its lights were off.

I moved to the side.

The car slowed. It was a long, dark, older model sedan. The window went down and I heard a male voice say, "Hi, honey."

"Hi, Mr. Bradley."

"Did you have fun at the 4-H meeting?"

"Yes," said my tween voice, while the real me wondered what a 4-H was.

"You need a ride?"

The little girl said, "Thanks, Mr. Bradley."

She reached out for the handle, and the world froze. Light, Serena's light, glowed to the left.

"It's time to go, Madison," said Serena. "Your grandmother is waiting." She held out her hand.

Madison took it.

"Go to the light." A gentle tug, and Madison's spirit broke free.

I was trapped in her body, watching as Madison moved to the border between life and death, and stepped through.

Serena didn't leave. And she didn't let go of Madison's—my— hand. Instead, she began to shimmer, to break apart into glittering dust that sunk beneath Madison's skin. She took possession of the girl's body.

I felt her anger, her exhaustion. She was tired of taking the souls while evil was allowed to live. Sure, there was an end game for these people, a final reckoning, but it all took so long. In the meantime, there were more bodies, more devastated families.

Serena opened the door, and I got images of what she had planned for this guy, what she was about to do.

Oh, my god.

CHAPTER EIGHTEEN

"It's okay," I heard Deputy Andrews say. "It's just shock. Get her in the car. I'll let Nancy know you're taking her home."

I blinked and found myself back in Dead Falls.

"Don't say anything," Craig whispered in my ear. "Not until we're back in the car." His arms guiding me, I stumbled to the car and fell into the front passenger seat.

"Was it Serena, again?" he asked as he climbed in behind me.

"Yeah, but it was different this time. She went after the guy. I saw what she did to him—it was—she was enraged."

Craig didn't say anything.

Nell started the car, but didn't put it in gear. "Craig?"

"I'm such an idiot," he said. "If I hadn't tried to mess with the system, I would be able to cross to the other side, and get some answers—the right way."

"You were trying to help," I said.

"No, I was trying to find a shortcut because I was scared for you and Serge. Now, I'm in the dark and stumbling around." He took a long, slow breath. "I can tell you the obvious. It's bad. Serengti aren't supposed to interact with anyone other than their charge. If she's stepping into their skin to exact revenge—"

"She's breaking the rules. So is the soul-eater," I said. "I'm no longer surprised they're both here, now. On some level, they must be calling to each other, connecting because they've pulled away from the system."

"Do you think they're working together?" Nell turned the car around and headed back to town.

"No," said Craig. "Serengti are isolationists."

"This system is broken and stupid," I said. "There's a soul-eater on the loose, a serengti that's violating its protocol, meanwhile, someone's murdered my dad and no one's doing anything."

"The other side is complicated," Craig said. "Things may not make sense right now, but—"

"I don't want to hear it!" I lowered my voice. "I don't want to hear it. I've been hearing that crap all my life. This is never going to make sense."

Craig leaned forward and put his hand on my shoulder. "I'm sorry."

"Let's get you home," said Nell.

"I don't want to go home. I can't." That was true. But at the same time, untrue. I didn't want to step into a house that didn't have my dad. Didn't want to see the chair he'd never sit in again, or the shoes he'd never wear. But I needed home. Needed to grab all his stupid flannel shirts and put them in airtight containers before time erased the smell of him from them.

"Take her home," I heard Craig quietly say.

No one left after they walked me through the door. We moved in unison, to my bedroom, where Nancy found us. The five of us stayed together, lights on, the animals tucked between us, waiting for the light that would never come.

CHAPTER NINETEEN

I woke the next morning and, for a split second, I forgot Dad was gone. Then it hit, and an icy cold took over the warm confusion.

Serge was on the computer, Ebony on his lap. "Craig is downstairs making breakfast. Nancy went to the station, and Nell's walking Buddha." He didn't bother asking how I was doing, and I appreciated that.

"I found out some stuff." He turned away from the device. "The cops already questioned Principal Larry, Mrs. Sinclair, and Mrs. Pierson. Especially Mrs. Pierson. She'd left forty messages at Hank's work. Some of them about Rori's funeral and headstone, some of them rambling incoherence. A few of them were angry. I don't think there's much to it, neither did your dad."

"If he'd told me, I could've—"

"You couldn't have done anything," he said. "Your dad was military. If anyone could take care of himself, it was him."

"Until it wasn't."

"We should search his room," said Serge. "There has to be something of your mom's in there. He couldn't have destroyed everything connected to her." He stood and stretched. "I asked Nancy, but Hank never gave her your mom's name, either."

"Obviously, the army was great for training him to keep his mouth shut."

"Go have a shower. We'll have breakfast, then we'll tear apart your dad's space." He smiled but he looked as sick as I felt.

"Can you hang out for a bit?" I asked. "I'm scared I'm going to space out in the shower and—"

His grin was a pale imitation of itself. "Hubba hubba."

"You're not coming in the bathroom with me. Just wait outside. If you hear any sudden thumps, get help." I headed into the shower, intending to be quick. But there was something about the drone of the water, the heat and steam, that left me incapable of leaving the tub. It was as though if I stepped out, Dad's death would be permanent.

I tried to remind myself of what Nell said, that I was lucky because once I found the soul-eater, Dad would be freed. And we'd be a family, again. But the soul-eater went after a certain kind of spirit. Common sense said Dad had been taken because the thing was out of control.

A small part of me wondered about the secrets Dad hid. His military background. The calls from Mrs. Pierson, Mrs. Sinclair, and the other townspeople. What else had been going on that I didn't know about?

And even when Dad was freed, I didn't trust Hera and the powers on the other side to leave my dad on this plane of existence. But my biggest fear was me. My emotions were all over the place, leaving me vulnerable to the serengti and terrified that I wouldn't find Dad's killer.

The knock boomed on the bathroom door and jerked me out of my reverie.

"Mags," Nell called. "Do I need to come in?" There was a brief silence, then, "Serge is hoping you don't answer and I have to go in there and effect a soapy rescue. I'm not sure if I want to support or shut down his fevered dreams."

"I'm okay. I'll be out soon." After I got dressed, Serge caught me up on what he'd found out when he'd crossed the police barricades and gone to Dad's crime scene. It wasn't much, but it was enough to keep hope alive.

"Homemade donuts," Craig said as we came into the kitchen. He stood over a pan of frying dough. Golden rings of pastry lined a silver tray that sat next to him.

"Homemade donuts." Serge's eyes went wide. "Craig, turn me solid—" His skin blanched. "Sorry, I forgot."

"Me too," he said and lifted his hand. "Managed to give myself a serious burn from the oil."

"How have you not inhaled everything on the tray?" I asked Nell as I sat down.

"The sauce isn't ready," she said.

"Sauce?" asked Serge.

"Simmer the blueberries first, then add honey. When it's shiny and jam-like, we pour it over the donuts, then drizzle Greek yogurt on top."

"No kidding." Serge peered into the pot.

Not that I wasn't loving the domestic calm, but grief rippled under my skin. Maybe anger. Whatever it was, I had to clamp down the urge to scream at everyone. I kept my mouth shut and let their conversation wash over me.

Craig plated the food and brought it over. "Eat."

"I'm not—"

"I know," he said. "But you have to. Especially you."

I took one, but it tasted like paper and sawdust. I put down my donut.

Craig caught the gesture and smiled. "Well, it was worth a try." He dusted the crumbs off his hands. "Nancy said she told the school you'll be out of commission for a while."

I nodded.

"My dad did the same thing for me," said Nell. "I'm yours till we solve this."

"Nancy also told them you'd stop by to pick up your homework for the week," said Craig.

"What do I care about homework?"

"You don't," he said. "But she thought it was a good cover in case you wanted to check out the principal for any supernatural clues."

Great thought, except my supernatural talents were failing me.

"Do you want to go right now?" asked Nell. "I can drive."

"Maybe later." I wiped my hands on my jeans. "The sooner we look through Dad's stuff, the faster we can get on track with his killer."

Nell shovelled the donut and sauce in her mouth, and stood.

They followed me to Dad's door, where my strength suddenly failed, and I seemed incapable of lifting my hand to grip the handle.

Craig put his hand on my shoulder. "Do you want me to open it?"

I shook my head.

"I can go through it," said Serge. "And check the room."

"No, I'm just being stupid—"

"No, you're not."

"Yeah, I am," I said. "The sooner we free Dad, the sooner he and I are Team Johnson again." Screw the fears about the future, and screw the worries about his secrets. When I freed him, we'd have a long talk about all of it. I gripped the doorknob and twisted.

The door swung open, and the room yawned before me. Greys and blues, the clean lines of his furniture. A hoodie he'd tossed on the bed, the sleeve lying on top of Nancy's flannel pajamas.

"We can do this," said Craig. "You don't have to—"

"I do it for strangers," I said. "I'm doing it for my dad." I stepped through. "Let's divide this up. Craig, you and Nell check the drawers. Serge and I will check for hidden areas."

We broke, each moving to the corners of the room.

"I wonder if your dad had any secret compartment spaces," said Serge.

"Mr. Johnson?" asked Nell. "That guy was chill. He wouldn't have secrets."

I stared at her.

"Okay, so he had one or two."

"Everyone has secrets," said Craig. "Go through the walls, Serge, and tell me what you see."

Going on my toes, I tapped at the drywall, listened, then dropped my hand and rapped again. The process was slow, the rhythmic knocking hypnotic.

Halfway down the length of the room, I hit a hollow section. More knocking revealed the area to be about a square foot. I turned, looking for Serge, but he must have been in a wall. If he could do it, maybe so could I. Not go through a solid surface, but since I seemed to possess the ability to travel in time, maybe I also possessed x-ray abilities.

I took a breath to steady myself, closed my mind to grief and anger, then concentrated. Imagined the layers of wall flattening, stretching. Visualized my gaze—"Oh, crap!" I jumped back as the wall caught on fire.

Whipping around, I yanked the nearest piece of clothing and smacked at the flames until I snuffed it out.

"You have to be careful when you're channelling your energy," said Craig, taking the shirt from me. "Or else you can set things on fire."

I shot him a dirty look.

"What?" he asked mildly. "I'm mortal. I'm allowed to say the blatantly obvious. It's probably the only time I'll ever be allowed to do it."

"Do you have any relevant pieces of advice?"

"Yeah," he said. "Don't do it again."

It was a good thing he'd taken the shirt because I was tempted to wrap it around his neck. I stared at the charred smudges on the wall.

"What?" he asked.

"I was thinking I'd give anything to have Dad storm in here and yell about the cost of fixing this."

"Leave it," said Craig. "He'll be back soon, yelling."

"I don't know. My powers are all messed up. There've been consequences to the things I've done. I've got this crazy serengti shadowing me—"

He took my hand. "Slow down, Mags, and breathe. Yeah, everything's messed up. Everything's always messed up. That's life."

"Your mortal pep talks suck."

"I'm doing the best with what I've got."

Serge emerged from the wall. "So far, nothing." He frowned at the soot stains. "Was that always there?"

"Do you think this is weird?" Nell was on all fours, peering under the bed.

"I'm not sure what the question is," said Serge, staring at her backend. "But I agree with anything you say."

"Focus," I said.

"I am focused," said Nell.

"Not you, Serge."

"What did he say?" she asked.

"Serge is back?" Craig pulled out his phone.

"Don't repeat what you said," I told Serge. "We don't have time for your hormones."

"Oh," said Nell. "I don't know what you said Serge, but thanks."

"What's weird under the bed?" I asked.

"There's a rug," she said. "It's the only thing here."

"I'm not the decorating type," said Serge. "Why is this weird?"

"Because you don't need a rug under there," I told him. "Craig, help me move this." I took a position at the headboard.

"Hold on She-Hulk," said Nell. She wriggled under the bed. A few seconds later, she pushed the rug into view. "Look familiar?"

"No," I said. "Should it?"

"Not really," Nell said. "I'm just making conversation to cover my panic. There's far less room under the bed than you'd think, especially given the small, amazing package that's me."

"I didn't know you were claustrophobic," said Craig.

"Until this moment, I didn't know either," she said. "Hold on."

I frowned, trying to orient to the sounds coming from under the mattress.

"Tell her I'm coming in," said Serge. "I can stick my head under the boards and see."

I relayed his message as he waded through the mattress, then sank from view.

"Mags, you need to see this," Serge said just as Nell said, "Oh holy crap. Maggie, you need to see this."

CHAPTER TWENTY

The bed pushed off to the side, we sat in a circle in the middle of the room, staring at the hole in the floor, and the guns hidden in its depth.

"I don't know what's worse," I said. "That my dad had a stash of guns, that he had guns and never told me, or that he kept them oiled and ready. You can smell it. You can see it. He was prepped for something."

"Maybe he was at the ready for when you finally started dating," said Nell. "Or the zombie apocalypse."

I rubbed my eyes and felt the faint thrum of the headache behind my lids.

"He couldn't have been a survivalist," said Serge. "He couldn't even boil water. Maybe this was because of what's been happening the past few days. All the threats and phone calls."

"This wasn't because of Maggie," said Craig. "These guns have been here for a while."

"Besides, he had Nancy," said Nell. "He didn't need any of this for Maggie. This was for something else."

I stood, wanting to bolt, wanting to run and never stop. "Someone pass me their cell."

Nell handed me hers, and I phoned Nancy.

"What's up, kid?" She sounded tired.

"Did Dad ever tell you anything about the guns he kept under the bed?"

The silence was short. "*What?*"

I repeated my question.

"I always figured there was nothing under his bed but old socks. Why? What did you find?"

I told her.

"Don't touch any of them," she said sharply. "In fact, get out of the room. I don't want any of you near guns."

"Seriously—?"

"Listen to me, kid. Get out. I'll be home as soon as I can." She softened her tone. "Go get your homework."

"Someone murdered my dad, probably because of some whacked-up hatred of me, not to mention the soul-eater that has my father's soul, and maybe my mom's, and Zeke's and Homer's, and you want me to collect bio and chem sheets?"

"I don't give a damn about your schooling," she said. "You're already smarter than half the teachers there. What I do care about is that I'm not your legal guardian. Hank and I weren't married, and we haven't lived together long enough to be considered common law. Which means I don't have full legal custody over you. Which means if I don't keep that moron of a principal happy—"

"He can call in social services and put me in care," I said.

"You could fight it," said Nancy. "You're old enough to file for emancipation from the government and be declared a legal adult, but that's going to take time. I'm filing the guardianship paperwork but we have to be smart—"

"Enough said. I'll go get my homework."

"Thanks, kid."

"And maybe I'll pick up some burgers for dinner—"

"They'll be gross by the time Nancy gets home," said Craig. "Nell and I will make something."

"We got you guys handled," Nell leaned in and spoke into the phone. "You two just work both sides of the living and the dead, and get this thing solved."

"I'm smart enough to not mess with Nell," Nancy said drily. "I'll see you at home."

"Have you found anything?" I asked and hated myself for the pleading tone in my voice.

"Not yet."

I heard the hesitation in her voice. "What aren't you telling me?"

"We'll talk about it at home."

I did not like the sound of that.

✦✦✦

I left Nell and Craig at home, fought through a band of reporters, and went to school by myself.

"What kind of guy makes you do homework when your dad's just died?" Serge kept pace as I ran up the icy steps to the front doors.

"The same kind of guy that called the reverend his friend."

"Good point."

Classes were in session, which meant I didn't have to deal with the entire student body. But some kids had a free period and were lounging in the common areas or hanging out at their lockers. Their stares and whispers followed me down the hall. I cleaned out my locker, then headed to the main office, where a package of my homework was waiting.

"Maggie." The secretary looked up, pity on her face. "I'm sorry about your father. He did the funeral for my father-in-law and your dad was so kind about everything. He made it as good as it could be."

"Thank you," I said. "I'm sure he would have loved to hear that."

She handed me a manila envelope. "I hope—"

"Miss Johnson. Good. You're here." Principal Larry stepped out of his office. "Come inside."

"No."

Serge stepped beside me and wrapped his fingers around my wrist. "I'm here. He won't hurt you."

"Miss Johnson. I realize you're under some emotional strain. However, I'm still the head of this school and you are still a student. You will come into my office. Now."

"No."

A flush of red crept its way up from the base of his neck.

"I'll talk to you out here," I said. "Where there are witnesses."

"Miss Johnson—!"

"Everyone knows you hated me and my dad," I said. "If you think I'm going behind closed doors with you, then—" I caught myself. Nancy's warning rang in my head. "—I respectfully decline, sir." The words were polite, but all I saw was a scarlet haze. Was I standing in front of the man who was responsible for my father's murder?

"I only wish to share my sympathies with you," he said, with a tight smile at the secretary. "Your father and I had our disagreements, but I didn't hate him—"

"That's not true," I said. "You tried to have him arrested the night we saw you at the Tin Shack. You wanted him charged with assault."

"I was justified. He accused me of—"

"You accused him back. You said he was gossiping about you, trying to start a petition to get you fired."

"Your father had been to the board numerous times, complaining about me. It made sense that he was the one behind the petition."

"Did it make you angry?" I asked. "Knowing that people didn't want you in charge of their children? Knowing what the world thought of you because of your friendship with the reverend?"

"Mags, what's going on? Your light is shifting." Serge let go of my hand and stepped back to get a clearer look.

The scarlet haze thickened, swirled like fog on the night breeze. "You were in a position of power but you abused it."

"I did no such thing!"

"You let the reverend hurt Amber and Serge."

The haze turned in on itself, a whirlpool of red, and from its depths, a form began to rise.

"Maggie. Stop. I don't like this. Your aura's jagged and it's dark red, almost black. Wherever you're going, stop." Serge turned, caught sight of the shape from the corner of his eye, and moved to it.

"I didn't know what he was doing!"

Serena rose from the haze. She was more defined than I'd ever seen her. Still faceless, but with the faint outlines of a mouth and eyes.

Serge swore.

"You knew what Serge was doing to me," I said. "He hurt me because his parents hurt him. You let it happen."

"Stop saying that!"

The secretary stood, frozen.

"Maggie. Mags!" Serge grabbed my face in his hands, but he was transparent to me. All I saw was Principal Larry, and all the ways he'd failed me, Serge, Amber, and every kid who ever trusted him to protect them. "You told my dad you have to have protection. How does it feel, being scared all the time? How does it feel to be on the wrong side now?"

"Your eyes are gone." Transparent tears formed on Serge's transparent face. "Don't do this. Don't provoke him. That thing is here. You know why it comes. Don't let him hurt you."

Serena moved to me.

"Did you do it to make the reverend happy? To keep him on your side? Why? What did he do for you?" I stepped closer. The red was all around me. "Were you like him? Like that?"

"I am not!"

"Is that why you shot my dad?"

The principal jerked back. "I never did anything to your father."

"Where's your gun?"

"I—"

"If you didn't hurt my dad, where is it?"

"The cops took it."

I moved to him.

He backed up. "I swear! I didn't hurt your dad!"

I kept closing the distance.

I heard Serge say, "I'm sorry Mags," then a sharp pain shot through my heart.

CHAPTER TWENTY-ONE

I sat in the nurse's room, a scratchy, grey blanket over my shoulders. The secretary's watchful gaze kept me in place.

"I'm okay," I said.

"You dropped like a brick."

Serge, leaning against the wall, folded his arms and stared me down. "I'm not going to apologize for what I did."

Really? 'Cause that's the last thing you said.

"I was pre-apologizing in case I hurt you."

"Maggie?" Nancy came into the room. "You okay, kid?"

I nodded and stood. "Let's go home." I folded the blanket and handed it to the secretary, then walked out of the room.

"You passed out?" Nancy followed me into the hallway.

"I didn't pass out. Serge decided to be my over-active conscience."

"You were losing your mind," he said. "And I had to step in."

"I was dealing with the principal—"

"Give me a break, Maggie! I know when someone's going psycho." He moved through the door.

"He's got a point," said Nancy, holding up his text.

"Principal Larry's involved in what happened to my dad. He ambushed Dad at the funeral home the night he died, and Dad got him out the door by telling him they'd meet later."

Nancy froze in the threshold, her hand locked around the metal door handle. "How do you know that?"

Serge and I locked gazes.

"I'm glad I'm already dead," he said. "'Cause she looks ready to kill."

"Did you go through my files? My private report—" She stepped through the door and held it open.

"It wasn't Maggie," said Serge. "It was me."

Nancy read the text. "You went through my files?"

"No," he said. "The night we drove up to where Hank was found, I went past the barricade and heard the cops talking."

"I know you have to collect evidence and investigate," I said to Nancy. "But how can you let him be around kids? Around people?"

"He's a person of interest, but for now, Principal Larry isn't a suspect."

"Did he meet with my dad that night?"

"Kid—"

"You're not even supposed to be on this case," I said. "Don't give me policy and procedure."

"Larry and Hank arranged to meet at the funeral home, after it closed," she said. "The security cameras show Larry's car pulling into the lot. He says he phoned Hank to get him to open the front doors. When Hank didn't answer, he left a message and waited. When Hank didn't show up after a half-hour, Larry went home. An hour later, he showed up at the station, demanding we charge Hank with something."

"That's convenient," said Serge. "Him waiting in the car and not getting out. He could have had someone else drive the car there, while he was committing the murder."

"I agree," said Nancy. She started for my car. "But Larry showed me his phone. There was a call made. I've put a request into his cell provider to see if we can triangulate his location. We have to wait, and in the meantime, because there's no evidence to implicate him, he's free."

"That's not right," I said. "He's part of this, I know it. What about the gun?"

"It's not a real gun," she said. "It's a modified starter's pistol, which has its own complications, but it wasn't the weapon used on Hank."

"What if the principal is telling the truth, then who did your dad go to see that night?" asked Serge. "There weren't any messages, there's nothing to track."

"You had something," I said to Nancy. "You said you would tell me later."

"Let's get home," said Nancy. "We can talk about it somewhere warmer." She put her hand up, then dug in her coat and pulled out her phone. "Yeah?" She said to the person on the other line. "Hold on. Repeat that." She gestured for me to get in the car, but something in her tone said the call was about Dad.

Nancy swore, and looked my way. "God, I totally forgot." She swore again. "Give him my number. I'll take the call right away. You didn't say anything, did you?" The question was asked sharply. "Okay, good. Friend or not, nothing gets out." She rang off and turned my way. "Gregory Ryan."

I looked blankly at her.

"Your dad's friend in Florida."

"Oh. Oh, crap, I forgot about him!"

"Apparently, my calls to him weren't sufficient, and you not answering his texts added to his panic. He's freaking out, hard. He says he's got information we need on your dad's murder, and he's coming to town to help with Hank's funeral arrangements."

"Okay, but when he couldn't get ahold of me, why didn't he phone you? Why call the station?"

"I didn't pick up, so he went with option B, but I'll tap in. Maybe I can stall him from coming here. We have enough on our plate—" Her cell rang. "That's him. Go home. I'll be there soon."

I climbed in the car and let it run for a bit.

"You lost yourself back there," said Serge. "I wasn't going to say anything in front of Nancy, but Mags, you've got to watch yourself. Grief can do weird things to a person."

"If you mean what happened with Larry, I'm tired of his crap. He hates me—"

"Yeah, yeah, he hates your dad, and he hated me, too. That's not the point."

"What is it, then?" I put the car in gear and drove out of the lot.

"I saw Serena. You were pushing Larry too far."

"I could have handled it."

"Your dad was ex-military, and he couldn't handle everything."

My grip tightened on the wheel. "You're talking about a mortal person versus—"

"I'm talking about that thing stepping inside you. Didn't you feel it? Didn't you sense it?"

"I was fine—"

"It was *inside* you," he said. "And the fact you didn't sense it should be proof you need to dial it back."

"Larry has information on my dad. I feel it. Maybe he was working with someone else, like Mrs. Pierson, or Mrs. Sinclair, or one of the other idiots who hide their hate in the dark."

"Maybe. But losing your mind on this isn't going to help anyone. Serena's gone rogue, so if she takes out Larry, I'm not going to lose any sleep. But the only way she'll step in to do it is if you step out." He put his hand on mine. "We already lost your dad. Don't ask us to lose anyone else."

I pulled the car to the shoulder. "My emotions are all over the place."

"Excellent deduction, Sherlock. Mags, I'm positive saying the painfully obvious is step one of the grieving process, but we have two lunatic entities on the loose, and one of them is holding your dad's spirit. Can you hurry up to step two?"

"Sometimes, I feel so cold inside, like there's a yawning void between me and everyone else, and no matter how hard I try to cross it, my legs are stuck to the ground. And other times, I'm hyper emotional, and no matter what anyone says or does, it's the wrong thing."

"Yeah," he nodded. "That's called grief. Step one, telling me the blindingly obvious. Feel like trying for step two?"

"What's step two?"

"I don't know," he said. "I just blew up one night, and then everything was better."

"Maybe for you. I was the one who had to clean up the chunks you left behind."

"If you blow up, I'll clean it." He frowned. "I don't know how I'll do it, but I'll figure out a way."

"How did I not sense it? I'm supposed to be training to be a guardian, my powers are increasing, how was I not there—even in spirit—when my dad was taken?"

"Craig wasn't allowed to see anything that connected with us. Maybe it's the same thing."

"But it's me and Dad. We should have defied the normal."

"Your relationship was special," he said, "but I don't think anyone gets special treatment, in this life or the next."

"Maybe."

He slumped in the seat. "I only got Hank for a couple of months." His eyes misted. "I never had a dad, and then I had this amazing guy, and suddenly, he's gone. And I'm a ghost who sees auras and energies. How did I not see that something was shadowing him?"

"You've only been dead for a while. I've been psychic all my life."

"Yeah," he said. "But we're both training to be guardians. Plus, I've been to the other side. Of the two of us, I should be the one held responsible for not seeing what was coming."

"You can't be responsible."

"Neither can you."

I sighed. "Fair enough. I get your point, but…"

"It's okay, Mags." He squeezed my hand. "We'll get through this together."

When we got home, Nancy was already there in the kitchen. Nell and Craig were at the stove.

"Thought soup might be the trick," said Nell. "Even if you don't eat a lot, it has all the vitamins and veggies you need."

"What did you find out?" I asked Nancy, taking the bowl and spoon Nell offered. "What was the thing you wanted to tell me?"

"I spent a frustrating morning phoning the Canadian military offices, trying to find out about Hank's funeral arrangements," she said. "When I finally got through to the correct office—" Her eyebrows pulled together. "—They said there's no record of his service, or him."

I set down the spoon, swallowed the rising nausea, and closed my eyes against the spinning room. "What?"

"Don't freak out, kid. That might mean a lot of things. It could even be that the guy on the phone mixed up some letters in Hank's name."

"Maybe your dad was deep in the military," said Nell. "And they scrubbed his name from the records."

Impossible. "Dad could barely fix a flat tire, I don't see him defusing bombs underwater or running point on some black ops."

"He could've faked his incompetence," said Craig. "Downplayed his abilities in order to fit in. That's what I do."

The sick feeling wouldn't be pushed down. I'd spent my whole life trusting Dad, believing we were teammates against the world, telling him all my secrets. But it seemed his life with me had been a lie. And while I'd trusted him with my life, he couldn't trust me with the truth. "What is going on? First, he tells you he's military, but there's no record of him. He couldn't boil water, but he had guns stashed under the bed. Where's the lie and where's the truth?"

"Your dad loved you—"

"Love means being honest." What if the secret he hid was the true reason behind his murder? What if my dad was never the guy I thought he was?

"Love means protection, and when it comes to parents, sometimes they make the wrong choice because they're trying to keep their kids safe," said Nancy. "Your dad was military, I know it. Gregory Ryan said he served with your dad. He's coming here, he insisted on it." She flipped her braid over her shoulder as she leaned over the soup. "At first, I didn't want him here." She glanced at me. "I don't want to explain to an outsider why I'm letting you do what you do. But I figure it's also a chance to get information on your dad, and that might help our investigation into his killer."

"Did he say anything when you told him what happened?"

She shook her head. "He said he was taking the first flight out and—"

We turned at the knock on the door.

"Stay here, all of you." Nancy stood. "I'll see who it is."

"I'll go with her," said Serge. "Just in case."

They went down the stairs, and the three of us followed.

Nancy turned, hearing the creak of floorboards behind her. "What did I say?"

"I listen for subtext," said Nell. "And it said, back me up."

Nancy glared at us. "Stay back." Then she glared harder at Nell. "No subtext. Just stay." She went down the rest of the steps and peered through the keyhole. "Oh." She opened the door. Bruce and Tammy stepped inside.

"Hey." Bruce waved up at us.

We waved back.

"We heard about the run-in with Principal Larry," said Tammy. "Are you okay?"

I nodded.

"Come on in," said Nancy, reaching for her boots. "I want to get back to work, anyway. See if there's something I missed, or if the guys found something new."

"You didn't finish your soup," said Nell.

"Sorry," she said. "I don't have much of an appetite."

Nell headed into the kitchen and came back. "Head's up." She tossed a protein bar at Nancy. "Just in case."

"You're a good girl, Nell," Nancy told her.

Nell grinned. "That's what the boys tell me."

Nancy rolled her eyes but smiled. "Maggie, call me if you need anything. Don't open the doors to anyone, and make sure everything's locked down."

I nodded.

"We'll stay with her," said Craig. "It'll be fine."

After Nancy closed the door behind her, Tammy said, "Good, she's gone," and ran up the stairs. "I didn't want to say anything, but there're all kinds of rumours going around."

"Most of them are stupider than dirt," said Bruce. "Like your dad was selling body parts to medical universities. But—" He tossed his and Tammy's jackets over the railing and jogged up the stairs. "I heard one of the guys, Rob, was fired by your dad. No one's saying why he was let go, but word is that he was super pissed at your dad 'cause he couldn't get a job anywhere else. Your dad has a rep. If he fired someone, then no one in town was trusting that guy."

"When did this happen?" Craig asked.

Bruce sniffed the air. "That smells good." He spotted the crock pot and headed to the table. "Rob was fired a couple of weeks ago."

If there was a prize for worst daughter, I was in the running, if not the crowd favourite for the winner. How could my dad have been going through all this stuff and I never knew? Because I'd been too wrapped up in myself. Was that why he'd never talked to me about his past? Had he tried and I'd been too selfish to listen?

"Do you know why he was fired?" asked Nell.

Bruce shrugged as Craig handed him a bowl. "Everyone's going to the gross and disgusting theories."

"That makes sense," said Nell. "Rob's classless, and that's saying a lot, coming from me."

"Yeah, but Maggie's dad would never let him go down that road in the first place," said Bruce. He dished the soup and handed a bowl to Tammy, then took the second bowl Craig held out to him. "I think it was probably just Rob making jokes about the families of the dead person. Your dad would never have let something like that go. He was all about respect and being decent. Or Rob was stealing jewelry the dead were supposed to be buried in."

No one could wear a mask twenty-four-seven, for seventeen years. Whatever was in my dad's past, I had to hold to the man I knew, no matter what the future would reveal and no matter what weird puzzle pieces were coming my way. "Thanks. He was a good guy."

"I heard Rob got a job hauling junk to the dump," said Tammy. "I bet we could find him if we went there."

"He's not at the dump," said Nell. "He's working out in Fort Mac. Flew out last week and he won't be back for another week."

"How do you know all this stuff?" I asked.

"You have your superpowers, I have mine."

"One person, suspected, and cleared," I said. "The rest of the town to go."

"There's other stuff to deal with," said Bruce. "I didn't want to say anything in front of Nancy, 'cause you know how emotional girls can get—ow!" He rubbed his shoulder.

Nell shook her fist. "Be an idiot and I'll do it again."

"I didn't mean it like that. It's just women can get hysterical—ow!"

"You're doing it wrong," I said. I reached over and took his bowl of food.

"Aw, come on." Bruce held his spoon in mid-air. "I'm still eating."

"Choose your words carefully," I said. "And you can keep eating."

"I will, I promise."

I handed him back the bowl.

"Take it for what you will," he said. "But I heard your dad was doing some late-night visits to another woman." He held up his hand to ward off Nell. "Not that I believe it, but I'm just repeating what I heard. They said he met up with her a couple hours before he died."

"Dad wasn't cheating on Nancy," I said.

"He was seeing a woman," said Craig. "But not like you think. It was Mrs. Sinclair, and Nancy knew about it."

"How is it you know this, and I don't?" I asked.

"Because your dad knew you felt badly about what happened with Amber and her mom."

"It's been horrible," said Nell. "The church board fired her after everything came out about Amber and the reverend. They said there was no way she couldn't have known."

"Christian charity at its best," muttered Serge.

"And now they're filing for welfare 'cause no one else wants to hire her," said Nell, glancing at her cell.

"I didn't know about any of that," I said.

"You've had your hands full," said Craig.

Maybe, but Principal Larry's words came back, accusing me of leaving destruction and not caring. It wasn't true. I had cared, but had I cared more about the dead than the living?

"Your dad hired Mrs. Sinclair to come in after hours. She was cleaning the funeral home," said Craig.

"See what I mean?" Bruce helped himself to more soup. "Your dad was a decent guy, Maggie."

"If Mrs. Sinclair was working for him, what about the rumour about him meeting up with a woman the night he died?"

"That was Amber. She's spinning out of control. Both your dad and Nancy were meeting with Mrs. Sinclair, to see if they could help," said Craig.

"How do you know all that?" asked Tammy. "I thought Nell was good at getting dirt, but you're amazing."

"Great," said Nell. "You mean, Nell is great, not good. In fact she's spectacular, a diva—"

I smacked her.

Craig shrugged. "I get around."

"I'm going to make coffee," I said.

"No, sit—"

"I can do that—"

"It's fine." I waved them down. "It's good to do something, anyway."

Craig followed me to the coffeemaker.

"How did you know all that?" I asked. I filled the pot with water.

"Partly because Amber was my charge," he said. "Partly because Nancy and Hank knew she had been my responsibility. They asked me about what her future held, if there was any way—" He glanced over his shoulder. "—Any way the reverend could reach through to this plane of existence and do anything to her, or the baby."

"And?"

"You saw how the reverend died," he said. "That guy's not going anywhere for a long time."

"Hey, Craig," called Bruce. "Is it possible Mr. Johnson went to meet Mrs. Sinclair that night?"

"I don't know," he said.

"There's only one way to find out." I set down the pot.

"I can drive." Tammy stood.

"I'll drive," said Nell. "And we're not all going to descend on the Sinclair house together."

"Rock, paper, scissors?" asked Bruce.

"More like Maggie, Craig, and I are going," said Nell. "You and Tammy hang out, maybe you can clean up the kitchen."

"What? You guys get to investigate and we have to clean house?" asked Bruce.

"We can find a different way to help the investigation," offered Tammy. "You know, divide up our resources. I have an idea."

Please let it not include another Ouija board. "No one has to—" I held up my hand.

"Did you enjoy the soup?" asked Nell. "The soup that Craig and I worked hard to make?"

"Well, yes, but—"

"Good, then it's decided," she said.

Bruce rolled his eyes. "Why do I bother?"

She smiled. "'Cause you're plucky, and I like that. Promise we'll share all the information when we get back."

"Tomorrow," said Craig. "It's been a long day." He looked over at me. "We all need some sleep."

I didn't want sleep, I wanted answers, but I couldn't argue with his logic. Better to get her in the light of day than the dark of night. "It's a good point."

No one let me clean up, so I sat on the couch while everyone tidied. And that gave me time to come up with a workable plan. It was all good to ambush Mrs. Sinclair, but questioning her would only work if she opened the door. Chances weren't great on that since I was the one behind her family's humiliation. But she held a clue, maybe, to Dad's murder, and I wasn't going to let that get away.

CHAPTER TWENTY-TWO

The next morning, I snuck out the back of the house, while Craig and Nell went out the front door and distracted the reporters camped outside. A couple of blocks later, we met up and drove to the Sinclair home.

"What are the chances no one's home?" Nell asked after I'd rang the bell for the third time and gotten no answer.

"Serge, go through the door and check," I said.

He nodded and disappeared.

"I hate this," said Craig. "I have no powers and no answers for all the skulking I did on the other side."

I squeezed his hand. "You were trying to help."

"I should've been smarter about it. Used my connections rather than trying to go directly through the system," he said.

"Can you still do it?" asked Nell. "Using your contacts?"

He shook his head. "No, not until my powers—" He stopped and looked at Nell.

"What?"

"You think Tammy and Bruce still have their Ouija board?"

"It blew up when The Family came out of it," said Nell. "But I bet they have another one stashed somewhere."

"Maggie," said Craig. "You okay if Nell and I take off? If we can get to a Ouija board, I can use it to call my connections. I'm mortal now, so I can't pull anything through. And as long as you or Serge aren't around—"

"We can do it at my place," said Nell. "Mom's at some board meeting, and Dad's at work."

Serge came through the front door. "No one's around, but there's a family calendar on the fridge. Mrs. Sinclair's scheduled to be at the funeral home tonight at eight."

"I guess I know what I'm doing tonight," I said. "Let's go back home. I'll get my car, then Serge and I can go to the funeral home later. Nell, you guys can head out to the séance."

"Séance?" asked Serge.

"I'll catch you up later," I said.

"Tammy and Bruce will be thrilled to help with the séance," said Nell. "More the merrier, right?"

+ + +

It was a weird thing to drive to the funeral home and not see Dad's minivan in its usual spot. Even weirder to see the flowers, stuffed bears, and notes that had been left in its place, protected by a tarp overhead. Weirdest was the boarded-up window and the faint smears of graffiti that had been painted over it. Love and hate, living side by side.

"Come on." Serge unbuckled his belt and stepped out of the car. "Let's see what we can find out."

"I never thought to ask," I said. "But seeing Mrs. Sinclair won't be easy for you."

"She never liked me, which was just as well. I never liked her, either. She had this weird way with Amber, like they were friends and rivals, more than mom and daughter." He shrugged. "I don't think it will be hard to see her, though. She can't do anything to hurt me."

"Do you think she knew? About her daughter and the reverend?" I headed to the entrance.

"No. She was a lot of things, but she never would have let that happen if she'd known."

"Well if it isn't little Maggie Johnson, the girl who all the ghouls love."

Carl.

"I have nothing to say." I kept walking.

"How did he find us?" asked Serge.

He's probably been here for a while. At some point, he knew I'd come here.

"I didn't get a chance to fully explain myself," he said. "I'm with the—"

"I don't care where you're from. I just lost my dad to a violent death, and you're here trying to make money from it. Don't you have something—anything—better to do?"

"New age, cult, and supernatural elements are a big thing," he said. "People like the curiosities of life. You, Maggie, are the most curious of them all."

"I won't let you turn me into a side show," I said bitterly.

"A few questions, that's all I have."

"Good luck with them." I walked away.

"Interesting, don't you think?" He called after me. "How the murder rate of Dead Falls spiked since you arrived."

"Don't let him bait you."

Too late. "I've been here for four years. It's a little late in the game for me to spike anything, don't you think?"

"I think it's entirely possible for you to do a lot of things," he said. "Five deaths. Two murders, two suspicious deaths, and an accidental one. Funny how you're connected to all of them. Funny how they all happened right after your dad and the town sheriff started dating."

I laughed. "You think we got together to kill people? For what, an uptick in coffin sales?"

"I think there's a lot more to the deaths," he said. "There's a lot more to you and your dad. I've been investigating your family, Maggie, and there are unanswered questions. Strange things that happen when you're in town. Sudden disappearances of people." He peered at me. "All the midnight moves. Why all the moving around?" He walked towards me.

I wanted to step back, but I held my ground.

"Strange, the way you'd leave town when teachers and social workers started asking questions, when parents wanted more information on the weird kid in their child's class."

"If you're asking me to explain parents to you, you're asking the wrong person," I said.

"I don't expect you to understand parents," he said. "There was just you and your dad. No mom. Did he tell you what happened to her? Or did she tell you herself?" He moved closer. "Does she come to you? What is it like, being able to talk to the dead?"

Serge's eyes went silver. "There's something supernatural going on with this guy." He moved closer. "Not soul-eater level, but he's got a covering of some kind—supernatural protection, maybe." He reached out his hand, touched what must have been a barrier. "I could probably push through it—"

If this was a movie, this was the moment I'd harness my power and blast him back with a ball of fire or light. But this was no movie and he had me so terrified, I couldn't think, I could barely breathe. *Don't*, I told Serge. *He has to think I'm mortal. You do anything supernatural, and it's over. He's probably recording us.* I tried again to do *something*, to say or do the brave thing, but my brain was a sputtering lighter, a few sparks, no fire.

Carl reached out to me. "I'm scaring you, and I'm sorry. Let's do a reboot." He smiled but I didn't buy the act.

"Think about it from another point of view," he said. "Aren't you tired of holding on to your secret? Aren't you tired of always being scared the truth will come out? Think of what a relief it'll be to just be yourself, be out in the open. And think of how much you'll be able to help the living, not just the dead. There are a lot of con artists in the world, taking people's money and feeding them lies about what's on the other side."

The bitterness in his tone caught my attention.

"You could put an end to the liars and really help those who need answers from loved ones who've died."

"Who did you lose?" I asked.

"Someone important," he said. "I've been investigating those in the supernatural world to know you're the real deal. You're the person I've been waiting for."

"It's a line," said Serge. "Even if it's real, this guy's a reporter. He's going to use you for his career, he doesn't really care about you."

I believe it. More than that, I remembered Dad's warnings of what the world could do to someone like me, and I wasn't going to let sympathy or pity force me into a decision I'd regret. "I'm sorry for your loss, Carl, but I can't help you."

His expression turned ugly. "What about the reverend and that kid, Kent Meagher? What am I going to find as I continue my investigation? Am I going to find the sheriff fudged things on her report? Maybe on all of them?"

He'd caught me and he knew it. Nancy had smeared the facts, she hadn't had a choice. How could she explain half the things that went on with me and the supernatural? "Just a few questions. It won't hurt." He raised his hands in surrender. "Look, it's not about spectacle or turning you into a freak show. You have a talent, a gift. Don't be selfish with it. You have the answers for what's on the other side. You can help heal all those who mourn."

"Go away." Point to me. I sounded braver than I felt.

"Fine." He pulled up his coat collar. "I guess I'll have to turn my questions over to the cops at Internal Affairs. They can ask Nancy about the discrepancies in her reports."

"Are you blackmailing me?"

"Negotiating."

"I'm bored with this and it's cold. I'm going inside."

"What happened the night on the bridge with Popov? How did you find the body of that kid? Why is there no record of your dad's service?"

"Keep talking," I said. "Exercise those lungs." Big words, but my stomach was a bowl of acid. Nancy had walked a fine line, helping me and covering for me when I investigated. And now, she was facing a possible inquiry, and I had no idea how it would all end. It seemed like my search for justice for the dead wasn't doing anything but hurting the living.

He smiled. "Run, rabbit, run. I'll get you, eventually."

"Haven't you heard of a lucky rabbit's foot? And I'm doubly lucky, because both of mine are still attached." Thank you, Nell, for the witty comeback. The wind blew, bringing with it the smell of the old mill.

"Carl, what are you doing, man?" Another guy emerged from the shadows. Slender, pale, dark hair. "Don't harass the kid."

"You following me, Savour?"

The guy flipped up the collar of his wool coat. "You're kidding, right? You think you're the only reporter looking into this story?" He glanced at me. "I'm sorry. He shouldn't be on you like this—not all of us are this...dogged." He stepped to Carl, but the other man dodged out of his way.

"It's not going to be like last time," said Carl. "I'm not letting you steal another story from me."

"No one stole the story," said Savour. "Your car broke down so I got there first. Come on, how about I buy you a beer?"

"Don't patronize me!"

"Fine," he said. "Then how about you use your head? The kid's guardian is a sheriff. You think she's not above finding a reason to arrest you if she finds out you're harassing her child?"

"That's police misconduct."

"Yeah," said Savour. "And then you can write a story about it. In the meantime, go home, and stop giving the rest of us a bad name." He looked over at me. "I'm sorry. Go do your business. I'll make sure he doesn't follow you."

"A reporter coming to your aid rather than finding the story?" Serge folded his arms and squinted at them. "I don't buy it."

Tell me about it, I said to Serge. *I'm sure it's a game of good-re-porter-bad-reporter and they're working together.* I went inside. The familiar sight of the staircases and reception area hit me like a bullet to my heart. I almost ran outside because dealing with Carl and his partner was better than dealing with the grief.

"Doesn't look like anyone's around," said Serge.

That was okay by me. I needed a couple of minutes to keep myself together. "Maybe we shouldn't do this."

"Don't freak out over what Carl said. Nancy's smart, and she would never do anything to put you or herself in danger. I'll text and update her, so she's prepared for anything that might come her way."

"I don't like him poking around, and I'm starting to wonder—"

"Don't," said Serge. "I know where you're going, and don't. This is your destiny, and this is what you scripted for your life."

"Except my choices have consequences for other people."

"Yeah, and those people have chosen to side with you." He squeezed my shoulder. "You can't make other people's decisions for them. They have freedom, and so do you. So, come on, let's look around."

We checked the main areas for Mrs. Sinclair, then the prayer room and the private space for the families. No luck. I walked to the office.

The door was partially closed, and there was light coming through the bottom crack.

"Don't tell me that!"

Mrs. Sinclair's voice. I glanced at Serge and put my finger to my lips.

He cocked an eyebrow and said, "I'm dead, remember? You're the one who'll make noise."

Right. Traumatic situations turned me into an idiot. I dropped my hand and continued along the carpet.

"It wasn't supposed to happen," said Mrs. Sinclair. "You said no one would get hurt, and the truth—" She paused, obviously listening to the person on the other end. "—People are hurt, and there's no truth. That girl lost her father—"

"I'm going to get closer," hissed Serge. "Maybe I'll recognize the voice on the other line."

He disappeared through the door as Mrs. Sinclair said, "I didn't sign up for this. We have to go to the police—" A quick silence. "What do you mean *why*? You know exactly—"

"Saint Maggie."

I jerked back and whirled around. "Amber." She stood in front of me, wearing yellow gloves and carrying a bucket and mop. "How are you doing?"

Her contemptuous expression said it all. She set down the cleaning equipment and peeled off her gloves. "And people think I'm stupid."

"I'm sorry, it was a bad question."

"And not like you care."

That stung. "I do care."

"Yeah, you really checked up on me after it all hit the fan. I must have been too busy eating chocolate to read your texts."

What could I say to that? *Sorry, Amber, but a few days after we solved Serge's murder, another ghost showed up at my door. I was trying to figure out who killed him and prevent the town from being possessed, and I forgot to text you.*

"Didn't think you'd have an answer." She rubbed her belly.

"How are you doing?" I asked. "Really?"

"We're on welfare, the church turned its back on us, I'm the town's favourite gossip topic, and Principal Larry kicked me out of school. How do you think I'm doing?"

"Maggie?" Mrs. Sinclair came out of the office. "What are you doing here?"

"I wanted to talk to you about my dad," I said.

Serge came up behind Mrs. Sinclair. "I could hear you on the other side of the door. So could Mrs. Sinclair. She hung up when she realized you were there. I don't know who she was talking to, but it was a woman."

"Hank? Why?" asked Mrs. Sinclair.

"I heard he was helping you—"

Amber snorted. "Some help. Come to my funeral home and clean toilets."

"Amber!" Her mom shushed her. "Hank didn't give charity, and I appreciate that—"

"He didn't give a lot to anyone, did he?" said Amber. "He was all over the principal when it came to his precious daughter, but when she stuck her nose in things that didn't concern her and screwed up everybody's life, he was suddenly hands-off with the collateral damage."

"He didn't do anything wrong," said Mrs. Sinclair. "And neither did Maggie."

"I guess everyone's a good person but me," said Amber. She snatched up the bucket and mop.

I put my hand up to stop her, but she shoved me aside and stalked off.

"I'm following her. Amber always went for the drama when she was planning something." Serge went after her.

"I'm sorry," said Mrs. Sinclair. "She's been—"

"It's okay," I said. "I know she's going through a bad time." God, what an understatement. "I'm sorry for what happened. I'm sorry for what—"

Her eyes filled with tears that spilled over, unchecked. She grabbed my hand and shook her head.

"Why don't we have a seat?" I led her into Dad's office, ignoring the twisting of my heart. It wasn't his office, anymore. I took her to the sofa.

"I can't believe this is happening," she said.

I handed her a box of tissues.

"This isn't your fault," she said. "What's happened to us, it's not on you. It's my fault."

"No, it isn't." I sat beside her. "It was the reverend."

"How did I not see it?"

"Because he was in a position of power and you trusted him."

"When I think about how much—" She broke down.

I put my hand on her shoulder.

"—I was happy with the time he spent with her. I thought he was like a father to her, a strong presence." She reached for a tissue. "The worst part is hindsight. I think Serge had tried to tell me." She began to cry again. "I shut him down. I thought he was rebelling. He was such a horrible kid—now I know why."

"He's in a better place," I said. "I know it. He's happy now, at peace."

"I wish I could believe that."

"I believe it. Dad did, too."

"Your dad was a good man," she said.

"I had wanted to talk to you, to ask if maybe you were supposed to meet him that night—"

"No." She gestured to the room. "He helped me get this job, swore the employees here to secrecy. Most of them were good about it. Rob, he got into it with me one night. Your dad let him go, but I heard your dad also helped him get that job up north in Fort McMurray." Her hand fell to her lap. "It's been good, being here. We've been getting harassed—phone calls, rocks through the window, spray paint on the house. At least here, it's quiet."

"I couldn't help but overhear the conversation you were having earlier, on the phone."

A flush of red stained her cheeks.

"Was there something you wanted to tell me?"

"It was nothing. I was arguing with someone about some debts."

"It didn't sound like that," I said.

She stood. "I can't help what you think you heard—"

"You were talking about me. Please, Mrs. Sinclair—"

"It wasn't you. It was Amber. She lost the only dad she knew—the reverend." Her face crumpled. "But then again, it's good he's gone. He hurt my daughter and I thought he was a good ma—" She reached for more tissues. "That's who I was talking about."

"Mrs. Sinclair—"

"It was a private conversation. Not everything is about you, Maggie!" She collapsed on the couch. "I'm sorry," she whispered. "I've gone from my life making sense to having everything in shambles."

"You said you didn't sign up for this," I said. "You said people had been hurt."

She didn't respond.

"Mrs. Sinclair?"

She glanced sideways. "You can't tell anyone this." She pushed up the sleeves of her pink sweater and wiped her palms on her jeans. "I have to think of Amber and the baby. I'm suing the church, the deacons, all of them."

"Mrs. Sinclair, you didn't see the abuse. If you didn't, then why do you think they did—"

"I don't, but in a few months, I'm going to have another mouth to feed. Those people didn't just abandon Amber and me, they left us with no money. Look what they did to our house. I don't have money to fix the windows or repaint those walls. They don't care. One way or another, they need to pay. All those who hurt her need to pay."

I couldn't tell if she was lying or trying to deflect from what she'd really been talking about on the phone, but her words held an essence of truth I couldn't shake.

"I need to find Amber," she said. "She's always been quiet and secretive, but now it's worse than ever. It's almost impossible to get her to put down her phone. She's addicted to reading what other people are saying about her on social media. I've tried to get her to stop, but she can't. It's like she has no value except for what other people give her, even if it's abusive and destructive value. I'm sorry I can't help you, now." She hurried out of the room just as Serge materialized.

"Any luck?" he asked.

I shook my head. "You?"

"Sort of. Amber's part of some online group that's all about supporting and promoting adults in relationships with young girls."

"That's sick."

"But one of the people must be here, in town, because she was texting with them. I didn't recognize the number, but I know it's local."

"What were they talking about?" I asked.

"Nothing. Just that she's the victim of a society that doesn't understand true love, and her mom's too controlling, blah, blah, blah. I don't know who she was talking to—their handle is Pygmalion—"

"That's not weird or creepy," I muttered.

"—Anyway, they said they'd meet up with her in fifteen minutes."

I was already heading for the door. "Where?"

"All they said was 'the usual place.'"

I stopped. "You've got to be kidding me."

"I wish."

"Psychic magnetism," I said. "You and Amber had a weird connection. I bet if you concentrated, you could locate her."

"I don't know," he said.

"I'm going to try too, but it's easier for you to get around town than it is for me. I'll have traffic lights and dead ends."

"This idea is a dead end."

"Don't make me beg," I said. "Mrs. Sinclair shut me down, but I know she's hiding something. If I had something on Amber—like maybe her getting into another destructive relationship or plotting to hurt someone—I bet she'd trade my silence for what she knows."

Serge watched me.

"It makes me feel like a slimeball just to say it, okay? I'm doing to her what the reporter did to me. And you staring at me like that just makes it worse, but we need answers and I'll do whatever it takes."

"I wasn't judging you," he said. "I was just thinking about what Craig had said one time, about how people thought destiny was this great thing, but it was one of the worst things." He started for the door. "We have to do all of this—follow Amber, blackmail Mrs. Sinclair—but it sucks."

"Yeah," I said. "It does, but there we are. Come on, let's go and get this over with."

CHAPTER TWENTY-THREE

Between me visualizing Amber and Serge using psychic magnetism, we located her at the high school.

"This feels like a weird place to meet with someone," he said.

"Not if the someone is the principal and an old friend of the guy you've been manipulated into believing you loved." I pulled on the door, but it was locked.

Serge knelt and peered through the keyhole. "I bet if I concentrated, I could unlock it."

"And what will you do when that works?"

Serena.

I turned and found her behind me. Her face held faint outlines of eyes and a mouth, though I didn't need her to have those features to know she was angry and full of contempt for me.

"You already had your chance to bring him to higher justice and you let him go free," she said. "What do you think opening the door's going to do?"

"You're talking about the day in his office?" I asked. "When the principal and I got into it?"

"You're crazy," Serge told her. "No way was I going to let him hurt Maggie just so you could find justice."

"I would never let him hurt Maggie," said Serena. "I was there to help her focus her power."

"You mean her anger," objected Serge. "And there's no good in that."

"The red," I said. "That was you."

I sensed her sarcastic response, though she said nothing.

"Why are you here?" I asked.

"Him." She nodded at Serge. "The night on the bridge, you caught my attention."

"If I had skin, it would be crawling," he said.

"I meant right now," I said. "Why are you here, at the school?" But I wasn't her focus, anymore.

"Don't be an idiot," she said to Serge. "You showed potential. You proved you had what it takes when it comes to a higher form of justice."

"Yep, definitely crawling."

"But you." Serena turned my way. "All this hand-wringing. You're supposed to be a guardian—"

"Not yet," I said. "I'm still training."

"A guardian," she repeated like I hadn't heard her. "A gatekeeper. Life and death, the eternal cycle of souls is on your shoulders, and you're fretting over police and social services. The bad people are bad people, and there is no helping them. There is only saving their future victims. I tried to show you that with Matty, Zach, and Madison, but you're as obtuse as ever."

"And what you did, killing the man who had Madison, that was better? You took their souls at the lowest point—"

"They don't deserve a higher point," she said. "And you're naive if you think they're worth a second or third chance."

"Hurting them hurts you—"

"But it saves the other souls," she said. "There's a cost to being a guardian. You do what's right for others, even if it hurts you. If you can't do that, then go do something else."

"I'd love to keep arguing with a faceless entity," I said. "But I have to nab a killer." Great. My irritation with Serena turned me into a cliché. I turned to Serge. "Get out of the way, I'm going to try to melt the lock."

I did my best to ignore the serengti, took a breath, and concentrated. "I feel something—"

There was a small *bang*, a blast of fire shot a hole through the door. Serena snorted.

"Close enough," I muttered. I used the hole to unlock the door. "Stay here," I told her.

"Whatever," she said. "You need me."

"No one needs you," said Serge. "Especially if you're sending Maggie down the wrong path."

"What is she, Little Red Riding Hood?"

"I'm not the only one noticing your fangs," he said.

"I'm pointing out the obvious. The higher-ups interfere when it suits them, and stay quiet when it doesn't. Interesting, don't you think, that Hera showed up on the night Serge died?"

"So?" asked Serge.

"So, why didn't she show up with your dad, Maggie? Why didn't she warn you? Why didn't she prevent Hank's murder?" Anger throbbed in her voice. "Did he deserve to die? And why did Hera rein in Craig when all he did was try to help you?"

I didn't have the answers, and I didn't like the questions. And I super didn't like that I agreed with her.

"You know I'm right," she said. "They have an agenda, one they're not sharing. They don't care about who dies and who gets hurt."

"Don't listen to her, Mags," said Serge. "There's got to be more than that to the story."

"Let's go," I said. "We're wasting time."

"Where do you think Amber and Pygmalion will be?" Serge pushed himself between me and Serena.

"I'm not sure. Maybe his office?" In the dark and alone, the school seemed bigger, containing more secret spots than I'd remembered.

"Why don't you follow the energy trail?" asked Serena.

Serge and I glanced at each other.

"Amateurs. Focus on the principal and Amber—"

"It's creepy, isn't it?" Serge whispered. "To think all this time, she's been shadowing both of us—" He spun to face her. "You must have known something bad was coming, why didn't you warn us?"

"I don't know everything," she said. "And I tried to protect everyone the best I could, but multitasking is tearing me apart. I have charges too, and souls that need protecting. I can't be everywhere at once." She pointed to the floor. "Look for her energy. Imagine who and what she is, and let it come to you."

I thought about Amber, the things I knew of her. A faint pink trail lit the hallway, a wobbly line that led to the principal's office. "Why do you care about me and Serge? You have access to anyone you want."

"I want you," she said. "And him."

I tried to get her to say more, but she refused. Which irritated me. "If you're going to be here," I said, as we moved into the main office. "The least you can do is be helpful. Shutting down when I have questions is nothing but you acting like a jerk."

"Shut up," she said. Serena pointed at the principal's door. Light leaked out from the crack in the doorway. She moved toward it. "Looks like he and Amber are in there. No one can see us but you. Stop talking before everyone starts calling you the undertaker's crazy daughter."

"Thanks for nothing," I muttered as she moved ahead.

"Let me go first," said Serge. "In case there's something bad or gross going on inside. You don't need to see it."

"And you do?" I asked.

"I can explode and put myself back together. According to Nell, you can barely dress yourself."

"Now is not the time to criticize my fashion choices."

He put his finger to his mouth.

Great. Everyone was telling me to shut up. I stifled a sigh and snuck toward the door.

"You want me to help you with answers," said Serena. "Here's my help. Call the cops." She moved from the light.

"Why? What's going on?" I pushed open the door. Amber and the principal lay in a crumpled pile. The bullet holes in their bodies told me they'd never rise again.

CHAPTER TWENTY-FOUR

Mrs. Sinclair sat in one of the chairs in the main office, a blanket wrapped tightly around her shoulders, with only a hint of her blue sweater peeking through. She rocked, moaning and muttering, tears falling unchecked.

Nancy went up to her and held out a paper cup. "You want some coffee, May?"

She stared at the cup for a long moment. "Yeah, I guess. Is Amber okay?"

Nancy glanced at me. "Amber's *body* is safe," she said gently. "The team is with her now, collecting as much evidence as they can." Nancy sat and took May's hand. "We'll get whoever did this."

"She was shot. So was Larry. Is it the same guy who killed Hank Johnson?"

"It's too early to say." Nancy shifted. "You went in and saw Amber?"

"When—" She licked her lips. "When I got the call, I couldn't believe, I couldn't—I had to see for myself."

"The deputy said you took some of her things home with you?"

Mrs. Sinclair nodded. "The scarf, her phone and earbuds. She's always misplacing them. Her wallet and keys. She wouldn't like to lose those."

"I know," Nancy said gently. "But right now, we need those things. Someone hurt Amber and Larry, and we need all the help we can get. There might be a clue in Amber's phone or in her car. We need the keys."

May nodded, the movement chopped and painful. "I'm sorry. I should've—"

"It's okay," soothed Nancy, taking the items May held out. "Drink your coffee. I'll be back in a minute." She stood and, noticing me, came over.

"How much tragedy can one woman take?" Nancy asked.

"I hope this is it," I said. "Mrs. Sinclair's been through enough, I'd hate to think of the gossip getting worse now that Amber and Principal Larry were victims of a double murder." Nice one, hypocrite. An hour ago, I was hoping for something juicy so I could exchange my silence for May's knowledge.

"Death has a way of shutting people up," said Nancy. "They'll focus on Amber's good qualities and forget about the other stuff."

"I hope so."

"You want to go through it with me, one more time. Why were you here?"

I hedged the truth. "I wanted to talk to Amber. I had a feeling there was stuff going on."

"Stuff?"

I shrugged. "Truth? I was hoping to find something that could connect her with my dad, or at least help me figure out what was going on." If Dad had been here, I would've confessed fully, but he was gone, and I was alone in the dark with my conscience.

Nancy gave me a hard look. "Maybe you were hoping to find something you could flip into a clue or an answer? Looking to blackmail her for information?"

"How did you know?"

"Because I know you. It's okay, kid."

I shook my head. "This whole thing is…it's either turning me into a terrible person or it's revealing that I was terrible to begin with."

"Flipping information is a common investigative tactic," she said. "Don't beat yourself up over it." Nancy squeezed my hand. "In fact, stop beating yourself up over everything."

"I miss him," I whispered. "I wish Dad was here."

"Me too," she said. "So bad it hurts." She put her arm around my shoulder. "Let's make a deal. We'll hurt together. Okay?"

I nodded.

"Don't shut yourself off and don't start keeping secrets. You have people to talk to. If not me, then Craig, Nell, and—" She glanced up to see if anyone was listening. "—Serge. Where is he, anyway?"

"In the room with the bodies. I tried to get a reading, but I almost set fire to the desk and papers. There're some marks—"

"That'll mess with forensics."

"Sorry."

"It's okay, I'll take care of it."

Which reminded me of Carl. I told her about his threat.

"We'll be fine," she told me.

"But he knows things—"

"We'll be fine," she repeated. "I'll take care of it. He doesn't know anything you can't find in an Internet search, and he's testing you to see if you'll cough up information. It's Basic Interrogation 101. When Serge's done, I want you to go home. The media's starting to gather outside, and I don't want you around. Especially if Carl's in the mix. He's not a threat, but he's a nuisance and neither of us needs that right now."

"I can go now, if you want."

"I'd rather have Serge with you," she said. "In case one of the reporters gets handsy. He can step in and upset their electrical systems."

"For the record, I know how to take care of myself."

"If you do it, it's assault. If Serge does it, then there's no paper-work." She gave me a tired smile. "Give a girl a break, would you?"

She left to take care of the investigation and Serge found me a couple minutes later.

Did you find anything?

He made a face. "Sort of. There's a weird liquid in the blood. I want to ask Craig about it."

Let's go. Nancy wants us out of here.

He started for the door, then stopped and stared at me.

What?

"I'm an idiot." He looked back at the office.

They say admission is the first step to recovery.

He shot me a dirty look. "I was standing there like a chump, listening to the cops talk, but I'm energy. Why am I listening when I could hack Amber's phone? Give me a second, let me see what I can find out."

My presence was going to be noticed, but I made my way over to the crime scene. The door was wide open. Frank and a female deputy were there. I took a spot by the frame, did my best imitation of a potted plant, and listened.

"Grab a baggie," said Frank. "Let's make sure we cover their hands."

"You think it's the same calibre that killed Hank?"

"Forensics will tell us." Frank grunted. "Just what this town needs, a serial killer."

"Bound to happen. All this fixation with social media and celebrity worship. People are losing common values."

Yeah, guns and psychos don't kill people. The Internet kills people.

"Tragedy," said Frank. "Amber's baby never stood a chance."

"Maybe that's a good thing." Her voice dropped. "The way people were talking about her and May. Some folks were a match away from lighting their torches and pitchforks and burning down May's trailer."

"No one's going to burn anything now. Poor woman. She used to be such a good-time girl, now look at her life. How much crap can a body take? Your boss seduced your teenage daughter and gets her pregnant—"

"Not just a boss," she said. "May trusted Popov, thought of him like a co-parent with Amber."

"Tragedy, all around," said Frank. "Hey, look at this." There was rustling, scraping. "Well, look at what we got here." Silence. "Just fired. Same calibre as the bullet wounds. Looks like we got the murder weapon."

"Hey, Nancy, come here and see this!"

I bolted from the doorway, a guilty flush on my face. It took me a second to realize it wasn't Frank or the female deputy. The voice was coming from the hallway. I sped toward the commotion.

Serge stood by the phone, the deputy next to him. "I need another second."

"What's going on, Andrews?" Nancy ran up.

"Something's wrong with Amber's phone," he said. "The thing's opening and closing apps, scrolling through texts. It's like it's possessed."

Nancy gave me a long look. "I'm sure it'll settle. Like *right now*."

"Even dead, I know not to mess with that tone." Serge stepped back. "I got some stuff that might help."

"Maggie," said Nancy. "Go home."

And I knew not to mess with that tone. Nancy had warned me about reporters, so Deputy Andrews came with us as we snuck out the rear exit. "She thought the reporters were out," I said. "But I only saw a couple of people at the front door."

"Maybe they'll be out later."

Famous last words. As we got closer to the car, the reporters emerged from the shadows, manifesting like lingering spirits.

"Just a few questions—"

"Is it true there's been another body—?"

"Did you discover the bodies—?"

"Do the dead talk to you—?"

"Do you have powers—?"

"If I had powers," I shot back. "Don't you think I'd use them on you and get myself some space?"

I dived into the car, locked the door, and ignored the questions they hurled at me.

"That wasn't the smartest thing you ever did," said Serge.

I let the engine warm up and rested my head against the steering wheel so none of them could see me talking to him. "I know. Ten bucks says tomorrow the headlines will be about how I'm a threat to society because of what I said."

"It was a good line."

I heard the smile in his voice. "Thanks."

The deputy chased off the reporters, then waved at me as I pulled out of the lot. I headed home. Craig and Nell were in the house. The smell of tomato soup and grilled cheese sandwiches scented the air.

"Not that I'm ungrateful for dinner," I said, as I took off my coat and boots. "But how did you get in my house?"

"My skills are more than supernatural," said Craig. "I have street abilities you can't begin to fathom."

"Yeah," said Nell. "He said, 'hey, Nell, where do they keep the spare key?'"

"Skills are skills. I fed Ebony and Buddha," said Craig. "And walked the big man."

"Thanks." I sank into one of the kitchen seats. Buddha came over for a tummy rub. "Did you learn anything with the Ouija board?"

"Other than that Tammy has a stash of them and Bruce isn't nearly as macho as he'd like to think when it comes to spirits?" Nell shot Craig a frustrated look. "I wouldn't know. Someone didn't want to share his information."

"Only because we weren't all together," said Craig.

"He wouldn't tell me," said Nell. "The whole Ouija board was them communicating telepathically. I asked but he said I had to wait."

"See what I'm saying?" Craig said. "I have street skills."

"We're together, now," said Nell. "Anytime you're ready to help—"

"There's a disruption on the other side. Whatever and whoever this guy is, he's done a great job of hiding."

"He's number one on the supernatural fugitive list," said Nell. "I bet that's why they couldn't protect your dad, Mags. They didn't see this guy coming."

"There's more to it than that," said Craig. "Let's dish the food, then dish the news." Nell grinned. "You see what I did there—"

I held up my hand. "Please, don't. I haven't had enough food or sleep for this."

"Bruce and Tammy said reporters are hounding the kids at school for info," said Nell. "Loser Larry was loving it, though. He was always out there, talking about what a menace you are. He let the reporters talk to any kid who was willing to back him up on his lies."

"Great, like I wasn't already a social outcast."

"No worries. Bruce and Tammy got it handled. I guess Bruce put some kid in a headlock for talking—lying about his connection to you—word spread. No one's talking now."

Craig shuddered. "That would do it. Bruce is a great guy, but who wants to be trapped in his armpit?"

Once the food was laid out, Craig took over the conversation. "Nell's right about the soul-eater being on the supernatural fugitive list—"

"Nell's right. Two words I can't hear often enough," she said.

"This guy's been around for a long time, and he's got the power of all the souls he's trapped. The other side's been looking for him for years. But he's made a mistake. He came here because of his link to you. The hunters know he's connected with you, so they're surrounding the town, watching and waiting."

I gave myself a second to consider what bounty hunters from the other side could look like. "His connection to me, via our past life or via my mom?"

He nodded. "No one's sure, but I asked a couple of friends to look into it. In the meantime, this guy has it out for you—"

"And we're sure it's a guy," said Serge. "He's not using the ghost energies to hide or change his gender."

"It's a male, but with his powers, he can hide under the guise of a woman," said Craig. "But I doubt that's the case. It takes an immense amount of work to hide your gender, and it's exhausting. My bet is he's stayed true to his birth gender. My contacts think it's not just you he's after, Mags, it's Serge too."

The ghost's eyes went wide. "Did Maggie and I do something with him in a previous life?"

Nell read his text. "If we knew that, Casper, we wouldn't be having this conversation. We'd be out there with holy water and silver bullets."

"That's for vampires and werewolves," I said.

She took a bite of her sandwich, and her response was lost to the bread and cheese.

"We're not sure why he's coming after you and Serge," said Craig, raising the soup to his mouth. "But, Mags, we think your dad was targeted by him to take you down."

Serge and I looked at each other. "Take us down?"

Craig swallowed and set down his bowl. "From what my contacts could tell me, you and Maggie will be the ones who capture him, bring him to justice on the other side, and free the souls. You're his retribution. They figure that's why he's here. He's trying to stop you."

"So why didn't he just come at me directly?" I had the answer as soon as I asked the question. "Because Serge and I are a team. If he came at us, that might be the moment we stop him. Permanently."

"But if your dad's dead and you're locked in mourning, you can't track him," said Nell.

"And if she goes rogue or starts doing her own thing because she's angry that the powers-that-be didn't protect her dad, then he also goes free," said Serge. "You have to watch your anger, Maggie, before any of those lunatics goad you into doing something you can't come back from."

"I think that's my cue to tell you what's going on on our side," I said. I gave them the lowdown on Amber, Principal Larry, and the appearance of Serena.

"My head's spinning," said Nell. "Amber's dead?"

"Shot."

"Shot to death?"

"Shot to death."

"Like with a gun and bullets?" she asked.

"No, Nell," I said. "With vodka and scotch. Of course with bullets and guns! What else shoots?"

"Well, you're shooting your mouth off right now, and you'd better check yourself and understand the seemingly simple questions are because I'm trying to sort it through in my mind. And you know better than to question the girl with straight As."

I blinked. "You're right. That was out of line, and I'm sorry."

She grinned. "Did you see what I did there, with the word 'shot,' how I turned it into shooting and—"

"I'm feeling less sorry."

"Don't worry about it." She stood. "Your clothes make all the apology you need."

I tossed a napkin at her.

Craig pointed at my sandwich. "Eat while we think this through."

I took a bite.

"The soul-eater swooped in and stole Zeke and Homer. We think it's because he was trying to throw Maggie and Serge off their game," said Craig. "Strike one for the soul-eater. Rather than disrupting your destiny, the two of you start looking hard for him."

"Then he kills Maggie's dad," said Nell. "And takes his soul."

I set down the sandwich.

Craig noticed. "At least eat the soup."

I reached for a spoon.

"That's strike two against the soul-eater," continued Craig. "Because now the two of you are buckled in for the ride."

I gave him a weak smile. At least one of us thought I was fierce.

"In the meantime, Serena's showing up—"

"Which is good and bad," he said. "Your power is growing but your anger is also calling her to you and creating a destructive bond—"

"I bet all that power and supernatural energy rolling around is why you could reach back in time and warn us about what was happening—" Nell snapped her fingers. "Wait a second, why are we worrying? Maggie obviously figures it all out, or else she wouldn't be in the future sending a message back."

"We're worrying because future Maggie has the answers and was smart enough to give the warning, but not smart enough to give the answer to this mess," I said.

"We've been through this—"

I waved down Craig. "I know, I know. Metaphysical differences between the dream world and this reality."

"I share your frustration. None of the pieces fit the puzzle. Especially the serengti," he said. "Something's off about Serena, but I can't figure out what it is."

"What could possibly be off about a faceless creature?" asked Serge. He turned. "Hey, Nell, see what I did there?"

She read the text and said, "Where are you?"

"Beside you."

"Fist bump. "She held out her hand.

"He did it," I said. "Now back to Serena."

"Serge nailed it," said Craig. "Serengti aren't faceless."

"You hide your face if you're trying to hide yourself," I said.

"Yes," said Craig. "But I feel like there's more to it than that."

"Didn't you say she's going vigilante, and it's not in their nature to do that? Maybe the loss of her features is literal," said Nell. "Maybe she's losing a part of herself."

"She's trying to gain it back with Serge and me," I said. "I get the feeling she's given up on me, but she's still trying to create a vigilante partnership with Serge."

"The soul-eater's coming for both of you," said Nell. "Serena's coming for Serge, and all the souls in the town are up for grabs." Nell ticked the list off on her fingers. "What I don't get is how Amber and Principal Larry play into all of this. Are we sure they're connected?"

"The bullets from Amber and Principal Larry's murders and Maggie's dad might be the same," said Serge. "I heard the cops talking about it." He pivoted to Craig. "There's a weird liquid in the blood. It's floating on top and it's metallic, but shimmery and green, and it looked like stuff was wriggling in it."

Craig read the text. "Shimmery?"

"Yeah, like it sort of changes shade but it stays green. What does it mean?"

"I don't—" He stared out the window into the dark night. Craig stood and shut the drapes. "I can't think of it. Stupid thing's just out of reach. It's—" He squeezed his eyes shut. "Green. Green is healing, green is life, grass. Blood and life, grass and death." He opened his eyes. "Let me think on it. The harder I reach, the more it's out of my grasp. It'll come to me, I just have to relax."

"Why would the soul-eater kill Amber and Larry?" I asked.

"There has to be a connection," said Nell. "What of it, Casper, are you the missing link?"

"Me?"

She read his text. "Yeah, you dated Amber, you had the connection to Larry. Anything you're not telling us?"

"Like what?"

"You secretly loved her?" asked Nell.

Serge shook his head.

"He's shaking his head," I told them.

"I really miss having my powers," murmured Craig.

"Then maybe it's something different, deeper," Nell said. "Maybe it's about guilt."

"Guilt?" asked Serge.

"For not helping her, for not stopping the reverend," said Nell. Her tone was gentle, devoid of accusation, but Serge's face flushed.

"I tried," he said. "I tried to tell Mrs. Sinclair, tried to tell the deacons at the church." He stopped to take a painful breath. "What do you do when no one wants to listen?"

"You do what you can and when that fails, you do what's necessary," said Nell.

Debbie-Anne, her aunt, had said the same thing the night we'd gone to her trailer, trying to solve the riddle of who'd murdered Serge. She told us about the abuse Serge had suffered at the hands of his parents, that she'd tried to report it, tried to get help, and all of it had been ignored or trivialized. She turned to alcohol to cover the pain of failing Serge, and I hoped that should I meet failure on the road, I'd be strong enough to turn to my friends instead. "We should talk to your aunt," I said. "She knows everything about everyone."

Nell grimaced. "Great. Can't wait to get drunk from her breath. Are we sure she knows things?"

"She knows things." I glanced at Serge. "She knew about Serge when no one else did."

"Jealousy! Possession!" Craig grinned. "I knew it would come to me. Jealous blood, that's what made the green liquid. But it's more than that—it's trying to get something that's not yours to have—trying to take the thing, even though it's not yours to take—" He made a frustrated sound. "I can't explain it, but it's not a regular kind of jealousy. It has psychic fall-out."

I took a second to catch up. "Who was jealous?"

"Whose blood was it?" asked Craig. "The principal's or Amber's? Was the shooter injured?"

"I never asked," I said.

"It was comingled," said Serge. "What does that mean?"

"Not much," admitted Craig. "But it might help with motive about why they were killed. What about—" He stopped as someone knocked on the door. "You expecting someone?"

I shook my head. "You?"

"Nope." He rose. "Let's see who it is."

"Not all of us," I said. "We look like a bunch of four-year-olds chasing a soccer ball. Serge and I will go. The two of you stay here and grab a knife or something—" I looked over my shoulder at them. Nell already had a knife in each hand. Craig, too. "—Never mind." The knocking continued, more insistent with each rap.

"Coming, coming." I hit the bottom step, then waited for Serge to do his thing.

He pushed through the door. The lower half of his body on this side, his upper half on the other. A second later, he came back. "I have no idea who that is."

"Does he look dangerous?" I asked.

"We've had three people murdered in two days and over half-a-dozen people killed in the last couple of months. At this point, everyone looks dangerous to me."

"Maggie," said the voice on the other side of the door. "Nancy, my name is Gregory Ryan. I was a friend of Hank's."

"Is that true?"

I looked up the staircase to where Nell and Craig stood and nodded in answer to Craig's question. "I don't know what he looks like."

"If Nancy was here, I bet she'd know," said Serge. "She looked him up on the police database."

"Maggie? Nancy? I know someone's home." His deep voice boomed through the wood. "I know—" His voice dropped. "I know things are weird right now, and I know you need help. That's why Hank called me."

"Do I open the door?" I asked my friends.

"I'm pushing my licence through the door so you know it's me."

Serge rolled his eyes. "Big deal. You can fake ID."

Gregory slid the plastic rectangle under the door. I picked it up. "No bad feelings off touching it," I said and flipped the licence so my friends could see it. "He looks okay."

"They always look okay," said Craig. "If bad guys looked like bad guys there wouldn't be any innocent men in jail."

"What do we do?" I asked. "I want to open it, I feel okay about him, but my powers are weird right now."

"I'm sure you're talking about this," said Gregory. "But it's cold on this side of the door."

"Let him in," said Nell. "I've got two knives and a wicked high kick."

"Maggie, Nancy, I am who I say I am. I'm not a reporter or anyone else looking to make money off you," said Gregory.

I squeezed my eyes shut and wished for the right answer to show itself to me.

"Open up," said Gregory. "I know who you are, Maggie. I know *what* you are. I know about the souls you've transitioned, I know about your ghost-brother Serge and your ferrier-boyfriend, Craig. Let me in, and I'll tell you who Hank really was."

CHAPTER TWENTY-FIVE

I opened the door and crinkled my nose against the smell of the old mill. Gregory and I took a good look at each other. Serge checked for auras and energies while Craig and Nell gave Gregory a hard once-over.

The initial checks done, Gregory pulled out a worn photograph and held it out. Dad, him, and a bunch of other guys from the platoon, squinting against the desert glare, their skin browned from the sun. "He was a good man." He waved the photo at me. "Take it."

"Don't you want to keep it?"

"I have him in my heart," he said, bouncing on his toes to ward off the cold. "I don't need him anywhere else. It's more important for you to have these mementos—I brought it for you. I figured with everything going on, you'd want proof I knew your dad before you let me in."

"You met in the army?" Nell asked.

He nodded. "First day of basic training. "

The wind swept the snow from the porch to my feet. "Come in," I said. *Text Nancy, tell her what's going on. Use my phone so she can respond.*

Serge nodded. "Already ahead of you."

"You're your father's daughter, Maggie," he said. "Trust but verify." He stepped inside, stamping his feet against the mat. "Thanks. It's cold out there and dry. The weather's doing all kinds of things to my sinuses."

"I'll get you some coffee," said Nell. "Are you hungry? We have sandwiches and soup."

"That sounds good."

I took his jacket and led him up the stairs. Ebony and Buddha moved from their spots under the table and headed toward the bedrooms.

"Animals," said Gregory. "Did Hank ever tell you about the dog we adopted while we were on tour?"

I shook my head.

"Found her in the broken-down rubble of a building. We took care of her the entire time. There was a kid—Ali—who used to hang out with us. He loved that dog, too. When we left, Hank let Ali keep her. I think it broke Hank's heart to give her up, but he knew she was in a good place. But I didn't come here to tell you war stories, and your dad would be ticked if I was jabbering on instead of catching you up." He moved to the table.

I took a seat beside him. Nell took one on the other side, while Craig went to the stove for soup.

Gregory pressed the heel of his hand to his forehead. "I used to visit Hank—you were just a baby then, Maggie. I had to stop because of the weather. This dry air messes with me. Headaches, nosebleeds, and medication wasn't what it is, now."

"Do you want some ibuprofen or aspirin?" I asked.

He shook his head and grinned. "You wouldn't believe it to look at me or hear me complain, but I used to be the best in the JTC. Your dad and I, teammates against the world."

My heart contracted, and contracted again when he continued, "Teammates until you, Maggie. You were his everything."

"Thanks," I whispered.

"Boy, he and I loved taking risks. The more dangerous the operation, the more there was to lose, the more we wanted it." The smile slipped from his face. "When I found out what happened to Hank, I knew it was fallout from one of our tours."

Craig set the food in front of Gregory, then sat down.

"Your dad never talked about his time in the military with you," said Gregory. "It was one of the few things we disagreed on. I thought you deserved to know, but some of the things we had to do—Hank didn't want to relive those moments, and he didn't want you knowing about the things he'd done—" His lips twitched. "—He's gone now, so I'll honour the memory and not tell you, either."

Well, that was helpful.

"You don't need to know the specifics of our missions to know we dealt with dangerous people. It's enough to say that our methods weren't always pretty." He took a mouthful of soup. "Most of the bad guys are in prison, some of them dead. But one man, he escaped." Gregory winced and pressed his fingers against his temple. "I think I will take that aspirin, now."

Nell rose to get it.

"Nancy texted back," said Serge. "I guess Gregory gave her the secret code she needed to get to the guys who can verify him and Hank. It's all checking out. Your dad was part of the military, so was Gregory. She says she's taken copies of the photos so you can see what Hank looked like when he was younger."

Nell returned and I said, "Tell me more about the man who escaped."

Gregory popped two pills and swallowed them dry. "He wasn't a bad man—"

"Does he have a name?" asked Craig.

"It wouldn't matter,' said Gregory. "Like Maggie's dad, this man can blend in and knows how to change his identity. God only knows what he looks like or what name he's using now."

"What name did he use when you and Dad were looking for him?"

His mouth pulled into a flat line. "Lucien."

"What happened?" asked Nell.

"Opinions vary. He was either a madman or a man ahead of his time, but our team had our orders. It was our last mission and maybe that's why the operation went sideways," said Gregory. "Lucien escaped but his capture was the responsibility of another team. Your dad left the military, married, had you." Gregory leaned forward. He ran his finger along the scar on his cheek. "You can walk away and try to make a new life, but your old decisions have a way of finding you."

Tell me about it.

"The military assumed—or hoped—that he'd died. But when I heard Hank had been murdered, I knew Lucien was still alive."

"You think he found Dad?" I asked. It made sense. The bruises on Dad's knuckles, his sudden, violent death at the end of a gun blast.

Gregory nodded. "I'm sure he's behind your dad's death, but it gets worse."

I wasn't sure how that was possible.

"Lucien vowed his revenge would be the ultimate payback. He didn't just come for your father. He came for all of you. I can't let anything happen to you or Nancy. I made a promise to Hank and I won't break it."

"How do we find him?" Nell asked.

"If I could talk to Nancy—damn—!" Gregory dipped forward, pressing his hand against his nose. "This weather."

"How did you survive the desert?" I asked as I handed him a tissue.

"I was younger then," he said. "Nosebleeds were a sign of a man's virility."

"I'm glad I wasn't alive then," said Nell.

"We have to figure out who Lucien is pretending to be," said Gregory. "Is there anyone in town who's acting strangely?" he asked.

"It's Dead Falls," said Nell. "Everyone acts strangely."

"What about new people, guys who're hanging around?"

"Two reporters, Carl Reid and a guy named Savour—I don't know his first name," I said. "But the town's overrun by new people, and Lucien could be hanging in the shadows. But Carl—" I thought of the supernatural protection that surrounded him. "He's the one I'd bet on."

"Him?" said Gregory. "Why?"

I shrugged. "He's been pushy and he said he's been researching my family. He says he has information on my powers and he's threatening to go public if I don't do what he wants. The problem is that I'm sure he wants me to contact someone from the other side, someone he lost. He didn't believe me when I told him I can't do something like that."

"Go on," said Gregory. "What is he doing?"

"He's been following me—really following me—and he threatened to leak information to Internal Affairs and have Nancy investigated for any covering up she did on my behalf."

"Maggie! He's been following you!" Nell smacked my arm.

"Why didn't you tell anyone?" Craig asked.

"Mags, I love you," said Serge. "But you can be a real deadhead sometimes. How could you not have told anyone he's stalking you?"

"He's a reporter, I thought it was part of the job." I gestured to Gregory. "I didn't know about his possible connection to Dad."

"I really wish I was off suspension," muttered Craig.

"But there was something else…" I thought back to our conversations. "He knew about Dad being military, but Dad didn't talk about his service."

Craig stared at me. "You have a guy who's following you, who knows information about your family that's not part of the public record, and it didn't occur to you to say anything?"

"I really thought it was part of his job as a reporter. Maybe he'd bribed someone in the department for information and found out about the tattoo."

"Or maybe he already knew about your dad's service because he was on the wrong end of your father's gun."

"I bet that's why Hank had the stash of weapons under his bed," said Nell. "That's who he was waiting for—Lucien."

"And maybe that's why there's no record of Dad in the military database," I said, looking at Gregory. "Because his real name was something else."

"Your dad and I worked the covert missions. We wouldn't show up on the regular channels. You'd have to know the right people to talk to and the clearance codes to find out anything. And it gets complicated."

Of course it does.

"Hank changed his identity when he realized Lucien was coming for him. He wanted to protect you."

Maybe that was why he wouldn't talk about Mom. Not because mention of her was painful, but because if I started connecting with her family, started looking for the other side of my family, Lucien could find us.

"The airport," said Nell. "The problem with your ID. If your dad was changing his identity, then he must have changed yours. No wonder you triggered the alert when you went through security."

"It's more than that," I said. "Dad wanted me out of town, fast. The video that was posted, the one that went viral, it showed the people at the gym that night, and Dad's at the minute-mark. I bet that's how Lucien tracked us here. He saw us."

"Use the right search terms, the right image parameters, and the internet crawlers will go through millions of bits of data to alert you to the thing you're looking for," said Nell. She turned to Gregory. "Who was she? What was their real last name?"

"I promised your dad I wouldn't say, and I won't, not until we know you're totally out of danger."

"But if Dad had family, they might be in danger, too."

"Lucien has the same tech as the military, that means listening devices that are state of the art, and he might have ears on you, right now. I've probably said too much. I wanted to bring my equipment. It would tell us if there are bugs in your house or near it. But I was in too much of a rush to get here. If there's time, I'll drive into Edmonton and see about picking up what I need." Gregory stood and pressed the tissue to his nose. "I'm sorry to cut our conversation short, but I should find a pharmacy and get something to help with this."

At the door, he turned and said, "I'll talk to Nancy and tell her everything I know. We'll get this guy, Maggie, I promise."

"What do we think of him?" I asked when I went back to the gang in the kitchen.

"The night we saw Rori on the road," said Craig. "You sent back a warning. *Beware the light, he comes in red.* The name Lucien means light, and red could be your dad's blood." He gave me a smile that had no humour. "Nice, isn't it? I remember what a name means, but it takes me forever to remember green liquid in blood."

"There wasn't just Mr. Johnson's blood. Amber and Larry are dead too. Not to mention Gregory and his nosebleeds," said Nell. "Lucien isn't just coming in red. He's coming in a lot of red."

"Not to criticize a military veteran," said Serge. "But Gregory wasn't that helpful. I get that he's trying to protect Hank's memory and to protect you too, Mags, but we don't need politeness. We need answers. We need to know exactly how the operation went wrong, what this Lucien guy used to look like, and what he looks like now."

"I think it's more than that," I said. "Don't you find it weird that Lucien and the soul-eater show up at the same time?"

"You think they're connected?" asked Nell.

"I think they're the same person," I said. "The soul-eater is a human being, and this Lucien guy has been hiding from the police for decades. What better way to hide than to use ghost power?"

"It makes a certain kind of sense," said Craig. "He withstands an army barrage that kills his family, but leaves him unharmed. That could be supernatural protection. And if he has all those souls at his disposal, he could be anyone. Even if he's caught, he could use the ghosts to break free, or manipulate circumstance."

"Carl had supernatural protection," said Serge.

"He's not the one," said Craig. "The soul-eater is coming after the two of you. If he's also Lucien, then he's not just coming for power, he's coming for revenge. Hiding under the identity of Carl is one thing, but hiding under his identity and allowing supernatural protection to be visible is too revealing. My instinct says Lucien is someone else."

"Savour's been around, too," I added. "Maybe he's Lucien and using Carl as his cover to get close."

"Or maybe it's neither of them," said Serge. "And Lucien is a mortal who's still in the shadows, plotting."

"Good point," I said. "This guy's supposed to be crazy smart. If I was him, I wouldn't come near me until I was ready to kill."

"But if it is Carl or Savour, then why didn't they kill you when they made contact?" asked Nell.

"Too many people around," I said. "It's one thing to kill me or my dad in the dark of night. The only time we were alone was in front of the funeral parlour. There's video surveillance there. He's not going to kill me when there's a trail for the cops to follow."

"You're right," said Craig. "If he's mortal, then he's spent a lifetime living in the shadows and being patient. If he's also the soul-eater, then he's one very old, very bad guy, and time has made him cagey."

Before I could respond, the radio clicked on, and the static hissed through the speakers.

"Maggie, oh, Maggie, he's coming. He's coming for you, Maggie."

Great, Mom. Tell me something I don't know. "Yeah, I know he's coming, but who is he? What does he look like—"

But she only wept and called my name.

"Any suggestions?" I asked Craig.

He shrugged, then turned to Serge. "Do you think you could reach through the static and make contact?"

"I could try." He moved to the radio and put his hand on top of it. He raised his other hand. Then he closed his eyes. "Maggie's mom—" He went quiet and I guessed he was telepathically talking to her.

She shrieked and his eyes snapped open. "Whoops."

"What did you do?"

"Nothing! I was—"

The static on the radio grew louder. So did her keening. The toaster and the coffeemaker, both beside the radio, began to vibrate.

"Exploding glass will be a bad thing." I shoved Nell behind me. "Get cover!"

The glasses in the cupboards rattled, the cutlery in the drawers shook. I turned, running for cover under the table. The explosion blasted me forward. I smashed my head against the edge of the cupboard, feeling something hard hit my stomach. Warmth bloomed from my belly as I crashed to the floor.

Nell yelled my name. I groaned and rolled over. Her gaze locked on to the red spreading from my torso, and she began to scream.

CHAPTER TWENTY-SIX

"**C**alm down," I said. "It's just soup."

"Why do you think I'm screaming?" she said. "That's homemade goodness, blended tomatoes and everything."

"I'll eat the sweater, okay?"

She helped me up. "Leave it. My soup's finally made it an item of quality."

I scanned the kitchen to figure out which mess to clean up first, then stared at what I saw. "It's fine. The kitchen's totally fine, no mess anywhere, except for the pot of soup."

"I noticed that too," said Craig. "I guess your mom just went after you."

"Someone needs to talk to this woman about appropriate displays of maternal love." I turned to Serge. "What did you say to her that got her so riled up?"

"Nothing," he said. "Just that Hank was dead and the bad guy was coming after you."

"We need to talk to you about your communication skills, Casper."

"I also told her that Nancy and Gregory were here and helping," he said.

Nell held her thumb and forefinger millimetres apart. "That's a little better, but—"

"I should have led with that. Her energy is fear. Pure terror." Serge rubbed his head. "I think she was going nuts by the time I got to that."

"We need to see what we can find about Carl and Savour, and if they're connected to the soul-eater," said Nell. "That should make your mom feel better."

I glanced at the clock. "It's too late to start hunting down bad guys."

"Tomorrow, let's start with my aunt," said Nell. "She's more likely to be sober—more sober—first thing in the morning."

I nodded. "Then Mrs. Sinclair and—did Principal Larry have any friends, other than the reverend?"

Craig folded his arms. "I guess we're about to find out."

✦ ✦ ✦

Nancy was at the coffeemaker the next morning. "Serge said you had a rough night."

I glanced over at the living room. Craig was crashed out on the big couch, Serge snored in the recliner. "Where's Nell?"

"She went home to check in with her folks. She'll be back."

"Communicating with my mother proved harder than I thought."

"Join the ranks," she said. "I feel the same way about mine."

I helped myself to a mug of coffee. "Did Gregory Ryan get in touch?"

She nodded. "Can't say I'm happy he showed up at the house unannounced, but I guess it's special circumstances."

"What's your read on him?"

She walked to the table and I followed. "Hard to say. He obviously knew your dad and he has military background, but I'm looking at everyone like they're a potential murderer."

I sat down. "Same."

"He asked me to give you his number, said he'd like to meet for breakfast and talk more about your dad."

"Where does he think we'll be able to talk without gobs of reporters surrounding us?"

"The police station. He said he'd bring pastries."

"Fair enough." I drained my cup. "First things first. Nell and I are visiting her aunt."

"Debbie-Anne? Why?"

"Because I think someone local did in Amber and the principal."

She nodded. "I do, too. But Debbie-Anne?"

"That lady knows everything. I'm sure she's got info." I gulped down my coffee. "Where are you on the investigation with Amber and Principal Larry?"

"Same place I am with your dad's," she said. "Nowhere." She glanced over her shoulder. "Is Serge awake?"

I shook my head.

"I didn't want to say anything because I don't want him to feel bad, I know he was trying to help. But when he hacked the phone, he accidentally reset it to the factory default. I have—Frank has—the tech guys working on it."

"If her stuff was stored in the cloud, then it shouldn't be an issue. It can be downloaded."

"Except Amber changed her password and May doesn't know what it is." She passed her hand over her face. "We have to do this by the book, but it's another delay we don't need. The more days that pass, the harder it is to find the leads."

"We have a lead with Dad: Gregory"

She snorted. "Hearsay from an ex-military guy who can't give out too much information because of state secrets hardly qualifies as a lead."

"Still better than going to interrogate an alcoholic." I stood. "But we do what we can."

"Take her some coffee and hazelnut creamer. She's a sucker for that stuff."

CHAPTER TWENTY-SEVEN

Half an hour later, I walked out of the house and into a confrontation. Carl waved at me from his spot at the top of the driveway. "Hello, Rabbit."

The slam of a car door was followed by Savour's running footsteps. "I'm sorry." He grabbed Carl by the arm. "I thought we handled this."

"I don't know what game the two of you are playing," I said. "But quit it. I'm not falling for the con."

"Working together? *Working with him?* You've got to be kidding," said Carl. "I wouldn't work with him if my life was on the line. Do you know what he did to me?"

"You did it to yourself," said Savour. "All the drugs and drinking—"

"I was grieving. You should have helped me, not called the cops and—"

"Take your history off my property. Nancy's home and she'll have no problem arresting either of you."

"How can you do this?" Carl asked me. "How can you be so selfish and deny the world your gift?"

"I haven't denied the world anything," I said. "But if you're looking for an answer about why I prefer my privacy, then look at how you're acting."

"I want answers—" Carl yelped as Savour grabbed him by the back of the neck and hauled him to his car. There was a scuffle, then Savour shoved him inside, leaned in, and said something. Whatever the conversation was, it worked. Carl drove off.

"He's right about one thing," said Savour as he came my way. "We're not working together."

"You just magically show up to help me out every time he's around?"

He slipped on his gloves. "My sister had the gift," he said. "Nothing like yours. She never dealt with the kinds of ghosts you do—"

"I don't—"

"I saw the video," he said. "I grew up with a psychic. I know what is real and what isn't. My sister—she tried to do what Carl wants you to do. She tried to help. But she couldn't withstand the skeptics, and she was consumed by those who were never satisfied by the answers she gave. She killed herself."

"I'm sorry—"

"We're on this earth for a reason," he said. "The world destroyed my sister and took her reason for joy away. I'm here to report, and I have a personal stake in anything paranormal. If the subject wants to make their gifts public, fine. But I've seen what the world can do, and I'm not going to let Carl hurt anyone. One girl's life destroyed was enough." He took out his business card. "You want to talk to me about anything, fine. You want to keep quiet, that's fine, too."

I took the card. Before I could say anything, he turned and walked away as Nell drove up. "Everything okay?" She pointed at his retreating figure.

"Yeah."

"Sure?"

"Yeah."

"Then let's talk about something important. If you're going to entertain people," she said. "You really should start stocking hair products. I had to go home and shower."

"I thought you went home to check in with your folks."

"Shower, show my face." She shrugged. "Same thing." She grinned. "But the priority was the hair."

"The drugstore has fewer hair products than you." I gave her a once-over. "But you look amazing."

"Tell me something I don't know."

"The skin of a female shark is much thicker than the skin of a male shark because the male bites the female during mating."

She shot me a confused look.

"You said tell you something you didn't know. Besides, didn't you ever wonder why you're so thick-skinned?"

She laughed. "You're such a weirdo."

"Yeah and you're my best friend, so what does that make you?"

"A girl who knows how to make good decisions." She grimaced. "Except right now. Sure I can't talk you out of seeing Debbie-Anne?"

"We need answers. She's got them."

Nell put the car in gear and pointed at the sheriff's car down the street. "Word is, Nancy's given them permission to shoot and arrest as they see fit, and not in that order. Word's spread."

"Not fast enough." I updated her on Carl and Savour, then texted Nancy with the information.

The drive to Debbie-Anne's was short. She was still at the trailer park, in a double-wide. Nell grew tenser with every passing mile, and by the time we reached the house, her shoulders were hunched by her ears.

"I remember when she was sober," she said, slamming the car door shut. "I remember when she loved us more than her addiction." She turned up the collar of her jacket. "Come on, let's get this over with."

It took a few knocks, all of them hard, before Debbie-Anne came to the door. She barely glanced at me. "What do you want?" she asked Nell.

"Information." Nell pushed through the door.

I followed and closed it behind me.

"The last time the two of you came to my house, it blew up. Now I'm stuck in this dump."

This dump, unlike her previous house, had white walls, instead of nicotine-stained ones, and the faint scent of new carpet.

She turned an accusatory stare my way. "You wanted information on Serge."

"And it helped us solve his murder."

"He blew up my house," she said. "Because he didn't like me talking about what he'd gone through as a kid." She took a long drag of her cigarette. "And when I told that to the cops, you refused to back me up."

"The police don't believe in ghosts," said Nell.

"No one believed in microbes until a microscope proved their existence." Debbie-Anne took another puff. "You've always been a weird kid," she said to me. "I know you see them. I know Serge came to you."

"And how do you know that?" asked Nell. "You have a ghostscope?"

"Because Maggie and Serge are connected, and anyone with a brain can see that. No coincidence you solved his murder. No coincidence you figured out who killed the Meagher kid, too."

"That's our Maggie," said Nell. "Connected to all the ghosts in Dead Falls."

Debbie-Anne ground out her cigarette in the ashtray she carried. "Definitely connected to the recently dead, aren't you? Does your daddy visit?" She smiled. "You didn't want to be up front about who and what you are. You didn't want to back me up. Now look what happened."

"You're such a whack job," said Nell. "You think that's why her dad was killed?"

"I think truth outs," said Debbie-Anne. "One way or another, it outs. Now, get out of my house." She flashed yellow teeth. "See what I did there?"

"I'm sorry for what happened to your place—" I said.

"I don't give a crap about my place. I care that you bailed on me. On Serge. This town doesn't take me seriously anymore. You had a chance to—"

"Give me a break," Nell said. "The town doesn't take you seriously 'cause you haven't walked in a straight line since 2001."

She flinched.

"I'm sorry for what happened to you," I said. "But people are dying, and you can help."

She shuffled away, toward the living room. "Your dad was a good man. If I knew who hurt him—"

"What about Amber and Principal Larry?"

"What about them?"

"What was going on?" asked Nell.

"What do you think? They had both lost the centre of their existence—" She nodded at me. "—Thanks to Maggie." She pulled out another cigarette and flicked on her lighter.

"Was Amber thinking of running away?" I asked.

Debbie-Anne held the lighter steady. "She was living with May. Wouldn't you consider running away? That woman never met a mirror she didn't love or a man she wasn't sure was Mr. Right."

"You must know something," said Nell.

"I know you're wasting my time."

"Who had it out for Amber and Larry?" I perched on the edge of the couch and tried not to disturb the confetti of broken potato chips on its surface.

"The church. It's not every day you find out the man you trusted to get you closer to God liked to seduce teenage girls," she said.

"Larry's family probably hated him, too," said Nell. "He was an embarrassment to them. Their ancestors started this town, they were pillars in the community, and he upends it all by being best friends with a creep." She gave her aunt a long look. "It's hard for a family when one of the members lets down everyone else."

"Save it for therapy." She snapped, then remembered she had a cigarette to light and put the flame to it.

"We know the person who killed my dad isn't the same one who murdered Amber and the principal," I said.

"And how do you know that?" Debbie-Anne's question held an edge.

"Intuition."

She snorted.

"Can you help us at all?" I asked.

"I've helped you all I'm going to help you," she said.

Nell dragged me up and pushed me toward the door. "I told you this would be a waste of time."

"Do you still see him?" Debbie-Anne called after me. "Is he still here or did he move on?"

"Just keep going," muttered Nell. "Not like she'll remember any of this in another few hours."

"Tell him I'm sorry." Debbie-Anne's voice broke. "Tell him I tried."

"Don't—"

I ignored Nell and stopped. Turned. "Wherever Serge is, I'm sure he's happy and at peace."

Serge appeared beside me. "I feel like you're talking about me."

I glanced at him, then went back to talking to Debbie-Anne. "No one can hurt him anymore. And I'm sure he knows there were people who tried to help."

Serge frowned. "She's talking about me?"

"I tried." Debbie-Anne cast a confused gaze at the ashtray in her hand. She stubbed out the cigarette then shoved it on the table. "You can't always save people, no matter how hard you try. No matter what you know." She looked at me. "But I guess you know that." Stretching out her hand, she reached for the bottle. "Not that it matters, the knowing. You still blame yourself, you still wonder if there was just a little something extra you could have done." She raised the bottle and drank.

"I wish I could appear to her the way Serena comes to you," said Serge. "I wish I could tell her it's all right now."

"Let's go," said Nell. "She doesn't need us anymore."

I started for the door, then stopped again. "Truth outs." I turned back to her. "Truthouts45. You're the one who posted the video of me."

"It can't be," said Nell. "Her hands shake because of the alcohol."

"Not when she was lighting her cigarette," I said. "Maybe she had help? Like Mrs. Sinclair. That was you she was talking to on the night Amber died."

"May's a wuss. She wanted my help to deflect the attention Amber was getting, then she cried like a baby when she saw what the video was doing to you." Debbie-Anne smiled. "You can't hide forever, Maggie. I made sure of that."

Nell rushed her, and I had to grab and pull her back.

"Psycho! This is all your fault! If you hadn't posted that stupid video, her dad would still be alive!"

"That's not my fault!"

"It is your fault!" Nell was crying. "Mr. Johnson spent his whole life protecting her, hiding her, and you posted her face online."

"I didn't—" Debbie-Anne looked at the bottle in her hand.

Nell broke free of my grasp, grabbed the alcohol, and flung it against the wall. "You're the reason my best friend's dad is dead. You're the reason she's an orphan."

I pushed her out the door. "Come on, it's too late now. Let's go."

We stumbled into the cold, leaving Debbie-Anne standing among the broken glass and spilled alcohol.

CHAPTER TWENTY-EIGHT

Nancy had listened as Nell told her about Debbie-Anne, held her as Nell cried about her family's involvement in my dad's death. Then she pushed her to arm's length so she could look her in the eyes. "You are not your family's decisions," she told Nell. "You are only your own, and I'm proud of everything you are and do."

Another hug, then we moved to Gregory who waited in the interrogation room.

"I'll be there in a second," Nancy called after us. She spread the slats of the Venetian blinds. News vans filled the visitor parking spots. A few brave reporters huddled together in the cold. "I'm going to bring them some coffee."

"Actually bring them coffee?" asked Nell. "Or dump a hot carafe on their heads?"

"Actually bring it." She sighed. "We all have a job to do. Besides, as long as I play nice, give them some info, they'll be good about leaving Maggie alone. That's the agreement, anyway." She frowned. "Most of them. You seen either of the reporters around?"

I shook my head. "Not since this morning."

She grunted. "I don't like this. Every confrontation takes us closer to the final confrontation."

"Why don't we get started?" asked Gregory. He sniffed his coat and winced. "Anywhere I can air this thing out? The old mill stink is settling in."

"Let me." Nancy took his jacket while Nell and I led him to the interrogation room.

"Donut?" He held out the box.

"No, thanks."

"Me either." Nell sat across from him. "You don't look so good."

"You spend a lifetime throwing your body into freezing water or running through a desert and tell me how you fare." He smiled. "These days, I worry when I'm not hurting."

"Nell's right," I said. "You look pale."

"Airplane food, airplane air. I'll be fine."

I didn't say anything.

We watched each other for a moment, then he sighed and leaned back in the chair. "Truth is, I don't have a lot of time left."

Five minutes into this relationship and I was already going to lose the one guy who had my father's—and my mother's—history.

"Should you even be here?" I asked.

"What's wrong with you?" Nell leaned forward. "My dad's a doctor. Maybe he can help."

Gregory shook his head. "There's nothing wrong with me but a lifetime of decisions, some good, some not so good. I've got all the medication I need and I'll be fine until I go back. But right now, you need information, and so do I. Lucien is here, and we have to stop him." He grimaced and clutched his stomach. "Do you have a photo of the reporters?"

"No, but I'm sure there are pictures of them online," I said.

Nell pulled out her phone and searched. "Got it."

"Air drop it to me," said Gregory. "I have an app on my phone that can run facial recognition." He turned his cell our way. "This is what Lucien looked like when your dad and I knew him."

"Wow, he's hot," said Nell. She gave me an apologetic smile. "I expected him to look like a bad guy. Sheen of sweat. Bristly moustache. Chomping on a cigar."

She wasn't wrong. Lucien was broad-shouldered and red-haired with a thick beard and intense blue eyes. He looked like he belonged back in time, commanding a Viking ship, not murdering my father.

"You said the operation went sideways, and Lucien blamed Dad—" I said.

"Got the photo, thanks," said Gregory. "Let me run it through the software. It should take a few minutes."

"What happened? How did the operation go sideways?" I asked. "And don't tell me this is about national security. I know how to keep a secret."

"I know you do," he smiled. "You've been keeping a big one your entire life." He jerked his thumb. "And those jokers in the news are about to out your secret to the world."

My panic must have shown on my face because he said, "Don't worry. When your mom left and you started showing your abilities, your dad and I had a long talk about how to best protect and raise you. I know how to keep them off your trail."

"You knew about me? You knew my mom?"

He nodded. "She was a sweet lady, and she loved your dad." He pointed at me. "She loved you, too."

"But she left."

"She was unhinged by the end. Her powers were too strong, and she couldn't see reality anymore. All she saw was the fracture of past, present, and future. It's an amazing ability, to exist in many points of time, but it proved too much for your mom. She almost hurt you."

My entire life, the only thing I'd known about my mom was that she was Indian and we shared skin colour. Now, I shared something else with her—the ability to jump in time. Would it drive me insane in the same way it did her? "Almost?"

"Hank came home, found her clutching a knife in one hand, you in the other. She was babbling about having to bleed some of your power. That you were too strong. You could overpower her and be a danger to the world."

Nell took my hand and squeezed.

"Your dad talked her off the ledge, but they both knew she was the real danger. No matter how much she loved you, she had to leave you." He wiped the sweat from his forehead. "You started manifesting your powers soon after."

"My mother's dead."

"I know."

"I don't understand," said Nell. "If you and Mr. Johnson were such good friends, why didn't he ever talk about you to Maggie?"

"Same reason Maggie's mom left. To protect Maggie."

"The operation," I said.

He nodded.

"What happened?"

"You know your dad," said Gregory. "He was a good man, but he had strong opinions, and he wasn't above doing what he thought was necessary." He smiled. "Something you and he have in common. He was fearless, wading into any fight if he thought it was the right thing to do."

I thought about the argument he'd had with Principal Larry at the Tin Shack, and nodded.

"Lucien, according to our commanding officers, was a bad guy." Gregory chuckled. "Funny, how we decide who's good and bad. Lucien crossed a few lines, but there were parts of him we all understood. He had a vision for his country, for his people. I've seen our government do worse." Gregory closed his eyes and I gave him a couple of minutes to catch his strength.

"We rolled out the operation and, at first, it went like clockwork. But just before the kill shot, we were told to hold off, to wait. But Hank thought there was a danger in delaying, so he moved on Lucien." Gregory pointed to himself. "With me and the rest of the guys following. Hank was a leader and we trusted him. There was a firefight, a lot of bullets. Lucien got away, but his wife and kid..." He passed his hand over his face. "Life went on for your dad and mom. Then you were born. When you were two, we got word Lucien was moving on the team, exacting revenge. We went underground, and your dad went deep underground. New identification, cut all ties to everyone he knew. He and I had a way of communicating, and as time went on and Lucien didn't surface, we got lax."

All the moving we did when I was a kid, I'd always assumed it was because of my power, because we were making sure no one could track my secret. Now, I was left wondering how much of my dad's past had played a factor. "Lucien's here, avenging his family."

"Revenging his family is more like it," said Gregory. "Your dad was a charmer. He got into the wife's head. Even if she'd lived, she would've left Lucien. I don't know how much of your dad's murder was motivated by Lucien's wife and kid dying, and how much of it was because they'd left him long before their hearts stopped beating, and their abandonment of Lucien was because of your dad."

His phone beeped. He turned it to us.

Lucien and Savour, side by side. The check points on their faces blipping, the text at the bottom leaving no doubt. They were the same person.

"Are you sure?" I asked. "Carl's the one with the psychic protection."

"Science doesn't lie," he said.

"But he had a sister—" God, I was gullible. He'd been feeding me lines, and I'd believed every word.

"Do you think he and Carl are working together?" asked Nell.

"Doubt it. Lucien doesn't trust anyone. He's probably manipulating Carl, and the guy doesn't even know it."

"Now what?" I asked. "How do we stop him before he hurts someone else?"

Nancy came into the room. "Catch me up."

We did. "We need evidence." She gestured to Gregory's phone. "None of this will help. Gregory starts giving up classified information by talking about black ops, and he's in jail and we still won't be any farther along in the investigation. I doubt national security will allow us to bring any of this to light."

"We get him the old-fashioned way," said Gregory.

"Not that old-fashioned," said Nancy. "We bring him in alive."

"How do we do that?" asked Nell.

"Police work, collect evidence," she said.

"What about getting a confession?" I asked. "He wants me to do an interview—"

"No way, kid," said Nancy. "You're not going into the belly of the beast."

"I won't go anywhere private," I said. "I'll meet him at the Tin Shack, talk to him—"

"You're your dad's child," said Gregory. "Take charge and take initiative. But Lucien is a bad, bad man. You can't trick him into confessing," he said to Nancy. "He's fast and he's deadly."

"We're running low on time," said Gregory. "And he's going to be getting desperate." He looked over at Nancy. "I appreciate your thoughts, but the time for talk is over. I came to tell you who killed Hank, and I came to take out his killer."

"Gregory—"

He bent over, coughing and retching. Gregory grabbed a tissue and held it to his mouth, but drops of blood spattered the napkin.

"You can barely stand," I said. "You can't take down a guy who eluded an entire black ops team."

"I don't need to fight with him hand-to-hand," he said. "I just need camouflage and—"

"Stop." Nancy held up her hand. "Just stop. Whatever you're about to say, don't."

"Don't tell me you disagree," he said. "I see it on your face. If you could get away with it—"

"It's about doing what's right," she said. "And this conversation is over." She looked at me. "Take him home."

"No one's taking me anywhere—" He broke down in a fit of coughing.

"Come on." I put my hand on his shoulder and felt the connection between us. "Let's get you home."

For a second, I thought he'd argue. Then he clutched his stomach and nodded. "For now."

"Take my SUV," said Nancy, handing me her keys and hitting the remote car starter. "It started snowing and the roads are bad."

"I hope that Claxton's not shut down again," said Gregory. He walked out the main entrance and stepped into a crowd of reporters. Deputy Andrews came out and cleared a path for us.

As we walked to the SUV, I searched the crowd for Savour, but came up empty.

"He's not here," said Gregory. "He would've seen me and known to stay away."

"Why doesn't that make me feel better?"

"Because, if he's not monitoring you, it's because he has all the information he needs. The danger is greatest now."

I helped him into the passenger seat.

"Thanks." He grimaced as he settled into the seat.

"What's wrong with you?" I asked. "Is it cancer?"

He smiled. "No, it's something with a long, complicated name that science can't cure."

I caught the hint. He didn't want to talk about it. "Did you know my mother's family?" I eased the vehicle from the curb, checking to make sure no reporters were in the way.

He snorted. "Her family is a bunch of lunatics. The smartest thing your dad ever did was to keep you away from them. They were a mean bunch, especially your grandmother. When Hank met your mom, she was beaten down. No exaggeration, he saved her life."

"What was her name?"

"He never said?"

I shook my head. "Dad never talked about her."

Gregory sighed. "I understand that, but it must have been hard for you."

"Her name?"

"Sundari, but everyone called her Sunny."

Sundari. I rolled the name in my mind. Sunny.

"She didn't cross over peacefully," I said. I wasn't sure why I was telling him this, maybe because he was a bridge to my dad and my history. Maybe it was nice to talk to someone who *knew* my history but with whom I didn't *have* history.

"You sense she died a violent death?"

"She comes to me."

He jerked in his seat and turned wide eyes my way. "You talk to her?"

"Not exactly. She's a warning voice when I am in danger." I blinked at the flashing light in the sideview mirror. Someone's high beams. I adjusted the rearview so I wasn't blinded.

Gregory leaned forward and opened the glove compartment. "Are there tissues here?"

"Try the middle console." The flashing happened again. I glanced in the rearview. Nothing was there. Frowning, I telepathically called Serge.

He appeared in the backseat. "What's up?"

Were you experimenting? I was seeing lights.

"No. Where are they?"

I looked around. *They're gone.*

"Winter lightning?"

Maybe, but I thought they were headlights.

"I'm staying. Savour might be following and using the headlights to mess with you."

"She doesn't talk to you—" Gregory gulped. "She doesn't—I'm sorry—can you pull over? Pull over!"

The car skidded to a stop on the shoulder, and he launched himself out of the vehicle. A second later, I heard retching.

"I don't miss that."

"Tell me about it," I muttered.

"We got some interesting stuff on Amber and her mom."

What kind of stuff?

"Someone put a lot of money into her account. A lot. When you're done with him, meet Craig and me back at the house."

Hold on. I called him back. *Which her?*

"Mrs. Sinclair."

I blinked. *What?*

"She got a job with your dad because she said she needed money, and no one would hire her. But she had three deposits in the last week, ten grand each time. The last one happened on the night Amber and Larry died."

Who put thirty grand in her account, and why?

Serge smiled. "You'll never believe it."

CHAPTER TWENTY-NINE

"I should have you arrested for trespassing." Mrs. Sinclair took a long drag of her cigarette. "Then I should have you charged with hacking my bank account."

"Go ahead," I said.

She snorted and took another pull of the cigarette. "With Nancy as the lead investigator in the case? Bet she'll sweep it under the rug."

"I think she'll be more interested in how you got thirty thousand dollars and who gave it to you." I'd made Nell and Craig stay home, but brought Serge as backup. I was ambushing Mrs. Sinclair. I didn't need her to feel overwhelmed by the number of people crashing her house.

Her place was startlingly clean. Maybe everyone grieves in their own way and her method was to declutter. Dad would've gotten a kick out of me scrubbing the house as a way to grieve him. I could almost hear his voice, "Geez, why didn't I think of dying sooner? Hey, my girl, you missed a spot."

"I don't have to tell you anything."

"You don't," I said. "I already know it was Principal Larry."

"So why are you here?"

"Why did he give you the money?"

She smirked. "From the generosity of his heart." She ground out the cigarette.

"I don't remember her smoking," Serge said.

Neither did I. "When did that start up?" I pointed to the ashtray.

"There are a lot of things you give up when you're a parent." She rubbed her eyes. "I don't need to give them up anymore."

There was no good place to go with that. "Why did he give you the money?"

"Get out of my house."

"I know he tried to hide the source of the deposit," I told her. "But I know it was him."

She watched me. "And how do you know any of this?"

"I have my connections."

Serge smiled.

She said nothing.

"Don't you want to know who killed Amber?"

"I already know." She turned her contemptuous gaze on me. "You did. With your nosing around. Just like you're doing now. Digging up things that should stay buried."

"Mrs. Sinclair, someone murdered your daughter—"

"And you think Larry's pity donation is connected to it? Don't be stupid."

"A teacher doesn't have thirty thousand dollars to just drop on someone else."

"Maybe he likes to save." She ground out the cigarette. "The money showed up in my account, okay? I don't know how or why, but I don't care. I need out of this town, and it'll help."

"If the money was from his family," I said. "There's no way they'd be happy about the way he spent it."

She stood. "Get out of my house. Next time, I'm calling the cops."

✦✦✦

"Have you lost your mind?"

I turned down the volume of the hands-free phone app in the SUV.

"No, Nancy, but—"

"You have information on Amber and Larry's murders, and your solution was to go to May Sinclair instead of me?"

"I thought—"

"No, you didn't," she interrupted. "And I'm disappointed."

Ouch.

"You're not a dumb kid, Maggie. Why would you do such a fool-hardy thing?"

"It's just Mrs. Sinclair and—"

"Get your butt home," she said. "And don't go near May, again."

"But—"

"I don't want to hear it. Do you even realize you're opening up the department to a lawsuit, not to mention opening me up to a personal lawsuit?"

"No," I said, contrite. "I didn't."

"May Sinclair's a lot of things, and vengeful is on the top of the list. No one crosses her and gets away with it. You know she's suing the church. Did you know she's suing the reverend's estate?"

"I didn't know he had an estate." I looked over at Serge.

He shrugged. "I didn't know either. Not like he and I ever talked."

"Stay away from May," said Nancy. "Get home and—"

"And what, play video games? Lucien is stalking my family, a soul-eater might have my mom and dad, and you want me to stay home and do homework?" I didn't add the other stuff, that Lucien was coming for her, too.

"I know, kid," she sighed. "And we have eyes on Savour. He won't get near you. Maggie, you need to be smart about this. Don't let grief cloud your decisions."

"Yeah, I know."

"Go home," she said again, her voice soft. "I'll talk to May. We'll figure it out. I promise."

I nodded, then realized she couldn't see me. "Got it." I signed off and turned to Serge. "Did you know the reverend had money?"

"It makes sense. Look at how he dressed."

"You never knew your grandparents, right?"

Serge nodded. "It was just the reverend and my mother."

"So, if they came from money—"

"I wouldn't know," he said.

"But maybe there would be evidence somewhere?"

"Probably the lawyer's office." He frowned. "Why? What are you thinking?"

"Principal Larry gave money to Mrs. Sinclair, but we don't know where he got the money from."

"You thought it was his family," he said.

I waved away his words. "I was just doing that to see Mrs. Sinclair's reaction. Can you imagine his family giving him money to do anything? He worked as a principal and look at his clothes and car. If he had money, he would've lived better."

"You think the money came from the reverend?"

"Maybe. But if their families didn't have money, then where did all the cash for Mrs. Sinclair come from?"

"You're talking about the reverend stealing from the church."

"You're the one who told me that, months ago."

"Except no one's said anything."

"Because he's dead. His entire family's been wiped out. Plus, there's fallout for the church. If the reverend had been stealing from them for years, then they'd be liable."

Serge's eyes widened. "Mrs. Sinclair's suing the church."

I nodded. "If she went ahead with the suit, then they'd have to open the books."

"Which means a whole bunch of people could be in trouble," said Serge.

"Right. They may not have stolen with the reverend, but they covered it up."

"And the principal uses the stolen funds to...buy off Amber and Mrs. Sinclair?" asked Serge.

"Maybe, or maybe he was doing something else, just him and Amber. Either way, someone from the church found out he had access to the money."

"And that someone went to the school to kill Larry, but why kill Amber?"

"Maybe for the same reason the soul-eater took my dad's soul. If Mrs. Sinclair's incapacitated with grief, then maybe she doesn't go ahead with the lawsuit."

"We should tell Nancy all of this," he said. "It might get us out of the dog house."

"Text her. I'm going to get us home. Ten bucks says she's timing my commute."

✦ ✦ ✦

Tammy's minivan was in the driveway when I got home. She and Bruce were in the kitchen with Craig and Nell.

"I got to thinking," said Tammy.

"Always a dangerous thing," murmured Nell.

I elbowed her into silence.

"I thought if we could access the other side directly, through a psychic, maybe we could get some answers."

"There's a bunch of them in town," said Bruce. "And one of them found us at the market. She said she knew we'd be there, and that we'd be the key to helping with the supernatural stuff going on."

"Isn't that amazing?" asked Tammy. "She knew we'd be there—"

"Talk about a genuine psychic, right?" said Bruce.

"Were you there handing out the flyers for your club?" Nell asked.

"Yeah," said Bruce. "And she—her name's Cora—said she knew we'd be there, doing that."

"Amazing," said Nell. "Talk about psychic power."

I leaned into her and whispered, "Could you try not to enjoy this so much?"

She didn't stop grinning. "These two are better than cable and streaming combined."

"Plus, Cora's a palm reader," said Tammy. "Things are so crazy for you, Mags. She can read the lines on your hand. Maybe she can tell you when it'll all end and then you'll know." She squeezed my hand. "You'll have an end date."

"Uh—"

Nell whispered, "What's more astonishing? Tammy having all those thoughts in rapid succession, or being ambushed by a plan for you to talk to a so-called psychic?"

I elbowed her in the ribs. "That's really nice of you, Tammy, but I'm not sure—"

"Great!" Tammy dragged me to the table. "Let's start. She gave us her email and cell number, and said to text as soon as we were ready."

Tammy and Bruce looked so happy, and I had no idea how to shut them down. I'd been dealing with enough hateful people, I wasn't prepared to lose two friends.

"Maybe we should do a quick check of her," said Craig. "Just in case."

"Already done," said Bruce. "We went to her website and checked out her bio and testimonials, and we checked the consumer sites too. There's nothing but positive comments about her."

"Nothing but positive comments?" I asked. "No one hits a hundred percent. Show me her website."

Bruce took out his phone.

"Wait," I said. "Not her site. Pull up her name in the search engine."

He did, and handed his cell to me. I went to the images section and scrolled through her photos.

"Why are you suspicious?" asked Tammy.

"Because it's too convenient. She finds you handing out flyers on the supernatural, so she targets you for her con, butters you up by saying you're key to the investigation—" I glanced up at them. "—And of course you are, but still...did you tell her you knew me?"

They glanced at each other.

"I should have known it was too good to be true," said Bruce. "We just wanted to help."

I stopped on an image and turned the phone to face them. "You did. Look at this. See the guy next to her?"

"Who is it?" asked Tammy.

"A very bad guy," I said. "We need to get this to Nancy."

"Cora chick was psychic after all," said Nell. "Tammy and Bruce just helped with the investigation."

"Yeah," I said as I opened the web page and texted the link to Nancy. "Too bad she's not psychic enough to see they were going to land her in jail."

CHAPTER THIRTY

"**C**ora, aka, Michelle Sandu," said Nancy. "Con artist."

I was at the police station, Cora was in the interrogation room. Serge was with me in the main office. Craig and Nell were back at the house with Tammy and Bruce.

"She's talking, which is a good thing. Savour hired her to make contact with you. Her job was to make you believe you had supernatural abilities, then use your belief to manipulate you."

"Little did she know…" muttered Serge.

"She was supposed to get you to the old mill," said Nancy.

"Why?"

She made a face. "To meet up with Savour."

A chill rippled along my skin. "Get me alone to do the deed."

"You're never alone," said Serge. "I wouldn't have let anything happen to you."

"It wouldn't have happened, anyway," Nancy said, reading Serge's text. She looked at me. "You're too smart to have fallen for her BS. The fact she's in custody proves it."

"Are you working late tonight?" asked Nell. "Maybe Maggie should stay with me."

"I'm signing off now and coming home," she said. "I think we all need some quiet time. The guys will bring in Savour, and I've got Frank watching our place, just in case." She pulled on her jacket and put in a phone call. "Craig, do your folks need you home?"

She listened to his response.

"Then how about you take a break and I'll make dinner tonight?"

Another pause, then she grinned at me. "He wants to know if you're helping with the meal."

"What's with the smirk?"

"To quote him, 'I love Mags and I'll go to the mat for her, fight demons and lost souls, I just don't want to eat anything she's made.'"

"Everyone's a master chef," I muttered.

"You're a lot of things." Nancy patted my arm. "But you're not meant to be in the kitchen. That's one thing I doubt you can change."

"Don't say it like that. I can practise and change my dismal—"

Change. I grabbed her hand. "The night I saw Mrs. Sinclair, the night Amber was killed, she was wearing a pink sweater. I remember it, but when I saw her later, her sweater was blue."

"So?"

"We were at the funeral home, talking to May. Then she left to find Amber. Serge and I drove around, looking for Amber too. We found her and Larry at the school, then we called the police right away," said Serge. "By the time Mrs. Sinclair showed up, maybe half an hour had passed."

"I'm going to ask again," said Nancy. "So?"

"What if she found her daughter and the principal before we did," I said. "What if she killed them, got blood on her shirt, and had to change."

"She cleans a funeral home. Maybe she spilled something on her sweater and had to change," said Nancy.

"Everyone says she looked at the reverend as a surrogate parent for Amber," I said.

"Maybe it was more than just the reverend as a co-parent," said Serge. "Maybe she saw him as a partner for herself."

"Debbie-Anne said May fell in love with every guy she saw. Maybe she created a fantasy around all of it. She was in love with the reverend."

"She would have felt betrayed and disgusted when she found out what he was really doing with Amber," said Serge.

"Maybe she was even a little jealous of her daughter?" I added.

"Playing along with this. Now the townspeople are talking, gossiping about her," said Nancy. "She's lost her fantasy man, her job. She's got a pregnant daughter, times are tough—"

"And Amber's making it worse by that online group," I said. "And by her turning to the principal, getting money from him. The deputies were talking about Mrs. Sinclair the night of Amber's murder. They called her a good-time girl... What if Mrs. Sinclair was out of her depth with Amber? What if she couldn't stand the gossip and the judgement from the townspeople anymore?"

"And there's the money that was embezzled from the church," said Serge. "Principal Larry wasn't a smart guy. It would only have been a matter of time before he screwed up and the secrets the board was hiding came out. They can't afford more scandal, but there would have been more gossip and whispers. Everyone would've been tainted by the town's judgement."

"And we all know how that hurts."

"May has issues," said Nancy. "But murdering her daughter?"

"Maybe there was an accident," I said. There's only one way to find out."

"It's a nice theory," said Nancy. "But there's no evidence."

"There could be," said Serge. "I know Amber stored her phone information in the cloud."

"We've been through this before," said Nancy. "The guys know the phone's been cleared. I can't suddenly make a move based on evidence no one has but me. May says she doesn't have the password. It's going to look suspicious if I can suddenly access Amber's account. Let the tech guys handle it."

"She may have killed her child and Principal Larry," I said. "What else do you think she's capable of?"

Nancy sighed. "A midnight move, that's for certain. But my hands are tied, kid. Do I want to find the killer of Amber and Larry? Yes. Do I want to protect you more? Yes. If I start pushing and crossing lines—I'm not part of the investigation. I can get into a lot of trouble if I play this wrong."

"There must be a way," I said. "Serge, what are your skills like? Can you find out the password, without touching the files?"

"I guess."

"So, maybe, if it's a common-sense password, you can make up a story for it," I said to Nancy. "Like, if it's the reverend's name, you say you just wondered if maybe that was the way Amber was trying to remember him."

"And I saunter in, start a conversation with the tech guys and casually drop it into conversation?" she said.

"Any woman that can make pear and chocolate frangipane tart can rock the art of subtle."

"Are you complimenting me or asking me to bake?"

"Both."

Frank came in. "You want to take a look at this." He held out a sheet of paper.

Nancy took it, read. Her face tightened. "Get May Sinclair in here. Now."

He nodded and left.

"What is it?" Serge asked.

"The money transfer to her account. It didn't happen automatically. Someone manually moved the money. Amber was under eighteen, which means her mom had to sign for her account, which means May was lying when she said she never touched the account or knew what was going on."

"Sure you don't want me to hack the cloud?" asked Serge.

"No," said Nancy. "I don't care what the procedures are, it's my turn, now."

CHAPTER THIRTY-ONE

We waited in the outer office while Frank questioned Mrs. Sinclair. Nancy watched from the other side of the mirror and fed the deputy questions.

"Nancy and Frank will get the truth," said Deputy Andrews. "They're a good team."

I nodded.

He began to speak, hesitated, then said, "On the one hand, I hope if May killed the principal and Amber, she was also behind your dad's death. I'd like you and Nancy to have answers. On the other hand, I can hardly believe May would do any of it."

Forty-five minutes later, Nancy came out. "Andrews, get Amber's phone and bring it to Frank."

"Did Mrs. Sinclair give up the password?" I asked.

"No," said Nancy. "But I know what it was."

Twenty minutes later, Frank led Mrs. Sinclair out in handcuffs.

I stood as Nancy came my way.

"The cloud had it all, and more," she said. "Amber was planning to run away, to go to Edmonton and start a new life. Principal Larry was helping. He used money the reverend stole from the church to fund their great escape. I read the texts and it's like a junior-high fairy tale. They were going to be together, he was going to help raise the reverend's baby, and she was going to go back to school."

Craig had said the green liquid in the blood had been a sign of possessiveness, jealousy. The more Nancy spoke, the more it felt like those emotions had been Principal Larry's, wanting what he couldn't have, and Amber playing him to get the life she wanted.

Nancy sat down. "May installed spyware on Amber's phone. She'd been monitoring all of it." Lowering her voice, she continued, "It wasn't Serge who reset the phone, it was May. She didn't want us finding the apps."

"But she never said anything to Amber? Never confronted her?" Serge asked.

"It's like sneaking into your kid's room to read their diary. She just wanted to know what was going on. When it looked like she was going to lose Amber, that's when the confrontation happened."

"Was it an accident?" I asked.

"According to her. May showed up, they argued. Amber wanted out of the town, but didn't want May coming with her. The plan was for her to run that night. Larry was to join her later, help set her up in Edmonton. May and Amber fought, and when it looked like Larry was going to side with May, her daughter pulled the weapon."

"Amber had a gun?" Serge asked.

Nancy read the text. "After their house was vandalized and the harassment started, May bought the gun for protection. She didn't realize Amber had taken it. There was a struggle, the gun went off." She rubbed her eyes. "She didn't mean to kill her daughter, and once it was done, she snapped. She was mad at the town, the church, furious with Larry. Blamed him for Amber's death, and decided to act as judge, jury, and executioner."

It was all so sad. May wanting to protect her daughter from the mistakes she'd made and driving Amber farther away with every attempt. Amber, wanting a sense of autonomy and finding it in all the wrong places. And all of it mixing into a toxic stew that boiled over and burned everyone. "What happens to her, now?"

"Jail. Trial. God knows what a judge will say to any of this."

"There are no happy endings in this town, are there?" I asked.

She gave me a tired smile. "In this life, sometimes there are just endings. Come on, let me grab my coat, then let's get home."

"Hey, what was the password?" asked Serge.

"The one thing Amber wanted and the thing her mother and this town could never give her," said Nancy. "Freedom."

✦ ✦ ✦

Nancy went to get her coat, and I started for the truck.

"Hold up," said Serge. "Something she said's got me thinking."

Does it hurt?

"Ha ha."

I rubbed my eyes. *How about if I wait in the car for you guys? I've had about as much as I can take of all of this. I want some quiet and a place where no one's watching me.*

"Fair enough. See you in a couple."

Deputy Andrews kept watch as I stepped into the black cold of the night and pulled my scarf tighter. The headlights of the SUV glowed in the snowfall, a warming beacon I needed. Amber, Mrs. Sinclair, Principal Larry, the reverend, it all left me feeling sick. All these people trying for their happiness and consuming everything good in their path. I hit the unlock button and heard the vehicle chirp in reply. I waved to the deputy as I opened the door. He waved back and went back into the station.

"Did the mom do it?"

I jerked back. "Carl!" I fumbled for the panic button on the fob, but he was faster. He grabbed and, twisting my wrist, wrenched it away.

"Don't worry," he said. "It'll only hurt for a second." He pulled his hand back, into a fist, and smashed it into my jaw. I slammed into the SUV's door. There was a dull thunk of my head hitting metal and I pitched into blackness.

CHAPTER THIRTY-TWO

I was, hands down, the stupidest psychic in the history of supernaturals. This was the second time a bad guy had knocked me out. I kept my eyes closed and listened. Judging by the hum of tires on the road and the smell around me, he'd taken Nancy's vehicle. Point for me—at least this time, I hadn't ended up next to a decaying corpse. And based on my position, the feel of the cold window pane against my head, I was in the front passenger seat.

"If you're going to pretend to be passed out," he said. "Do a better job. I know you're awake."

I didn't respond.

He grabbed my shoulder and shook me hard. "Stop pretending!"

"I was doing you a favour," I said, opening my eyes. "Figured if I stayed still, it would give you time to rethink what you're doing and take me back."

"And what?"

I shrugged. "Leave me in the truck, engine running, maybe crack a window so the animal rights folks don't get mad." I stuffed my hands in my pockets.

"You're pretty funny for a girl in your position. I know what you're doing, but stop searching. I took your cell phone. Dumped it."

"I can afford to be funny, I'm not the one who kidnapped a minor," I said as I buckled into the seat. I sensed Serge's presence manifest in the seat behind me.

"Maggie! We came out and you were gone—oh, holy crap!" He took in the scene and leaning forward, squinted at the windshield. "Where are you?" He scanned. "Claxton, heading west."

"Where are you taking me?" I asked Carl.

"Your psychic talents can't tell?"

"They're stunned by this display of your stupidity. How do you think you're going to get away with this?"

"Don't worry," said Serge. "I have a general location. I'll get Nancy and come back to you."

"I'm not trying to get away with anything," Carl said. "I need your help, that's all."

"And then you'll quietly allow yourself to get arrested?"

He touched his pocket. "I have a plan."

It was too dark to make out the shape of whatever he'd touched, but I got the sudden sense that his plan involved a final, deadly solution. "All this for an interview?"

"Interview? You think this is about some article?"

"Isn't that what you've been harassing me about? 'Tell us your secret. Admit to the truth.'"

"Not for some stupid story. I need your help." He reached into his jacket, felt around for something, and I tensed. But the object he pulled out was a photo, laminated against dirt and time. "This is my ex-girlfriend. Julie. She died in a car accident." He turned left on Miller's Ave.

I pulled on my harness, reached across, and took the photo. "And?"

"You have to contact her. We had a big fight the night she died. That's why she was in the car. She was driving around, trying to clear her head. I need to know if she forgives me. I need to know if she blames me for the accident."

Serge reappeared.

Tell Nancy, change of plans. He's on Miller's—smart money's that he's taking me to the old mill. No witnesses, lots of deserted area.

"Okay, I'll be right back—" Serge stopped. "I'm an idiot. I'll text her." A second later, he said, "What next?"

Don't do anything yet. I have a plan.

"That's not how this works," I told Carl. "I'm not some spooky version of the cell company."

"You have to do it!"

"I can't—"

Carl smashed his fist into the steering wheel. "I didn't risk all of this to have you say no." The speedometer climbed higher. "You're going to help me. One way or another, you're going to help me."

"I'm sorry for your crappy planning," I said. "But I don't have the power to call the dead back from the other side."

"You're psychic—"

"I'm not that kind of psychic." I tossed the photo at him. As he fumbled to catch it, I took my chance.

I leaned over, hit the button of his seatbelt, and unlocked it. At the same time, I grabbed the wheel and wrenched it toward the shoulder.

Serge pushed through the driver's seat, put his hand on the wheel, and aimed it for the lamppost. "Get in your seat, hold on!"

I shoved myself back into the seat, grabbed hold of the handle, and braced for impact. The SUV skidded on the ice and careened for the light post, and this time, there was no ferrier to save me.

CHAPTER THIRTY-THREE

The airbag exploded, metal smashed into metal, and I swore I heard my dad's voice saying, "Just hold on, my girl."

"Are you okay?" Serge touched my head.

"I think Dad warned me."

"Your dad's here?"

"Maybe. Maybe I'm just hallucinating. My compliments to whoever designed the safety system of this car," I said. "Might be nursing a cracked rib, ringing in my ears, and definitely got cuts, but mostly good." I pushed the airbag away. "How's our psychotic friend?"

"Out of commission," said Serge. "Maybe permanently. Smart move, undoing his seatbelt. But you should've let me just kill the engine, though. It would have been safer."

"You weren't here for all of it. The best plan was to knock him out." I unbuckled myself and reached over to Carl. His pulse was steady, but he was a bloody mess. I reached to his jacket and felt the lump he'd been touching. After I pulled on my gloves, I reached into his pocket and took out a gun. "A stalled engine would have agitated him, and he came with a friend."

"Point taken."

I hunted around, found Nancy's spare set of handcuffs, and locked him to the wheel. Then I got out of the car, my gait wobbly, my vision blurred. A vehicle approached from the other direction. The driver stopped, got out. "Are you okay?"

I didn't need perfect vision to know who I was dealing with, and now I knew why—if I wasn't having auditory hallucinations—I'd heard my dad's voice: "Savour. Stay away."

"What's going on?" He moved toward me.

I shook my head, trying to erase the ringing. "I know who you are. The police are on their way."

"What are you talking about?" He kept moving.

"I can put him down," said Serge. "At least until the cops get here." He moved forward but I pulled him back.

"Don't," I said. "If he's also the entity, then he can eat you. Literally."

"We have to do something, and that gun won't do anything."

"Neither will you. Just give me a second to think."

"We don't have a second," said Serge.

"Maggie, I don't understand why you're acting like this," Savour said.

"I'm not the one who's acting. You are, Lucien."

He stopped, tilting his head. "You know."

"I know."

"Gregory blabbed. If he wasn't already dying, I'd kill him." He smiled. "I still might."

The wind blew stinging snow across my face. "What happens, now?"

"I end the threat." He reached into his pocket, pulling out a pair of leather gloves. "I'd be lying if I said I wasn't disappointed. I've been watching you, monitoring your movements. There's not much super in your supernatural, is there?"

"There's enough to take you down," said Serge.

"I like your style, ghost," said Lucien. "I look forward to adding your energy to mine."

One theory confirmed. Lucien was the soul-eater.

"No one's adding anything," I said. "We're here to subtract one bad guy from the world."

Serge winced. "Seriously? That's your best line?"

"Leave me alone. Once he unleashes his ghosts, we're done," I told him. "We have to keep him talking for as long as we can."

"Where's a car sliding out of control when you need it?" Serge muttered.

"Are you done formulating your game plan?" asked Lucien.

"We were laying odds," Serge said. "About how scared you are of us."

The soul-eater grinned. "Hardly."

"Sure," said Serge. "Maggie figures you're scared enough to use half your ghosts on us. I figure it'll be all of them."

Lucien laughed and held up his hands. "Waste ghost power on the two of you? Why do you think I wore gloves?" He flexed his shoulders. "Your daddy was very naughty with me, Maggie, and he's here now, watching."

"Prove it," I said. "Let me talk to him."

But Lucien smiled. "I could harness his energy and use him to kill you, but that's too quick a death. I want him to watch, to be helpless just like me, as someone takes his family from him. But first—" He stretched out his hand. Energy flashed from his palm and struck Serge.

Serge flew backwards, high into the treetops. He hit the branches and ricocheted down the trunk.

Lucien raised his hands, again, as Serge stumbled to his feet. Orange light emanated from the soul-eater's fingers, forming a bubble around Serge that held him immobile. Forks of white electricity flashed inside the dome and took hold of the ghost.

Serge's body began to vibrate; his hair stood on end. The vibrations picked up speed until he was nothing but a blur in the centre of the circle. A final flick of Lucien's hand, and Serge exploded into supernatural confetti.

I wanted to scream but I kept my mouth shut.

"He's fine," said Lucien. "I want to savour the moment I consume him, but I need him out of the way so I can enjoy our time together." He waved his hand again. "A little boundary spell to keep our time together private. Wouldn't want any cops, ferriers, or ghosts ruining the fun, would we?" He winked. "We both know Craig is mortal now. He'll make a delightful treat when I'm done with you."

For a second, I considered running, but marathons were never my thing. Besides, Lucien wasn't a guy I'd ever want to turn my back on. I waited for him to come to me and wondered why my life seemed to be endless moments of waiting for the bad things to come to me.

I thought of the gun in my pocket, but I didn't know how to use it. Besides, with my marksmanship, I was more likely to shoot myself in the foot. I took it out and tossed it aside.

Lucien's gaze followed its trajectory. He closed the distance between us. "I like a girl who comes prepared, but you should have kept it. You'll need all the help you can get." He balled his hand into a fist and punched me.

In the movies, the hero gets hit in the face, but they keep going. I'd give anything to live in a movie, right now. His fist connected with my cheekbone, and I heard the crunch of bone on bone, felt the world rock and tilt on an axis of pain I hadn't known existed. I dropped to the ground, gasping for breath. In my head, my mother's voice sounded. *He's coming, Maggie, he's coming for you.*

I wished she was more of a doer than a talker, because I could have used one of her poltergeist moments right now.

"How could they have ever thought you were destined to be a guardian?" Lucien asked. "How could they have ever believed you could do anything but annoy me?" He lifted his foot and swung.

I caught his boot, twisted.

His reflexes didn't allow me to bring him to the ground, though it made him stumble and gave me time to scramble away. From the corner of my eye, Serena's form flickered, trying to get into the space and failing.

I swept the landscape for the gun—not to shoot, but if I held it, then it gave my punch more weight. And I wasn't worried about Lucien using it on me. He'd been clear: I was to die at his hands.

I spotted the weapon, tucked by the wheel of the SUV. I ran for it and heard Dad yell "Duck!" and I dived for the ground. The swish of air over my head, followed by the sound of Lucien's boot hitting the door panel.

I tucked and rolled. Dad.

Dad was here.

Warning me.

Protecting me.

Nothing mattered anymore. Not the cold, not the ache in my jaw, certainly not the fear of what Lucien could do to me. My only focus was what I could—would—do to him. He had my dad, maybe my mom too, and I was getting them back.

CHAPTER THIRTY-FOUR

I circled back to Lucien.

He smiled. "I see the spark, I see the light." He raised his hand, waving me over. "Come, give it to me."

"Hardly." I lifted my fists. Waited. I didn't have to wait long. He rushed me. Punches. Jabs. Kicks.

I did my best, but I was no match for him. He pummelled me, his knuckles breaking skin, his feet cracking bones. I couldn't hear Dad anymore, but judging from the sweat on Lucien, he was having a hard time fighting and controlling the ghosts, too.

Then I had it. A split-second. Lights, flashing in a sequence. It distracted Lucien and gave me the moment I needed. I drove my shoulder into his chest, and when he stumbled back and hunched over, I brought my knee to his face. He howled, doubled over, and I took my chance.

I jumped on his back and wrapped my arm around his neck. Then I locked my hold into a vice grip and squeezed as hard as I could. "Not as easy to take me out, is it?"

He wheezed, clawing at my arms and face, but I held on.

"I like a challenge." He dropped to his knees, bending over as if to pray. Light and heat blasted from him, shooting me up and away.

I bounced into something solid but yielding.

Serena stood on the other side of the barrier, using me as a shield to block Lucien from seeing her. "Keep going," she said. "I can find a way in."

"The barrier won't let anything in."

"I come at the violent deaths of children and animals, but I don't want your death to be the reason I break through the boundary." She pressed against the unyielding dome. "The longer you fight, the weaker the barricade becomes. Keep going until I can find a tear. Maggie—" Her voice cracked. "—Don't die."

I turned back to Lucien. "That was quite the hit. Felt like it took a lot more power than you thought."

He was wreathed in flame, and the fire burned the ground as he came closer. "I'm not worried. It'll take me ten minutes to kill you instead of five. That's okay. I have all the time in the world." His face twitched, pulled.

"Not as much time as you think," I said, pointing. "Looks like the slaves are revolting."

"Only one." He smiled. "And he's easily consumed." The fire exploded. There was screaming, the crackling and sparking of bone and flame. After a moment, the fire diminished. "See?"

"That better not have been my dad." I rushed him, and he ran to meet me.

More fists and feet. More punches and cracked bones. More blood. I hit and kept hitting. I bled until the snow under me was red. Lucien grabbed my arm, twisted, and threw me to the ground, then knelt on top of me. The stink of the mill surrounded us.

Putting his hands on either side of my neck, he squeezed. "Don't cry. You'll see your dad, soon enough."

Then, suddenly, he was off me. I coughed, gagging as air swept into my bruised windpipe.

Serge. He'd re-formed, and he was pummelling Lucien. I raced to help. Before I could reach them, the flames exploded. Green-purple. They reached out like hands and grabbed Serge.

Lucien stood. Smiling. "Nice timing. I was getting hungry."

"Serge!"

"Don't worry." Serge smiled at me. "I have a plan."

Lucien's lips parted and he unlocked his jaw. His mouth widened until his lower jaw touched the ground. He exhaled. His breath was wreathed in orange-red flame. He inhaled, the sound was like a category-five hurricane, and sucked Serge in.

"Now." He pivoted my way. "Where were we?"

I didn't have the strength to taunt him, didn't have the heart for bravado. He had my family. I didn't know what Serge had planned, but if my parents couldn't find an escape, I wasn't sure my soul-brother would.

Lucien stepped toward me. Stopped. Grabbed his stomach. Looked at me with a combination of shock and worry.

"Something you ate not agreeing with you?"

He took another step, but the ghosts inside him pulled back. Lucien strained for control of his body, but the rebel forces were rising within. A loud gurgle from his torso, then his body began to swell. Larger, wider, like someone had attached an air tank to him and turned it on high.

I pivoted and ran away from him. The explosion sounded, the detonation lit up the sky, and chunks of Lucien rained down, spattering the ground with flesh and blood.

CHAPTER THIRTY-FIVE

"Told you I had a plan," said Serge, wiping a chunk of bad guy off his head.

"Good plan. Much better than cutting an engine."

"You gave me the idea when you said you might've heard your dad. I realized the ghosts inside him must have a way to see out. They had to know what was going on."

"You decided to get eaten and lead a revolt."

"It's not my fault he didn't watch his diet." He lifted my chin, gently turning my head. "You look awful. Do you have any teeth left?"

"I'll count them later." Around us, the spirits released from Lucien's prison struggled to their feet. Orbs of light enveloped some and transported them to the other side. Ferriers came for some, and the rest were collected by an assortment of relatives and beloved pets. They moved along the bridge so fast, it was hard to keep track, though I didn't see Zeke or Homer among their numbers. "The souls are crossing over."

"Wouldn't you?" He froze. Looked at me. "Oh, crap. Your mom and dad. Maybe it's like Rori. They had to go and check in, but they'll be back."

"Maybe, but I doubt it." I tried not to cry. Dad and Mom had pushed through Lucien's walls to send me messages and warnings, but once they were free, they'd left without a word.

"I texted Nancy and told her exactly where to find us."

"That must be her," I said as the headlights of a car lit up the night. "Give me a second to check on Carl." A peek into the SUV showed he was still knocked out, and a quicker inspection verified his breath was steady, as was his heartbeat.

The car slowed, stopped, and Gregory got out. "Thank god! I was at the station and I heard the call go out. Are you okay? Where's Savour?"

"Dead."

"He can't be—not that easily. Get in the car," he said. "If he's not here now, he'll be back soon."

"Nancy's coming," I said. "And Savour's not a threat."

"You don't know—"

"We took care of him," I said.

He blinked.

"We're safe," I said.

"I still don't like this," said Gregory. "Savour is clever. He may have faked the injury to throw you off."

"Trust me, he couldn't fake it."

"Maggie." He put his hand on my shoulder.

From the corner of my eye, I caught the flashes of light, and the stench of the old mill swept my way. And then it all fell into place.

I'm such an idiot.

CHAPTER THIRTY-SIX

"**N**ancy's taking a long time," I said. "I should try her again." I pulled out my phone, unlocked it, and pretended to scroll for her number. *Serge, don't speak out loud. Pretend I'm not talking to you and get out! Get out now!*

Why? What's going on?

Later. Get out. Get Craig. Tell him we were wrong about everything. Savour's not the soul-eater, it's Gregory.

Gregory plucked the phone out of my hand. "The benefit of being me," he said. "Is my hearing. Your tone changed, tightened." He dropped the phone and brought his heel down on it. "Call Serge out from the SUV."

"He's gone."

"You're lying."

I shook my head. "Go, look."

He gripped my arm and shoved me toward the vehicle. "What gave me away?"

"I don't know what you're talking about. I don't know why you're acting like this."

Gregory twisted me around and slapped me with his free hand. "Don't lie, Maggie." He grunted, doubling over.

I pulled, but he tightened his grip. When he stood, he no longer looked like the man who'd called himself Gregory. He was Lucien.

"There," he said. "That's better. Disguising myself takes a lot of energy." He raised his gaze and swept his hand to the sky. A translucent dome arced overhead. The wind died, the snow disappeared, and I was left alone and in the quiet with a serial murderer.

"Are you dying? Is that why you came for me and Serge now?"

He laughed. "Never, my dear. Thanks to my ghostly helpers, I'm immortal. The nosebleeds and pain was the result of having to disguise myself. It doesn't usually hurt, but you are no ordinary person. There was Serge and your pet ferrier, too. Too many supernaturals and the energy required to hide myself was extraordinary."

"Let go of my arm," I said, pulling away from him. "We both know I can't run anywhere. The real Gregory. Where is he?" I knew the answer, but I needed to keep him talking, needed to keep him distracted until I could figure out a way out of this.

Lucien smiled. "Where do you think?"

"You killed him and kept his soul."

"How else would I know the details about his friendship with your father? How else would I know how deeply your father cares about those he loves."

We walked to the SUV. "I told you," I said as he scanned the interior. "Serge's gone."

Lucien put out his hand. "I don't sense him." He stepped away. "You didn't answer my question. What gave me away?"

"Your smell," I said. Not true. It was the lights. In the car the night I drove him home and again, just now. Sequential flashes that reminded me of the TV show Serge had been watching, the one where the characters had used Morse code.

I wasn't going to say anything about that, though. Maybe it was the ghosts asking for help and doing it in a way he couldn't track. If so, I wasn't going to out them. "You stink. At first, I thought it was the old mill. Then I realized I only smelled it when you were around." I rubbed the spot where he'd slapped me. "I didn't put it together, at first. When you took Homer and Zeke, that was the smell."

"That could have been anything," he said.

The pieces were falling into place, making me feel stupid for not seeing the solution sooner. "Buddha and Ebony left the kitchen as soon as you came into the house. They would never leave unless they felt threatened." The more I thought about it, the dumber I felt. "You talked about Claxton being shut down, but you couldn't have known about it unless you were already in town."

"That was smart," he said. "Observant."

"Not that smart or observant." I sat in the passenger side of the

SUV. "If I was really on it, I'd have realized what you were the night I told you my mom had died. You said you already knew. But how could you? Dad didn't even know."

"Smart girl. I'm going to enjoy us working together."

"I don't suppose I can turn down the job offer? Not sure I'll like the hours. For sure, I already hate my boss."

"Too late for any of that."

"So why haven't you killed me yet and taken my soul?"

"I make it look easy," he said. "But corralling souls into a united project takes energy."

"You're tired."

"I am not."

"Yeah, you are. You're exhausted. Why don't we call this off?" I said. "We can meet up again in a couple weeks, after we've both had a chance to recover."

He laughed. "I like your humour." His smile slipped. "I look at you, and I see your mother. You're like her in every way imaginable. Feisty. Funny."

"How do you know what my mother looks like?" None of it made sense. "Dad got married after he left the military. You wouldn't have known about his wife unless you were already tracking him, but then, why didn't you kill—" Wait. All my information on Dad's history was based on what Gregory—Lucien—had told me. Maybe he'd been lying about all of it.

"He stole my family. He stole my Sunny."

The world tilted. "My mother was your wife?" Oh, god. "You said my dad killed your wife and child—"

"He signed her death warrant as soon as he stole her heart from me." The skin on his face hardened. "No one takes what's mine."

"And the child—" I whispered.

Tears glittered in his eyes. "You were supposed to be mine. He took your mother, he took the possibility of me being your father. Can you imagine what your powers—your life—would be like if I had been the one to raise you?"

I almost threw up from relief that he wasn't my dad. "Not to trivialize your pain or the loss of your family, but in my entire life, my dad never hit me. I've known you for five seconds and not only have you hit me, you're about to kill me."

"I don't have a choice! If you'd been mine, if we'd been a family, it would have been different. I would have shown you all the world has to offer. We would have been a team."

The dynamic duo, eating souls, and using their power to get rich and stay forever young. I'd take Dad's broken down coffeemaker and flannel shirts any day.

"Instead, I'm forced to use these guerrilla tactics. It's a pity. There will be a recovery period for both of us, and that's nothing but wasted time."

I stepped out of the vehicle. "Take me. I won't fight."

"Don't lie."

"I promise, on one condition. You release my mom and dad, and you don't touch Nell, her family, Serge, Craig and his family."

"A negotiation?"

"If you want to call it that."

He walked with me, stopped, and turned back to the SUV. Stretching out his hand, he flicked his wrist. The vehicle exploded with Carl in it. Smoke and fire plumed to the domed barrier and with it, the reporter's soul.

Lucien's body shook. His human covering fell in dusty pieces as his soul-eater form took hold. Feathered wings, black and edged with the blood of the fallen, dark purple skin, tentacles reaching from his forehead, multiple rows of teeth, and fire for eyes. He reached out, caught Carl's soul, and pulled it to him.

Carl screamed and bucked, but it didn't matter. He howled, begging Julie for forgiveness. The reporter kept shrieking as Lucien swallowed him.

Then Lucien turned to me and said, "I don't negotiate."

"You must," I said. "The fake Lucien was working with you. He had to be, if he had those souls. Was he a soul-eater in training?"

"Fake Lucien," he said. "I like it."

"Who was he, really?"

He smiled. "Think it through, think of all you know of me, and you'll see the answer to your question."

Lucien was a loner, he didn't trust anyone. He thought of people as possessions, souls as power sources, and believed he was better than the supernatural system in which he worked. "It was you," I said, after a minute. "You used the soul power to create another entity and disguise yourself."

"The first rule to defeating your enemy is to know them. I had to find out how you'd kill me. It took some work and I had to give up a few souls, but now I know." He scratched the underside of his chin. "Serge will have to be destroyed. The two of you can't be together. Too dangerous. I have friends in low, low places. Do you know what they'd do for a chance to take his energy?"

I ignored his taunt. "How do you know I won't start a revolt?"

"Because I have Homer and Zeke, and I'll do terrible things to them if you don't listen to me. That tactic wouldn't have worked on Serge," he said. "He survived the terrible things that happened to him. But you, Maggie, you're still soft. You'll be easy to control."

"You only think so."

"I feel your energy. I know you feel badly for that idiot, Carl. How much more will you hurt for Homer?"

"The other side is coming for you. Even if I can't stop you, the hunters will get you."

"I *want* them here. This barricade is a lighthouse calling them. Look up, Maggie, and *see*. The dome isn't just for defence purposes. It's a network. The harder they try to breach the field, the more it will suck their energy. And all that power will go to me." He rolled his shoulders. "Come on, let's get this over and done with."

I was going to die, and I was going to do it at the hands of a murderer. But Lucien had given me the secret to his undoing. Power. Maybe I couldn't defeat him by myself, but I wasn't alone in this fight.

I sank to my knees and surrendered. Overhead, the shadows of the hunters covered the dome and threw their outlines on the ground before me.

"Giving up so quickly?"

Lightning flashed across the dome. The hunters trying to break in.

"Idiots," muttered Lucien, looking up.

Then I closed my eyes and called Serena to me. Called her *into* me. Her energy combined with mine.

The barrier took some of my power. I'm too weak to fight, she said, *I need time to regain my strength*.

I don't need you to fight. I only need us to survive long enough for the hunters to find a way in. Serena, you come when a child or an animal is going to die a violent death. Lucien's powers can't stop that. Hide in my energy and protect me, now.

Her energy and mine comingled, giving me flashes of insight into her life and making her psychic signature known to me.

Lucien's first strike came swiftly, rocketing me off my feet and into the trees. I smashed into a branch, grabbed hold, and hung on. Lucien ripped me off, launched me into the air, then hurtled me into the ground. Serena's energy was like bubble wrap, cushioning the blow, but she couldn't last forever.

"How are you still alive?" Fire sparked from Lucien's hands.

I closed my mind to him and opened it to the ghosts he imprisoned. They sped by me, flickering, flashing. I told them to revolt, told them to break free. But the damage, the endless years of abuse and torment from Lucien had taken their toll. They were too afraid, too weak to fight. I felt Zeke's presence, wrapped around Homer's, and promised I would save them. A bolt of energy sizzled through me, Zeke and Homer offering whatever strength they could.

Another round of Lucien's barrage left me with a bleeding mouth and cracked bones. I crashed into the ground, coughing and trying to get air back into my bruised lungs.

"Why aren't you dead, yet?"

Because a serengti's destiny was to protect the abused, to take the victim's place, and endure the beatings and violence. Which meant she could take anything Lucien dished out, and when she tired, she could take my energy to strengthen herself. Because a serengti lived the final moments of the victim, which meant she hid in their energy, which meant Lucien—the king of all abusers—would never sense her presence.

Are you okay, Serena?

I want to kill him and I'm feeling stronger.
Hold that thought.
Lucien raised his leg and kicked me in the stomach.
It's enough! I can't stand it! He must die.
Serena, no!
He's taken too much, Maggie. He's taken everything from me!
She separated from me and stood before him, faceless, burning, and with murder on her mind.

"A serengti?" Lucien stepped back. "I've never seen one before." He stretched out as if to touch her, then pulled back. "Later, my beauty." He turned to me. "Time to go, Maggie. Time to come home."

He brought his foot down on my head, and it all happened at once.

—Me grabbing his foot, channelling all the energy and power I had into blasting him from me.

—Serena's howl of rage and the ball of energy she hurled at him.

—The splinter of the barrier cracking.

—Serge slipping beneath my skin to bolster me with his energy.

—Craig, in ferrier form, grabbing Lucien from behind.

"No! It's not possible! My dome!"

"Your dome is powerful," said Craig, wrestling Lucien to his knees. "But it can't keep out a ferrier who has come to claim a soul."

Lucien struggled, but his wings gushed with the blood of all those he'd captured. Some of the souls were revolting and he was losing power. "She's not your charge. You can't claim her."

"I didn't come to claim Maggie," he said. "I came for you."

Lucien screamed, pushed, and wrenched himself free.

Craig raised his arm, stretched his claws to the sky, and raked holes in the dome. The hunters flew in, thick, dark shadows of muscle and purpose.

"I will not be ended, not like this," said Lucien. He swept his hands outward, clapping them together. Nancy appeared.

"What the—?" She spotted me. "Maggie!"

He grabbed and pulled her back into him. "Shh," he told her, pressing his face into her hair. "This is between me and Maggie."

"Let her go!" I grabbed and held on to Serena as she moved to him. "Don't," I told her. "Don't get close to him."

Two of the hunters flew at him. One of them separated Nancy from Lucien, and I ran to them. The other one grabbed and held him down as the hunters surrounded him. Lucien screamed as they tore into him, releasing the trapped ghosts. When they finished, they let him go.

"We have what we need," said one of the hunters to Craig. "He's yours to claim."

Lucien knelt on the snow as ferriers appeared to take the ghosts to the other side. They blipped in and out in sparks of colour, appearing and disappearing like fireworks.

"They took my power," he said. "They've made me mortal."

"I'll arrest him for Hank's murder," said Nancy. "But he had supernatural power then, and there's no evidence of his involvement in the crime."

"He blew up your SUV," I said. "With Carl in it. I'll be a witness."

"You will be a witness," said Lucien, moving aside to reveal the gun he'd hidden.

Nancy grabbed at her hip. "It's mine!"

Everything moved fast, but I was faster. Lucien raised the gun, and I knew who his target was. Not me. Nancy. Killing me would be swift and easy. Killing Nancy would be his final infliction of pain, forcing me to live a life without her.

I moved, shoving her aside as the flash of the muzzle flared.

A blast of light and energy swept over and through me—Serge...

There was the shock of the bullet tearing its way into my skin, the searing agony as it ricocheted, and the final burst of white light that engulfed everything.

CHAPTER THIRTY-SEVEN

I woke to find myself in a hospital bed. The room was dark and I tried to figure out what the weight on my chest was. I shifted and the weight moved.

"Mags!"

"Nell?" I felt a hand on my forehead. My voice sounded slurred and heavy.

The overhead light came on. Nell was in the chair by the bed, holding my hand. Nancy was in the other one. Serge on the window sill. Craig lay on the bed beside me. He smiled and removed his hand from my forehead. "You're back."

"I heard there was cake."

"They were worried," Nell said. "But I wasn't. I knew you'd be okay. Rori said it would all work out."

"I don't know if I would call it that," I said. "There was a ton of destruction and—"

"Don't be a diva. Rori said it would work out," said Nell. "She didn't say you were going to get a Hollywood happy ending."

I looked at Craig. "But you got a happy ending, sort of. They lifted your suspension."

He shook his head. "No, they didn't. Serge came, told me what was happening—"

"And he flashed into ferrier mode," said Serge. "It was awesome."

"Just like that?" I asked.

"I am what I am," said Craig. "No one gets to tell me what I can be and when I can be it, especially when the people I love are involved. Maybe that's what I had to learn, that no one can take my power from me."

"Mags, you did get a happy ending," said Nell. "You're here."

"Yeah, exactly how did I survive? The last thing I remembered was the bullet, and I know it was working its way to my heart."

"I ripped it out," said Serge. "But the bleeding was terrible."

"I cauterized some of the vessels to stem the flow," said Craig. "But the paramedics deserve all the credit."

"What about the mortal fall out?"

Craig glanced at Nancy. "The ferriers and any of the hunters who were still there worked to shift the evidence. To the mortal world, it'll look like we need it to look. Lucien took you and Carl hostage, shot the SUV, and blew it up. Nancy showed up, there was a fight. She got his gun away, but he got hers. He turned it on her, but you stepped in, taking the bullet."

"What about Lucien?"

"When you dived in front of me, there was a flash of light," said Nancy. "The combined energy of you and Serge. It blasted Lucien to smithereens."

"But everyone else was okay? Our energy didn't hurt anyone else?"

"Think of your energy like the world's best targeting device," said Craig. "It honed on Lucien and Lucien alone."

"And hell claimed him," said Serge. "I won't gross you out with the details."

"Thanks. Are the ghosts okay?" I asked.

Craig nodded. "All that were to be transported were transported."

"Did you see my dad?"

Craig and Serge exchanged glances. "No, sorry," said Craig. "But that can mean a lot of things."

"But why? What can it possibly—"

Nancy put her hand on mine. "Questions for later, kid, when you're stronger and can deal with the answers." She looked at my friends. "Let's go. I promise we'll be back in a couple of hours and we'll talk then."

+ + +

I dozed, then woke to a faint light in the corner. Carl. "Why are you here? You should have crossed over."

"I'm scared," he said. "No one tells you—no one tells you when you die, you see all the moments of your life. I wasn't a good guy. I took advantage of others, I was mean..."

"That's not what's holding you here," I said. "You're scared of what Julie will think of how you lived your life. She's the reason you kidnapped me."

"Kidnapped. God. I'm never getting into heaven."

"I don't know about heaven, but you're not as bad as you think."

"You don't know that," he said.

"I do. Hell took Lucien. It would have taken you too, if you deserved it."

He began to cry. "I'm so scared."

"Serge said you had supernatural protection," I said. "Someone on the other side must love you, and loves you enough to have covered you. Someone like Julie. Don't be afraid to cross over."

"What's on the other side?"

"Julie, for one." I was too tired and doped up with meds to take my time with his transition. The quickest route to him crossing to the other side was via his lost love. "Tell me about her."

"Julie? She was beautiful." He smiled as memories came to him. His energy glowed and radiated soft tendrils of pink light. "Sweet. She was my conscience. I feel like everything went wrong when she died and—" He looked at the point by my bed. "Julie? Is it you?" He listened, laughing through his tears. "Yeah, I'd forgotten about that." She said or did something that made his legs buckle. He sobbed, "I don't know if I deserve it. I've been so horrible."

The spot beside my bed glowed, moved close, then enveloped him. He cried, and cried harder, then disappeared in the fading light that left peace and love in his wake.

"Maggie?"

I turned as Zeke and Homer emerged from the other side of the curtain that separated my side of the room from the other.

"We didn't want to leave until we said goodbye and thanks for saving us," said Zeke.

"I'm so sorry," I said. "I'm sorry I couldn't prevent Lucien from taking you."

"Shucks," said Zeke. "No one can stop bad things from happening. I just appreciate you helping fix it. 'Sides, you gave me back my little brother."

Homer climbed on the bed. "You did real good, Maggie."

"Thanks for all your help. I felt you and your brother's energies protecting and helping me." I took his hand, trying not to cry. "I really am sorry. I'm so sorry for all the bad things you saw and did because Lucien trapped you."

Homer leaned forward and wrapped his arms around me. "Even in the dark," he said. "There is always love."

I sank into his energy, hugging him back even as he faded from my arms.

Zeke had Homer, and together they'd crossed over. But where were my dad and mom? Had they found each other, or had they fallen between the cracks into a dark so consuming that not even my love could reach them?

CHAPTER THIRTY-EIGHT

Nightmares woke me. I opened my eyes to see Serena sitting by my bed. "I don't have much time left," she said. "My decisions are catching up, but I wanted to make sure you were okay."

"I am. You don't have to go."

"I'm dying."

"You don't have to—"

She shook her head. "It's done."

"Mom."

She froze. "I'm not your mother."

"I think you are," I said. "I felt your energy."

"There could be a lot of reasons for that."

There was no hard evidence to prove Serena was my mother. All I had were bits and pieces of her words and a gut feeling I couldn't shake. "You're my mom."

"Prove it."

"You're losing your features. It might mean you're losing yourself. But it might also be a way for you to hide your face from me, so I can't see the resemblance.

"That's hardly evidence—"

"The Voice manifests as pure fear. You've shown me nothing but rage. Maybe that's because supernatural creatures can exist in multiple dimensions, and they can be multiple things at once. Craig is human and ferrier. I'm human and guardian."

"I'd know if I was your mother."

"You told me you'd been watching me from the time I was in a crib," I said. "Only a mom would do that."

She didn't say anything.

"Lucien and my dad both said I look like you, which makes me wonder if the vision Nell saw wasn't me but you. Protecting me in any way you could."

Her life-force flickered, a rainbow of colours spread from her centre and radiated out.

"Think," I said. "How did you die?"

"My heart stopped beating."

"Serena."

She was quiet. "I don't want to think about it. My death is done—it was painful—"

"For me, please. I need to know if you're my mom or not."

She didn't say anything for a while, then, "Your dad didn't want me to leave. He wanted us to stay together, but I was a danger to you and him. I loved—" Her voice broke. "—I loved you both too much to ever harm you. So I left. I told Hank it was forever, not to come searching for me, and he agreed. But that was never my intention. I wanted to heal myself, I wanted to come back whole, to come back to you. But Lucien found me. I don't know how, but he did. He murdered me and tried to take my soul, but he wasn't powerful enough. I split and hid myself in pieces. Part of me became the serengti, part of me became The Voice. I lost other sections of my soul, but I made sure some of me stayed with Lucien so he would never know the full truth. I was so angry at him, so full of rage that he took me from you and your dad. The two of you were my everything."

"And you watched over me."

"I couldn't let him hurt you," she whispered. "I tried to warn you."

"You protected me, and now he's gone."

She began to weep. The rainbow colours inside her intensified, pinpricks of light sparked inside of her. Serena—Sunny—my mother reached out to me. "Maggie, oh, Maggie. I love you so. I'm sorry I had to leave you. I'm sorry I wasn't strong enough—"

"You were strong enough. You left to protect me." I leaned forward, ignoring the pain of the stitches and folded her into my arms.

"I've made so many mistakes."

"No mistakes. Just learning. You're perfect. You're my mom." I was crying, now. After so many years of wondering, so many years of fearing why she'd left us, I had my answers. I had my mom.

Heat and light glowed from the points where our hearts met,

healing, calming. When I pulled away, I found myself looking at an older version of myself.

"The other side is calling me, I have to go," she said, wiping away the tears from her face, then mine. "I have to answer for the things I've done."

"Please don't. I just got you. There's so much I still need to know. They can wait."

"No, they can't. The answers you seek will come, and I'll return to help."

"You can't know that."

"I do."

"Dad didn't."

"There's a reason he's not here."

"I'm sick of the reasons, "I said. "I'm tired of the excuses. He's gone and now you're leaving. Why don't the higher-ups care?"

She held me close. "They do care, but existence is more complicated than you know. Somehow, someway, this makes sense." She pressed her kiss against my forehead. "Your dad would never leave you."

"But he did. When Lucien murdered him, he didn't come to me. When Lucien died and Dad's soul was released, he didn't come."

"Your dad was never in Lucien. I would have felt it."

"But—but I heard him. He was there, helping me." I pulled away. "Could he have split himself like you did?"

"I don't know. Where is his body?"

"At the funeral home."

"Let me check." She flashed from the room. A minute, two, and she still hadn't returned. Finally, she reappeared by my beside. "Did you not see the mark?"

"Mark?"

"On his forehead."

"The bug?"

"*The* bug. It's a scarab. The Egyptian sign of rebirth and regeneration."

"What does that mean?"

"It means he's coming back in this lifetime."

"When you say this lifetime—?"

"I don't have a timeline, but that's why he didn't come to you when he died, because he was already on the other side, booking his round trip back to you."

It wasn't an answer. He could come back tomorrow; he might not come back until the moment before I took my last breath. I was hoping for something concrete, hoping for a schedule for when I'd see him, again. Once more, I was left without a resolution.

She took my hand. "He's coming, Maggie, he's coming for you." She kissed my fingers, my face. "And so will I. My daughter, my girl. I love you. I'll be back." She flashed before I could tell her that I loved her too, but the warmth of her energy told me she already knew.

✦ ✦ ✦

"Why aren't you sleeping?" Nell came in the room.

"Why are you here if I'm supposed to be sleeping?"

"I came to check on you." She moved into the room as Craig, Serge, and Nancy walked in behind her.

"Why aren't you sleeping?" asked Nancy.

"Nell and I already had this conversation," I said.

"If no one's going to sleep," said Craig. "How about if Serge and I do a food run and smuggle it in?" He looked at me. "You've had stomach surgery, so you can't have anything. You can watch us eat."

"That's cruel."

"You should've been sleeping."

They gathered around my bed.

"Watch this," said Serge. Light flashed over him.

"What am I—"

"Oh, I can see you," said Nell. "Nice trick." She took his hand. "You look good, Casper."

He blushed.

"I took Gregory to the other side, he's safe now." Craig came and sat beside me. "You okay?"

"I saw my mom, and I helped her transition."

"That's good."

I reached out for Nancy and winced as my stomach stitches voiced their disagreement. "She said Dad's coming back, in this lifetime."

She blinked back her tears. "How soon?"

I shrugged. "There's no answer to that. Maybe tomorrow, maybe years from now."

"I wonder what he'll look like," said Nell. "It's not like he can return looking like himself."

"I don't care," said Nancy. "I'm glad he's coming back."

"All of this is good," said Craig as he kissed the top of my head. "But you didn't answer my question. Are you okay?"

"I don't know," I said. "Maybe. Probably. I'm glad Dad and Mom are okay, but this life is proving harder than I thought. I figured being a guardian would be solving problems, but the death, destruction, and the pain—"

"Destiny isn't a straight line," said Craig. "It's full of loss and pain. That's why it's destiny, because you pay a price for it."

"Maybe, but the price tag is higher than I thought." Dad was coming back, but who knew when that would be, and who knew how our relationship would evolve. He'd kept secrets from me. His motive was protection, but it had put me in more danger. Plus, I wasn't sure *who* I'd be when he returned and how time would affect us. Would he still be my dad? Would I still be his girl?

Mom was on a round-trip, too, which meant we'd have a chance for a relationship. But she was supernatural and so was I. Did that complicate or make it easier for us to forge a bond? And what about Nancy? How would she and my mother deal with their shared love of my dad? Plus, Dad could take a long time before he returned—maybe long enough for Nancy to find someone else. Once again, I was left with too many questions, too many threads, and no way to tie up any of them. "I've never thought about death as loss—I mean, I see the dead. But Dad's gone and so is Mom. They're coming back, but I don't know when, and I don't know what it'll be like when they return." I struggled to get out the next words. "And who's next? The higher-ups let a soul-eater take both of my parents. None of you are immune—"

And the biggest question loomed before me. Who was I going to lose, next? The soul-eater had taken both my parents, and sure, they weren't gone forever. But next time, the person I lost might not come back. Next time might be a forever loss. "I was hoping for resolution," I told Craig. "I was hoping for a clear view of the future."

He laughed, but it was not unkind. "Death is part of life, Mags. None of us are safe from it."

"But I have powers—"

"Everyone has powers," he said. "Yours just happens to be seeing the dead."

"I guess I was hoping for a happy ending."

"That's only for fairy-tales and movies," he said.

"Life is about loss," said Nancy. "And sometimes, even the most beautiful things come to an end."

I took her hand. "Maybe there are no happy endings. Maybe there are just endings, and it is up to us to make them happy."

"That's a good thought." Craig smiled and pulled me close, and I gave myself over to the warmth and the love of those who surrounded me.

ACKNOWLEDGEMENTS

Guyanese culture embraces the idea of the supernatural. It's not uncommon for your ancestors to visit you in your dreams (which is why you must always behave. No one wants Grandma or Grandpa coming for a midnight talk, and using their stern voice). In your waking life, you pay attention to what's going on around you because your deceased loved ones will do things—send a bird into your house, put a song on the radio—to let you know they are present and watching over you. It's one of my most favourite things about my culture—the idea that love is so strong, it can transcend space, time, and death.

I want to thank the amazing team at Great Plains Teen Fiction for giving me the chance to share a series of stories that embrace and celebrate both my Canadian and Guyanese culture, and for being fabulous in general. Steph, thanks for being a second pair of eyes and helping to polish the story!

Much thanks as well to my fantastic agent, Amy Tompkins, for all the chats and wisdom, to the Furies, Nikki Vogel, Kate Boorman, and Hope Cook for their insights to the craft of storytelling, and to Sven, thanks for all the late night talks, early morning chats, and keeping me well-stocked in tea and cookies.

Everlasting thanks to my readers. Thank you for sharing this journey with me!